Saving the Cowboy Billionaire

A Chappell Brothers Novel: Bluegrass Ranch Romance Book 7

Emmy Eugene

Copyright © 2021 by Emmy Eugene

All rights reserved.

No part of this book may be reproduced in any form or by any electronic or mechanical means, including information storage and retrieval systems, without written permission from the author, except for the use of brief quotations in a book review.

ISBN-13: 979-8509548109

Chapter 1

Conrad Chappell stared at his phone, willing a whole slew of texts to come pouring in. At this point, he didn't even care who they were from. He simply needed something to distract him from the frilly music piping across the whole ranch, the general excitement hanging in the air, and the suffocating tie around his neck.

Wedding number six.

Conrad loathed weddings as a general rule, mostly because they reminded him that he wasn't as happy as he pretended to be. For a while there, he thought he and Ian would live out their bachelor lives in bliss. They shared a house—a big one too—and they got along great.

Ian cooked. Conrad did dishes. Ian put in the laundry. Conrad moved it to the dryer. They'd worked together for decades, attending the same trainings and workshops, and they'd learned horse racing and equine training from their father, who'd been one of the best in the business.

Now, Bluegrass Ranch was one of the best in the business. They produced top-quality racehorses year after year. Every brother in the family had a job to do, and each one was vital to the success of the ranch.

He and Ian, though, had often thought their jobs were the *most* important. They trained the racehorses. The ones that won millions of dollars and then became assets to the ranch. They could then sell the stud fees, something Duke and Blaine handled.

Conrad had been learning over the course of the past few months that a racehorse would never keep him warm at night. He might be able to tell them secrets, but they never talked back. A horse never asked him how his day was, and a horse had never offered to bring him dinner when he wasn't feeling well.

He loved his job, but it didn't love him back. He wanted more. He wanted someone's hand to hold, a woman to talk to, and Ryanne's pretty face to light up when he walked in the door after a long day's work.

He looked up as boots came up the steps. "There you are," Ian said. "I figured you be up here." He took in the state of Conrad on the small couch at the top of the steps. They had a little landing here, and it was the perfect size for a loveseat and a tiny end table. Conrad loved to lie on the couch and read a fantasy novel in his spare time. Ian never touched it, as far as Conrad knew at least.

"Do we have to go?" Conrad asked.

"It's Lawrence, so yes," Ian said. "You usually love weddings."

"I do not," Conrad said.

"Sure you do. You find the prettiest girl, you flirt with her, and she comes to sit by you."

"Mm." He wouldn't be doing that this afternoon, though he supposed he had done something exactly like what Ian had described at other weddings.

"You're really hung up on this mystery woman."

"I am not," Conrad said, but the words held little power behind them. He hadn't told Ian who he'd gone to lunch with last week. Ian would know Ryanne Moon, as they'd all grown up together in Dreamsville, and for some reason, Conrad wanted her all to himself for a little while longer.

She's not yours at all, he thought. That was the whole truth and nothing but the truth. They'd gone to lunch together last week, with another date planned for Friday. One date didn't mean they were a couple, and Conrad knew enough about Ry to know she wouldn't want to be claimed even if they were.

She'd canceled on him on Friday morning, claiming she simply had too much to do to get ready for the grand opening of her first physical store for her clothing brand, Andy and Ryan.

Conrad had gone to the grand opening, but Ry hadn't had more than four seconds for him. He wasn't even sure they'd made full eye contact in the hour he'd hovered near or inside the building.

She'd rented a decently-sized space on the end of a strip mall that had a nail salon, a popular Mexican restaurant, a cell phone store, and a mailbox office. She'd had a lot of people at the grand opening, and she'd been busier than a bee, flitting here and there and everywhere to keep customers happy and make sure her employees knew what they were doing. He'd finally left without truly speaking to her at all, a ball of nerves stuffed somewhere in his chest.

Conrad looked back at his phone again. He and Ry had texted several times over the past week—about what they'd done for a month before he'd finally gotten a date and time lined up where they could meet.

Her last text to him had come in last night, right when Conrad was settling down to sleep. *I'm so sorry to do this*, it had said. *But I can't come to the wedding tomorrow. Something's come up, and I need to take care of it.*

He'd asked her what could've possibly come up. She hadn't answered.

Conrad flipped his phone over and Ian settled on the top step. "You know," his brother said. "You don't have to pretend not to like her for me."

Conrad looked at Ian, but he had his head bent toward the floor. The brim of his hat concealed his face. "I know," Conrad said, but he wasn't sure he did. Ian had a major aversion to women, and it didn't matter if they were nice, smart, kind, beautiful, hard-working, and nothing like his ex-wife.

To him, every woman was Minnie. Though they'd been divorced for a while now, Ian had not even so much as flirted with another woman. Conrad was impressed by his brother's blinders, as he didn't even seem to notice when there were humans of the opposite sex around.

"I'm okay," Ian said. "With whatever you choose,

Conrad. I've had some time to get used to the fact that my brothers are going to get married, whether I think it's stupid or not."

"You like Olli and Ginny," Conrad said weakly. "Lisa's great too. Tam constructed the best saddle you've ever sat in." He cleared his throat, because he really loved all of his sisters-in-law. "Beth feeds you every time you show up at her house, no matter what time of day or night it is. And Mariah actually made you laugh over the weekend."

Ian looked up, a smile on his face. "I know. I told you, I'm fine. I've made my own choices, and you should get to make yours. So just *call* this woman already. I *hate* it when you grump around the house, slamming cupboards and growling about how I've drunk all the cream."

Maybe Conrad had done that this morning. "I ordered more cream," he said.

Ian grinned at him, and Conrad couldn't stay mad at him for more than two seconds. He'd never been able to. As one of the younger brothers, he spent most of his childhood years with Duke, who was just younger than him, and Ian, who was just older. The three of them had been a real "troublesome trio," if anyone asked their mother, and Conrad was glad he still had both of them to talk to.

"It's…I went out with Ryanne Moon last week," Conrad said. "You know, the girl I took to my junior prom?"

Ian's eyes widened for a moment, and then he whistled through his teeth. "Wow, Conrad. Goin' back to your roots?"

Conrad lifted one shoulder in a semi-shrug. "I don't

know. It took over a month to even set up that date. She canceled on me for Friday, and then again last night for the wedding." He didn't want to say the next thought in his mind, but someone needed to. "Makes me think she's just not that into me."

At least, not the way he was into her. She'd consumed him, and Conrad thought only of food, horses, and Ryanne, and not always in that order.

"What did she say about today?" Ian asked. "Bringing a woman to a family wedding is a big deal, Con. Maybe she realizes that when you don't. Maybe she didn't want the pressure."

Conrad nodded and flipped his phone over again. He looked up and past his brother on the steps, to the big windows that filled the front of the house. They always cast sunlight on this couch, which was another reason he liked it.

Ian's phone sounded half a second before Conrad's. "That'll be Spur," Ian said, but neither of them moved.

"She said something had come up that she needed to take care of." Conrad tapped on his phone to wake it, and he navigated to her text. He handed the device to Ian. "That's it."

"Then she didn't answer." Ian handed the phone back. "She just opened a brand-new store. Maybe something really did come up."

"Maybe," Conrad said, but something felt false in her words. He wasn't sure what.

"After the wedding, go down to the store," Ian said. "Just ask her point blank: Are you interested in me or not?"

She'd already told him she'd be extraordinarily busy, and he'd thought that would be okay. Deep down, though, he wasn't okay with setting up dates and then getting canceled on. Maybe every once in a while, sure. Things happened. People got busy.

Ian's phone rang, and he cursed under his breath as he stood up. "No, Spur," he said in an acidic tone. "I haven't left the state. We're on our way." He started down the steps, and Conrad better get going if he wanted to ride around the ranch with Ian.

Since he didn't want to show up to the wedding alone, he got to his feet with a sigh and followed his brother downstairs. The weather had cooperated, and Conrad was glad he'd stop getting texts from his mother about how they all needed to pray harder that Mother Nature would curb the winds.

Pray for this, Mom always said. *Pray for that.*

Growing up, Conrad had done it. He did love the Lord, and he went to church every week. He just wasn't as convinced as his mother that prayer was all that powerful. God already knew what Conrad wanted; why did he have to ask for it?

Sometimes, he didn't get what he prayed for, and he had no idea what that meant. Did God not hear him? Did he not care about what Conrad wanted?

In Conrad's mind, it was simply a whole lot easier to be the best man he could be and let God take care of the rest. If he didn't pray for something, then he didn't have to worry if he didn't get it.

Ian drove the two of them from the house where they lived in the corner of the ranch toward the epicenter, where the homestead stood. With Lawrence getting married, and Duke already with the knot tied, only Cayden and Ginny would be living in the homestead. It was still the central gathering place for all the cowboys, cowgirls, and family on the ranch, and Conrad was glad he wasn't the one maintaining it.

There was no one better for that job than Cayden and Ginny, as evidenced by the huge hanging flower baskets that had been added to the porch since the last time Conrad had been here—which was yesterday afternoon.

Someone—probably Ginny—had hung a huge banner along the rooftop above the garage that read *Congratulations Lawrence and Mariah*, and Conrad could hear the music coming from inside the house the moment he got out of the truck.

If Ian could go inside, so could Conrad. Ian didn't even break stride, so Conrad squared his shoulders and put on his brave face too. They entered the house through the garage, and despite the noise, Spur appeared at the end of the hall immediately.

"You're here," he said, stating the obvious.

"Yes, *Mother*," Ian said. "And if you'll look at the clock, we're not even late."

Spur didn't even flinch at the hardness in Ian's voice. He just grabbed him in a hug and said, "I know this is hard for you. Thank you for coming anyway."

Ian hugged Spur back, and the two of them clung to one another in such a way that revealed to Conrad how very hard it was for Ian to be here. He'd done it, though, and he was such a good example to Conrad.

"Ginny's got a whole feast for us," Spur said. "We didn't want you to miss it." He released Ian and stepped past him to hug Conrad. "How you doin', brother?"

"Good enough," Conrad said, embracing his brother back. They all wore identical suits in navy blue, but no one looked as good as Spur. No one was ever as good as Spur at anything. The man exuded confidence, and he did have a lot of natural talent with horses, ranching, and people. What he wasn't good at, he could spot in others, and he made sure they were in charge of that around the ranch.

"Come eat," Spur said. "I managed to beat Duke away from taking seconds until you two got here."

Ian had already moved into the kitchen, but Conrad's chest pinched a little bit. They couldn't even wait until everyone had arrived to eat? How hard would that have been? Ginny had texted and said eleven-thirty for lunch, and as Conrad looked at the microwave above the stove, the numbers ticked to eleven-thirty.

His annoyance surged, but he tamped it down. He had plenty of experience doing that, and he knew eventually it would go away. That, or he'd go out on the deck and jump rope until all of the negative feelings inside him swirled way. Another activity that drove his irritation into the ground was chopping wood.

Since he and Ian lived in a house with a wood-burning stove, there was always the need for more wood. With summer only a month away, though, Ian would know why Conrad was out at the woodpile.

He told himself it didn't matter, because Ian let Conrad do what Conrad needed to do to feel better. They'd always done that for each other, and Conrad had endured plenty of Ian's ranting sessions, especially when Spur had gotten engaged and Trey had gotten married without telling anyone in the family.

Conrad filled a plate with food, and he enjoyed the company of his large and growing family. All too soon, it was time to take everything outdoors, where the men and women split up into separate tents to finish getting ready.

He'd never really understood the point of having separate rooms for the bride and groom, but everyone seemed to do it. He just wanted to wake up in the morning on his wedding day, get dressed, and pick up his bride-to-be. They'd get to the venue together, and they'd walk down the aisle together. She didn't need to be *given* to him. She'd be a strong, capable woman, and she'd *choose* to be with him, the way he'd choose to be with her.

Annoyingly, Ryanne's face filled his mind. She did have beautiful, brown eyes, with all that reddish-brown hair that he loved. He couldn't quite remember what it was like to kiss her, as he'd been out with a lot of other women in the past twenty years. He kissed almost everyone he went out with, because kissing was fun, and Conrad had previously dated for fun.

He wanted to have fun now too, but he wanted to be more serious as well.

Finally, the wedding started, and Conrad got in line. He hated lines; he hated suits; he hated weddings.

He put a smile on his face, because this was his brother, and he loved Lawrence. Mariah was the perfect complement to him, as he was quiet and she was literally the most personable and bubbly person Conrad had ever met.

She was blonde and pretty, and she was quick on her feet and super organized. She'd been one of the top marketers at her firm, but she'd left to become an event planner.

The moment he stepped out of the men's tent, Conrad could see how she'd excel in such a job. Not a single detail sat out of place in the large tent where hundreds of guests had arrived to witness the wedding.

Every chair had a light pink bow tied around it, and they all looked exactly the same, the tails of them billowing in the slight breeze blowing through the tent. Lights hung in the rafters, making the atmosphere magical. Pots overflowing with flowers hung from every post on the outer edges of the tent, and Mariah had put what looked like vintage street lamps down the center of it too. They marked the aisle, and they also held beautiful, fragrant flowers.

Conrad did his part by walking down the aisle to the altar, which was a trough from right here on the ranch that had been filled to overflowing with flowers. Roses, daisies, lilies, orchids, and every other type of flower imaginable. Flowers and more flowers.

Lawrence had said Mariah wanted flowers, and wow, she'd gotten them.

He took his spot on the left side of the altar facing the crowd, where he'd stay for the duration of the ceremony. Behind him, on the other side of the flimsy tent flap, another tent waited with tables and chairs for the dinner that would be served.

Conrad could smell the steak and salt, and his stomach grumbled at him, though he'd eaten only three hours ago.

Lawrence took his place at the altar, and he turned toward the back of the tent right as Mariah and her father stepped into view. She wore a gorgeous, lace-covered gown that accentuated her slim waist and all her curves.

The very air held its breath as she made the journey toward Lawrence. Conrad watched his brother as he took Mariah from her dad, and the happiness in Lawrence's eyes knew no limits.

He wanted that, and he swallowed hard against the rising jealousy. Just another reason he hated weddings. So many reminders of what he lacked, what he was faking about, and what he wanted but didn't have.

He may have zoned out during the pastor's speech, because he blinked rapidly when the people in the tent started clapping and cheering. He saw Lawrence kissing Mariah, and he saw them turn toward the crowd, their hands clasped as he lifted them skyward.

Conrad got himself in gear and clapped for the happy couple, even going so far as to whistle and catcall as they made their way back down the aisle.

The excitement and adrenaline subsided quickly, and guests started to file into the aisles. Mom always had a crowd around her, and Conrad turned away from that whole scene.

He just needed somewhere quiet to be until it was time for their early dinner. He'd be wearing his suit for the duration of that afternoon and evening's events, but all the women needed time to change into their party dresses for the dance and reception. That would be after the dinner, which would be served in thirty minutes' time.

Mom and Mariah had decided that would be enough time for anyone not invited to the dinner to clear out, and for Mom to get a few last-minute pictures in place for the meal and following reception.

He ducked past the break in the corner of the tent, stepping out of the wedding tent and into the dinner tent. The staff had gathered there, and the head chef was leading a meeting about the food, the order of service, and the expectations for that afternoon.

Conrad felt very out of place, but he was used to such a thing. He stood quietly in the corner, no one looking his way at all, which was also about how things went.

Across from him, he could see several waitresses as he scanned, and then a face caught his attention in a way no other had.

He pulled in a breath as their eyes met, and he said right out loud, "You've got to be kidding me," when Ryanne Moon's eyes rounded as she recognized him.

Every eye in the tent turned toward him then, and the chef stopped talking. Conrad felt wind blowing through his soul, and he had to work extremely hard not to bark a question at Ryanne about what in the world she was doing here, dressed like that, when she should be in some slinky, sexy gown on his arm.

Chapter 2

Ryanne Moon's prayers had gone unanswered. In fact, the Lord had downright blown them up. He'd done the exact opposite of what she'd been asking him to do—keep her invisible that day. Keep Conrad's attention somewhere else.

He'd be sitting at the front of the tent, and she'd specifically requested the back section. She'd be wearing all black, and waiters and waitresses were invisible. No one truly looked at them. No one even cared they were there, unless their food didn't come out.

Why in the world was he standing in her staff meeting?

Not your staff, she had the wherewithal to think. She had a staff down the road, in a strip mall, in her clothing store. This was a job for a friend to whom she owed a favor. Wendell had called, and Ry hadn't been able to say no.

She didn't seem to have a problem telling Conrad Chappell no, though faced with him in that suit, with flowers pinned to the lapel, and every line hitting his muscular body in exactly the right way...and Ryanne wouldn't even be able to speak.

Chef Lucas Wendall pushed through the crowd to Conrad and said something Ryanne couldn't hear from clear across the tent. She couldn't see Conrad, as Wendell had plenty of bulk on his frame too.

He turned a few moments later and said, "Ryanne, I need you over here."

All the eyes shifted to her, and she prayed that the Lord would open up the Earth and swallow her whole with every step she took.

Just another prayer that went unanswered, as she arrived next to Wendell and in front of Conrad only a few seconds later.

"He needs to talk to you," Wendell said. "You know what you're doing, but I need you back in ten minutes."

"Yes, sir," she said, though Wendell was one of her oldest friends. Technically, he'd been Andrea's best friend growing up, but Ry had known him her whole life. After Andy's death, Ry and Wendell had found some comfort in each other, and if there was anyone Ry couldn't say no to when he was in a pinch, it was Wendell.

Conrad indicated the wide open tent to his left, and Ry followed him in that direction. Her heart lodged itself right up in her throat, and she wasn't sure how to speak and keep breathing at the same time.

Conrad led her through the maze of tables to the outer edge of the tent, as far from the staff meeting as he could get. Cars and trucks had been parked along the lane in front of where the wedding events were taking place, as well as all the way down the dirt road that led toward a bend and back toward the main highway.

The Chappells had always known how to throw a good party.

"Remember when you guys hosted a New Year's Eve bash in the barn?" she asked, not sure why that particular memory had crept up on her. "It was our senior year."

"Yes," he said, his tone clipped and formal.

"I only came for a few minutes," she said. "I didn't stay until midnight or anything." She hadn't wanted to see Conrad kiss someone else, and he'd been there with his latest fling. She'd been the same age as them, and he'd found someone else by Valentine's Day.

No matter who he went out with, Ryanne hated that it wasn't her. She'd also learned that year that Conrad had wings, and she didn't think there was a woman alive who could clip them.

She wondered if that had changed in the years that had passed since then.

"It was a good party," he said. "Why'd you leave?"

She stared out at the blue sky, only a few wispy clouds floating through it. The air smelled half like the food she'd be serving soon and half like pure country. Sunshine, horses, and possibilities.

His sister-in-law should make a candle for that. *Pure country*.

Ryanne had done a little Internet digging of her own since her date with Conrad last week. The Chappell brothers and Bluegrass Ranch did very well for themselves. This was the sixth brother to tie the knot, and one of his brothers had won the Sweetheart Classic twice in a row.

Olivia Hudson had won a major internship with a huge retailer that had taken her perfumery from a mom-and-pop operation she ran out of her garage to an international company that sold perfumes, colognes, and scented candles in all fifty states—and now thirteen countries.

Another brother had snagged himself an award-winning leatherworker for a wife, and Tamara Lennox was known all over the South for her fine craftsmanship.

They had the best wedding planner in the state now that Mariah had married Lawrence, and Lisa Harvey owned one of the most prestigious stud farms in the area.

It was Ginny Winters who really crowned the Chappell family. She was the sole heiress to Sweet Rose Whiskey, which had been in business for over a century, and who had more money than the Queen of England.

Conrad's parents were well-respected in the community, and his mother had been heading up charitable organizations for fifty years now.

Not only would Ryanne not fit in this prestigious family, she couldn't even imagine herself at family parties and get-togethers.

"Do you want me to be honest?" she asked. In her heart,

she wanted him to say yes. She had things to say to him; things that wouldn't go away until she did.

"I would prefer that to a vague text about something coming up that you have to take care of," he said dryly. Maybe he was barely holding back his anger. She wasn't quite sure.

"Something *did* come up," she said. "Wendell needed servers for this wedding, and I've worked with him a lot."

"He was Andy's boyfriend," Conrad said.

"Yes."

"What about last Friday?"

Ryanne swallowed. "Last Friday was me freaking out," she said.

"About what?" Conrad tore his eyes from the horizon and looked at her. "I thought we had a great lunch on Wednesday. Well, at least after the part where I sort of yelled at you." He offered her a kind smile, and oh, she shouldn't have looked at him.

"We did," she said. "I...I'm so busy, Conrad. I just need to get Andy and Ryan off the ground. Then maybe we'd have a chance."

He studied her, and in high school, he'd simply accepted whatever she'd said to him. She could still hear herself telling him on New Year's Eve that she needed to get home to help Tyler with his party. Conrad hadn't questioned why her older brother couldn't put on his own party without her help.

He was questioning her now, and he hadn't even said anything.

She looked away, sighing. If she stayed here much longer, she'd tell him too much, and then she'd regret everything about this day, not just that she wasn't wearing her designer gown and hanging on his arm.

"Why'd you leave the New Year's Eve party?" he asked. "Honestly."

"Honestly." She took a deep breath. "Because you were there with Annette Lansing, and I couldn't stand to see you kiss someone else when the clock struck midnight." She looked at him, everything laid out between them.

"Why'd you cancel on Friday?"

"Because," she said. "I knew if I started seeing you again, I'd fall in love with you, and you'd break my heart all over again." She whispered the last several words. Tears filled her eyes, but they weren't the happy kind people cried at weddings.

She brushed at her eyes quickly, because she didn't want to ruin her makeup. She had a job still to do today. "Please, Conrad. Just leave me alone, okay? I'm opening my store, and I'm finally feeling like a normal person after Andy died, and I need my heart."

A storm raged across Conrad's face. She hadn't known the man possessed such strong emotions; in high school, he had a devil-may-care attitude, and he'd been larger than life. She could still feel that energy pulsing off of him, and she knew she'd do dangerous things to be with him.

"What if I promised not to break your heart?" he asked, each word carefully measured out. He swallowed after the question, clearly having trouble keeping everything tightly controlled.

"How can you make such a promise?" She shook her head, horrified when an errant tear splashed her cheek. She swiped at it and drew in a breath. "I have to get back to work. I'm sorry about Friday and today. I just need to focus, and Conrad, you've always been terrible for my focus."

"I'm not the same person I was in high school," he said.

"No," she said. "You're not. You're better."

He shook his head. "Not true. Please, don't say no all the way yet." He reached out and brushed her fingers with his. A whisper of a touch, the way she skimmed her hand across the tops of the blades of grass.

Instant heat filled her body, and Ryanne really wanted to say yes. "I can give you a halfway yes."

"I'll take it," he whispered, drawing her fully into his arms. He smelled like pine trees and leather, fresh air and a mountain fire. He'd always been the man of her dreams, and that hadn't changed about him. "I just want a chance."

He pulled away, his hands sliding down to her waist, where he held her as he looked at her. "Can you give me a chance to show you that I'm not the same? I'm not better, and I'm not worse. I'm just older. Different. I think we'd be really good together." Another swallow, and she liked that he was nervous. It made her feel more powerful than she otherwise would have.

She nodded, not sure what to say, and the next thing she knew, Conrad had placed one hand on the side of her face and lowered his mouth to touch hers.

She reacted like a dehydrated man who'd just found water, and she kissed him back with enthusiasm. She told herself that it was because she hadn't had a boyfriend in years. She hadn't kissed a man in so long.

Really, though, it was because he was Conrad Chappell, and she'd always failed at staying away from him.

Chapter 3

Conrad became aware of the eyes on him, but it still took a couple of seconds for him to pull away from Ryanne. Kissing her felt like the best decision he'd ever made, and as she stepped back and ducked her head, a new kind of chill entered his blood. The kind that didn't really exist in Kentucky this late in May.

"When can I see you again?" he murmured as he slipped his hand away from her. He stepped back too, putting the appropriate distance between them. He glanced over to Lucas Wendell, who had been Ryanne's sister's boyfriend. She'd seemed pretty chummy with him too, and instant jealousy flowed through Conrad despite the man-nod he gave the chef. Wendell clearly wanted Ryanne to get back to work, and Conrad fell back another step.

"I better get back to the wedding." He reached up and adjusted his cowboy hat, which had been pushed back during the kiss. "Which tables will you be working?"

"The back," Ryanne said, her voice throaty and muted. She cleared the emotion from her throat and glanced over her shoulder too. She then nodded toward the corner of the pavilion. "The three over there."

"Great." Conrad put a smile on his face, because he finally had a real reason to have one there, and ducked back through the white fabric separating the two spaces. He very nearly rammed into Ian, and sincere gratitude flowed through him that he hadn't been caught kissing Ryanne by his brother.

"There you are," Ian said, looking past Conrad. He forced himself not to turn around and look too, and instead, he met Ian's eyes a moment later.

"Here I am. What did I miss? Mom texting a mile a minute to make sure we have all the bows tied on precisely right?"

Ian grinned and shook his head. "That too, but really you missed Blaine and Tam rushing off to the hospital."

Conrad's heart jumped to the back of his throat. "Really?" He looked around, trying to find his older brother and his wife. Tam was due any day now, and it seemed like today was that day. "Mom's not going to like that."

"She's having a real dilemma," Ian said, and he sounded downright gleeful about it. "I told her I'd skip the dinner and go to the hospital to be with Blaine and Tam." His expression darkened. "She told me if I left even five seconds before the last chair was cleaned up, she'd shave my head in my sleep." Ian adjusted his cowboy hat, revealing his chestnut brown hair which had grown far too long.

Even Conrad had been after him to cut it, but Ian had started wearing it long as a badge of honor. Conrad suspected he didn't even like the long locks, but at this point, he wouldn't concede. Ian really did have a stubborn streak.

Conrad supposed he did too, but he definitely felt more moldable than Ian. His tenacity wouldn't allow him to accept Ryanne's non-answer to when he could see her again. He was going to see her again right now.

"Come on," Conrad said, turning away from the thinning crowd. "If we have to stay for this dinner, we'll want a seat at one of the back tables." He led Ian to one of the three tables in the back corner, and he'd barely sat down before Spur descended on the two of them.

"You can't sit back here." He pulled out the chair besides Conrad and sat down.

"You just did." Conrad gave Spur a look that said, *Mind your own business.*

"Mom wants everyone up front." Spur wiped his hand along his forehead. "It's so hot today."

"Spur," someone called, and Conrad's oldest brother got to his feet instantly. "Come turn on these misters."

Spur bustled off to do what his wife had said, and Conrad tried to duck his head so Olli wouldn't see him. Like that would ever work. She seemed to have eyes in the back of her head, and her heeled feet approached the table in sharp clicks.

"You two," she said. "You get up and go help your mother."

Conrad turned and looked up at Olli. "Oh, hey, Olli. Can I have Gus?" He stood and tried to take the little boy from his mother.

"No, you can *not*," Olli said, sharp disapproval in her eyes. "Your mother is hauling in the dry ice herself. You lazy cowboys. Get out there and help her." She threw a look at Ian, who hadn't moved. "Go on now, Ian. She needs you."

"All right," he drawled as he stood. He tipped his hat without a smile in sight and walked away. Conrad decided to do the same, and he got away from Olli before she could start in on the lecturing. He loved his sister-in-law, but once she got started... She was a force that couldn't be stopped.

Conrad wasn't sure why Mom was hauling in her own dry ice for the punch bowls. The Chappells had plenty of money, and she'd hired people to do far less than that. He found her struggling with a large block of the stuff, and he rushed forward to take it from her. "Mom, what are you doing?"

"Javier hurt himself on the first trip," Mom said, clear frustration in her voice. "This all needs to go in, boys."

"We've got it, Mom," Ian said, his voice much kinder than Conrad's had been. Conrad kept his face turned away from his mother, and he got the dry ice where she wanted it, along with every other detail. Thankfully, the two seats he and Ian had occupied earlier were still available once it was time for dinner to really begin, and Ian met his eye.

"Do you think we can really sit back there?"

"I say we try," Conrad said, looking back and forth between the open seats on the front family tables and the two at the back table. He then moved toward the back, determined to pretend like he'd gone deaf if anyone called his name.

No one did, which was surprising enough all by itself, and he and Ian sat down at the back table. Not thirty seconds later, Ry filled their glasses with pink lemonade, the sweet scent of her skin and clothes reminding Conrad of that kiss.

He wasn't sure what Ian saw on his face when he looked up at Ryanne, but it had to be something. She'd barely walked away when he asked, "When did you kiss her?"

"I didn't kiss her," Conrad said, but his voice sounded false even to his own ears.

Ian started to chuckle, and it was the low kind that would escalate if Conrad didn't put a stop to it.

"Shh," he said, glaring at his brother as Ryanne looked over her shoulder from the table next to theirs. "This is your brother's wedding."

Ian quieted and leaned closer. "Is this why she said she couldn't come to the wedding?"

"Lucas Wendall was Andy's boyfriend. He asked her to help. She said yes." Conrad watched Ryanne walk away, and he didn't mind that view at all. He tore his eyes from her with some degree of difficulty. He wasn't going to be Mr. Obvious, and he could wait until they could be alone to see her again.

Right now, he *was* at his brother's wedding, and his mother had just spotted where he and Ian had chosen to sit.

"Incoming," he whispered to Ian. "Get your game face on."

"You boys are not sitting back here," Mom said as she leaned her head between Conrad's and Ian's. "Now, I have a smile on my face, and I expect the two of you to stand up and follow me to the family table with smiles on your faces too."

"Mom," Ian said, his voice made of flint.

"*Now*, Ian," Mom said. "This is Lawrence's wedding, and heaven knows he's done unsavory things for you." She straightened and walked away.

Conrad looked at Ian, and he cocked his eyebrows. "Lawrence is the best of all of us."

Ian wore only darkness in his eyes, but he said, "Fine. I'll sit up front for Lawrence. Not for Mom."

Amen, Conrad added silently, but a wedding day was no day to get into all of their issues with their mother.

"Ch, ch, ch, ch." Ian made the noise as he worked the blue roan in the circle, getting her to come into the center just the way he wanted. If there was anyone more skilled with a horse than Conrad, it was Ian. Growing up, Conrad had worked his tail off to be as good as Ian, and he often found himself still trying to prove to Daddy and Spur and everyone else that he deserved to be one of the trainers at Bluegrass Ranch.

The ranch housed a lot of stables and boarded dozens and dozens of horses. Various trainers came to work the horses on the track where they'd hosted the Summer Smash last year, and Cayden, Ginny, Lawrence, and Mariah were currently in the midst of planning the second race in what they'd decided would be an annual event at the ranch.

"You almost done?" Conrad asked, leaning against the fence.

Ian barely looked at him. "Yep. Time to go?" He kept the cane tapping on the ground but had stopped vocalizing.

"Yes," Conrad said. "Duke said we could ride with him, and he has an appointment at four, so he won't be staying long."

"Perfect," Ian said. "Let's get Stars For Eyes put away." He slowed the horse, stopped her, and approached. He took a few seconds to stroke the sides of her face as he murmured to her. Conrad and Ian shared most things, but when Conrad had asked him what he said to the horses, Ian wouldn't say.

Conrad texted Duke that they needed ten more minutes, and Duke said he was on the way. He helped Ian put the horse back in the stall, and they got in the truck with Duke and Lisa.

"Howdy, Lisa," Conrad said, because he liked his brother's wife. She ran a stud farm on the other side of town, and Duke lived up there in the farmhouse with her. They seemed real happy together, and Conrad smiled at the dark-haired woman.

"Howdy, Conrad," she said. "I got that new saddle sealant in, and it's amazing." She twisted fully in her seat and grinned at him.

"We've got to get that," he said, glancing at Ian. His brother didn't answer, and Conrad frowned.

The wedding dinner hadn't been terrible. They'd eaten grilled cheese sandwiches back at home, and they'd enjoyed the morning training horses, like they usually did. Their afternoon trip to the hospital to see Tam and Blaine and their new baby was out of the ordinary, but Conrad couldn't see why that would upset Ian.

He looked out his own window, his thoughts oscillating between Ryanne and how soon was too soon to call and what could possibly be wrong with Ian.

"What did they name him?" Duke asked. "Does anyone know?"

"No one has said," Lisa said. "Even when I asked Tam in a private text, off the family group chat, she didn't say. She didn't even respond."

Conrad turned back toward the front seat. "Why wouldn't she? Is there something wrong with the baby?"

"Surely Mom would've said something if there was something wrong," Conrad said, looking to Ian for confirmation, the way he had so many times in the past. "Right?"

Ian wore concern in his face too. "I'd think so, yeah."

"We're here," Duke said, pulling into a parking spot. "Let's go find out."

Chapter 4

Blaine Chappell rocked his son in his arms, a feeling of pure contentment flowing through him. He leaned down and touched his lips to the baby's forehead, gratitude filling him for the blessings of the last twenty-four hours.

Beside him, the baby in Tam's arms fussed. He looked over to his daughter, who had been a complete surprise to him. The doctors had said she'd be a boy, and Tam had looked at him blankly when the nurse had asked what her name was.

He'd known instantly, though, and he'd said, "Caroline. Her name will be Caroline Shirley Chappell."

The little girl was definitely more work than her brother already, and the twins were only one day old. Caroline cried more. She took longer to nurse but didn't eat as much. She'd hardly slept last night at all, which meant Blaine and Tam hadn't slept either.

Right now, Tam looked at him with wide eyes that asked questions he didn't know the answer to. He got to his feet and handed her their son, saying, "Here you go, Georgie. You go see momma for a minute. I need to have a word with your sister."

He took Caroline from Tam and bundled her tightly in the pink blanket his mother had rushed right out to buy last night when she'd learned the supposed-to-be-a-baby-boy was really a girl. "There you go, sissy. No crying now."

"You can feed her," Tam said. "Maybe then she'll behave when your family comes."

"Knock, knock," a man said, and Blaine turned toward the familiar sound of Duke's voice. Spur and Cayden had already been to visit, and Blaine had sworn them to secrecy about Caroline.

"Is everything—?" Duke cut off the rest of the question and stopped in the doorway, his eyes sliding down to the pink bundle in Blaine's arms.

"Don't stop in the doorway," Lisa said crossly. "There are more of us coming, Duke."

Duke moved out of the way, a smile growing on his face. "You had a girl."

"This is why you wouldn't text me what you'd named the boys," Lisa said, advancing quickly toward Blaine. "Can I have her?"

"She's a diva," Blaine said, passing the white-blonde-haired baby to Lisa.

"She has so much hair." Lisa sounded like she'd seen the most wonderful thing in the world. She combed her fingers through the wispy hair and grinned at Tam. "How are you?"

Blaine left the two of them to chat as he embraced his brothers. "Thanks for coming." His emotions surged, and he did his best to swallow them down.

"A dad to two babies," Conrad said, plenty of warmth in his voice. "How are you feeling?"

"Honestly?" Blaine asked, keeping his voice low. "I'm afraid to go home. Here, I know if something happens, someone will know what to do." He ducked his chin. "I certainly don't know what to do with them when they cry."

"Just think about what makes you cry," Ian said. "And fix it for them. You'll be fine." He stepped away from Blaine, who was still reeling from what he'd said. "Can I have this one? What did you name him?"

"George," Tam said. "And that's Caroline."

"George is such a good, strong name," Ian said, and Blaine turned to face the bed where his wife lay. All he had to do was make the babies comfortable and they wouldn't cry. Food, warmth, naps. He could do that, couldn't he?

He'd spent the last nine months trying to make sure Tam was as comfortable as possible, and he could do the same for these two little humans that had come into his life.

"Who's got Jane and Jasper?" Conrad asked. "I could bring them to the corner house." He sounded hopeful, and Blaine grinned at him.

"Would you? They're just at home. Cora came to stay with them last night, but I'm pretty sure she has some wedding stuff to get done."

"I'll text her," Conrad said, pulling out his phone. "They can stay with me and Ian until you guys are ready to have them back."

"Thanks." Blaine did love Tam's corgis, but they definitely preferred her. He had no idea how the dogs would react to having two little babies in their space, but they were generally well-mannered canines. He'd spent so long worrying about things that he couldn't control, and he usually found he shouldn't have spent so much time and energy on them at all.

He cleared his mind. The corgis would be fine with the babies. The kids would love those silly dogs, just the way he and Tam did.

Caroline started to fuss a little, and Lisa shushed her and bounced her as she danced around.

"You can feed her," Blaine said, reaching for the bottle sitting in the plastic bassinet where the baby lay if someone wasn't holding her. She'd hardly been in it, as there was always someone willing to hold her.

Lisa took the bottle and settled down with the infant in the rocking chair Blaine had been in earlier. She seemed perfectly at-ease with the baby, and Blaine cast a glance at Duke, who stood over next to the counter and Conrad. Ian held George, and his face held a glow that Blaine hadn't seen very often on his brother's face. At least since his marriage had ended.

Blaine knew keenly how Ian felt, and he grinned at his brother, hoping that Ian's heart had started to heal. That process took time, and Ian sure had taken a lot of that, but

Blaine wasn't going to rush him.

He also wasn't the brother who asked questions about relationships, marriages, or babies, so he just crammed himself into the small space beside Conrad and Duke and listened to them talk about life on the ranch.

"When's Mom comin'?" Duke asked in a break in their conversation.

"She was here last night and this morning," Blaine said, glancing at him. "I suspect she'll be back. She said something about smuggling in fried chicken for dinner." He grinned at them, but only Duke smiled back.

"So we'll be gone," he said, and it was obviously not for Blaine.

"You just need to go talk to Mom," Blaine said, looking back at Lisa, who'd tamed and calmed Caroline enough to put her to sleep. He should've taken a video of it so he could rewatch how she'd done it.

"I don't want to talk to Mom," Conrad said.

"She'll never come to you," Duke said.

"As you've told me a bunch of times," Conrad said dryly.

Blaine agreed with Duke; he'd had some issues with their mother too, and while she'd felt badly about it, Blaine had been the one to approach her. Conrad would have to do the same if he wanted things to change.

He lifted his phone. "She wants me to come for my birthday."

Duke peered at the device. "That's a text from Daddy."

"That invite comes from Mom, though," Blaine said.

"Whatever." Duke stepped away. "I want a couple of

minutes with George," he said to Ian. "You go tell Conrad he has to go to dinner with Mom and Daddy for his birthday."

Ian passed over the baby boy, and he faced Conrad and Blaine. "Are you going to go? You could take—"

"No," Conrad yelled, which made Blaine blink rapidly a few times. "I'm only going if *you'll* come with me." He glared at Ian, and those two had always been close. Blaine had given up trying to know all the secrets between the eight of them.

"Mom will make those honeyed carrots I love," Ian said. "And chocolate cake. Of course I'm in." He grinned like that would annoy Conrad, which of course, it did.

Blaine looked at his wife and noticed how tired she was. "I'd take a cake right now. Maybe I'll ask Mom to bring us some food."

"Don't think your fridge isn't already full," Conrad said. "If I know Mom, and I do, that's where she's been all day. Your house, making freezer meals."

"You better start praying they're not freezer meals," Ian said. "Even hers aren't good." He sucked in a breath. "Don't you dare tell her I said that."

Conrad started to chuckle, and Blaine joined in. His mother was a good cook, but even he didn't think some things should be frozen and reheated later. As if on cue, though, his phone chimed, and Mom said, *I put a couple of meals in your fridge for when you and Tam come home. How are the babies?*

Chapter 5

Ryanne closed the filing cabinet where she'd just stowed her last invoice. She strongly disliked this administrative side of Andy and Ryan, and she missed her sister the most when she had to work in the office at the back of the boutique.

Having a retail space in a strip mall hardly counted as a boutique, but Ry was sticking with the term anyway.

She left the office and went next door to it, to a room she'd deemed her sewing studio. Here, she got to design. Here, the sun shone and birds chirped. Here, Ry felt at home.

She didn't hand-make every piece of clothing in the boutique. Such a feat would be impossible for a single person. But she did create each piece from the recesses of her own mind, and she made detailed instructions for how to replicate the designs so her seamstresses could do it.

Running her fingers along a bolt of shiny, black spandex,

Ry's pulse finally started to calm. Beyond the back of the store, the sales floor at the front of the space called to her. She liked interacting with the customers and talking to them about what they liked and didn't like.

Max, her assistant, was already out there though, and Ry had promised not to come out and procrastinate her work here in the sewing studio. She left the spandex and wandered down the wall of fabric. Most people put books in shelves like these, but she'd filled them with bolts of cloth.

She just needed to find the right one for the tunic she'd been envisioning for a while now. If she started on it this month, she could get the fabrics ordered and have it sent to the sewing floor by August, and they could introduce the tunic as part of their spring line next year.

Ry had learned in design school that garments needed lead time. She couldn't come up with the spring line in February and start selling it in March or April. She needed a good nine months to get things done, as she couldn't do everything herself. Working with big companies for fabric, notions, and construction required precise timing and planning.

Ry opened her sketch book, wishing she was clairvoyant. It was hard to predict color and pattern trends that would be popular in almost a year, but she'd seen some mustard and some sage coming out of the bigger design houses recently.

Mustard felt like an autumnal color, and she had an adorable fit-and-flare dress coming in a color she'd deemed *marigold* for the fall line.

"Designs are in for the July subscribers," Max said, and Ry looked up from her sketches.

"What do you think of doing a blouse bar for our spring line?"

"Only tops?"

This wasn't the first time Ry had mentioned such a concept, so of course Max would be able to continue the conversation where they'd left it previously. Ry thanked her lucky stars that she'd met the curvy blonde a decade ago, because she'd been an invaluable resource for Ry, and her very best friend.

"We could do some T-shirt style dresses," Ry said, flipping a couple of pages. "Baby doll stuff."

"Have you thought any more about expanding your line to include plus-sizes?" Max entered the room, the thick, three-inch binder in her hands. "You need to approve the style shots for the July subscribers, so Joel can get them on the website."

"Okay." Ry put down her sketch book and looked at the binder as Max slid it in front of her. A sticky note sat in the corner that read *Call Hyrum!*

"Who's Hyrum?"

Max plucked the note off the plastic sheet and stuffed it in her skirt pocket. "Just some man."

"Mm hm." Ry looked at Max, who wore innocence in those baby blues. She had more dates than anyone Ry knew, which had worked in both of their favors when they'd been in college. In the past five years, though, Ry had stopped doubling with Max and whoever she was seeing that week.

"So he's not The One," Ry said, focusing next on the patterned black-and-white skirt she was offering to her monthly subscribers. "This is fantastic. Did we get Franco again?" She could tell the photography belonged to Franco Monserrat. He had a particular style, and the way the legs angled in this picture showed maximum skirt while maintaining the femininity of the garment.

"He's the best, isn't he?" Max asked. "And no, Hyrum's not The One. But I met a new man, a cowboy named Jerry Jones, and I don't want any comments about the name."

"No, of course not," Ry said, checking next to the skirt. "I know so many Jerry's under the age of eighty, so that's a totally normal name."

"Stop it," Max said, bumping Ry with her hip. They laughed together, and Ry checked off all the fashion shots for the website.

"I've got a date with a man named Yarn too," Max said. "So I expect tons of teasing about that as well."

"Yarn?" Ry looked at her to see if she was kidding. She sure didn't seem to be. Her phone rang, and since she did so much business with the device, she checked it instantly.

"Conrad Chappell," Max said, her voice sing-songing. "Ten to one."

It *was* Conrad, and heat shot through Ry. "I should answer, right?"

"You kissed the man at his brother's wedding." Max closed the binder and pulled out her own phone. "I told you to answer him last night when he called the first time."

She swiped on the call and turned her back on Max. "Hey," she said.

"Ryanne Moon lives," he said, plenty of surprise in his voice.

She cocked one hip and rolled her eyes. "Okay," she said. "Of course I'm alive." She'd told him she'd be busy. She'd texted him last night that she had a call with a supplier out of Hawaii, and they were five hours behind Kentucky.

"Do you work every evening?" he asked. "You never said."

"Yeah," she said, pressing her eyes closed. "I fell asleep in the middle of texting you."

He chuckled, but the sound didn't seem particularly happy. "Wow, that's not exactly what a man wants to hear."

She cracked a smile, feeling the walls around her heart start to break down as well. The kiss had helped with that too, but she'd quickly rebuilt those barriers the moment she'd left the Chappell's ranch. "Yesterday was a long day."

"I understand that," he said. "Is today long? I could stop by with dinner."

Ry took a moment to think through what it would be like to have someone at home, waiting with hot food and a friendly smile when she got there. Someone to get the laundry washed, dried, and folded. Someone to pay the bills and get the groceries.

In truth, it wasn't all the tasks of life Ry wanted help with. It was the loneliness.

Conrad could help you with that, she thought, but she wouldn't let that come out of her mouth.

What she said was, "We need some rules, Mister Chappell."

"Rules?" he repeated. "For what?"

"Don't think because I let you kiss me at that wedding that you're going to get to do that every time you see me."

"No, ma'am," he said quickly. "I wouldn't dream of kissing you again. In fact, I haven't even thought about it once."

She giggled at the teasing tone of his voice. "I don't work every evening."

"Are you working tomorrow night?" he asked, and something rushed through the speaker. Perhaps it was the wind, and she reminded herself of how different the two of them were. She didn't particularly enjoy the outdoors, and he practically lived in them.

The idea to design a men's line nagged at her, but Ry was already drowning in Andy and Ryan as it was. They needed athleisure. They needed plus-sizes. They needed a men's line. There was so much more expansion to happen, but Ry could only take one step at a time.

"No, sir," she said. "But I don't want to go out," she added quickly. "I just want something quiet and intimate."

"I can do quiet and intimate," he said, his voice low and nearly hoarse. "But it's a little unfair to make a no-kissing rule and then say that."

Ry laughed again. "I'm sure you can handle it."

"I guess we'll see," he said. "Is six too early?"

"No," she said. "It'll help me get out of here on time."

"Great," he said. "Send me your address, and I'll be there at six tomorrow with dinner."

"Great," she agreed, and the call ended. She sighed at the same time Max said, "You made dinner plans with him."

Ry jumped, having forgotten that Max had entered the sewing studio. Thoughts of Conrad could scatter her mind so easily, and she hated that.

"You don't have to sound so surprised." She shoved her phone back in her pocket.

Max tucked her long, blonde hair behind her ear. "You haven't been out with anyone since Andy died."

Ry sucked in a breath. "I know." That had nothing to do with Andy, but neither of them said that.

"Do you?" Max stepped in front of Ry and put her hands on her shoulders. "Stop for a second, honey. Just stop."

Ry searched Max's face, seeing the surprise and vulnerability in her eyes. Max had been a very, very good friend. She hadn't left Ry's side for longer than ten minutes after Andy's death, and she'd only done that to shower.

"Who is this man?"

Ry sighed and took Max into a hug. "Remember that boy I told you about that night we were playing Truth or Dare?"

"Honey, I was hopped up on Starburst. I have no idea what we talked about that night."

"Conrad Chappell," she said. "The boy in high school who took me to our prom. Kissed me. Made me think I'd be a cowboy's wife one day. Then left for the summer?"

"That's him?" Max pulled back, her eyes wide.

"That's him," Ry said. "I ran into him a while ago." She turned away from her best friend. "I should cancel. I have tons of work to do here, and I can just drive through somewhere on the way home so I don't have to cook."

"Ryanne," Max said, and Ry lifted her head. They rarely used their full names with one another. Max really drawled hers out too, making it three syllables instead of two, turning it feminine instead of masculine.

"Maxine," she said back, a hint of sarcasm in the second half of the word.

Max cocked her hip. "If you like him, go out with him."

"Of course I like him," Ry said. "I kissed him, didn't I?"

"Mm, I think you let him kiss you." Max picked up the binder and started for the door. "This time, Ry—tonight —*you* try kissing *him*. Then see if you're worried about him breaking your heart." She walked out before Ry could respond. She didn't have anything to say anyway.

She also wouldn't be kissing Conrad that night. She'd just told him he couldn't do that every time they got together, and that was a very good rule worth keeping.

She needed others too, because she wanted to get to know the man Conrad Chappell was now, not exist with memories of who he'd been fifteen years ago.

"Oh, did you get that flyer I put on your desk?" Max asked, poking her head back into the room. "The one about your fifteen-year class reunion? I promised Jerry I'd make sure you got it, and I want to report to him that I did my duty when we go out tonight."

Jerry Jones...

"Wait a second," Ry said, marching toward Max. "You're going out with *Jerry Jones* tonight?"

Max's smile filled her whole face. "That's right, honey. And I want to kiss him, so I need to know if you saw that flyer about your reunion."

"I saw it," Ry said. "In high school, *Jerry* went by *Jerome.*"

"I guess he's a little more casual now." Max gave her a quick quirk of her lips and ducked back into the hallway. "And he's oh-so-good-looking. Probably just like your Conrad Chappell. Give him a chance, Ry."

Ry reached the door and watched Max return to her desk. She put the binder next to several others and tapped on her computer while Ry tried to figure out if she should give Conrad the second chance he'd asked for or if she should cancel for the next evening.

Chapter 6

Lights flashed on Conrad's phone the moment he was awake enough to see them. It was hard to get up before the sun in June, but he and his brothers sometimes still managed it. Today, he hadn't, though. Dusty light came through the blinds, and he sat up and stretched his back while reaching for his phone.

"If this is Ry canceling on me..." He didn't finish the sentence to himself, because what could he say? He'd go over there and demand she see him? He'd take her dinner anyway?

She hadn't sent her address after their call, and that alone had been enough to make him ignore Ian and sit on the tiny couch on the landing with a fantasy novel in front of his face. He hadn't read it, but if Conrad was good at anything, it was pretending.

He could also heat up anything from the frozen food section of the grocery store, make anything into a sandwich, and brew the best coffee on the ranch. If Ian didn't get a full thermos of that by six-thirty a.m., everyone he came in contact with that day would know about it.

So Conrad discarded his phone without looking at the texts and headed toward the shower instead. "You guys go on downstairs and see if Ian will let you out."

The corgis continued to lay on the bed, both of them looking at him without moving their heads.

"All right," he said. After he showered and got dressed, he pocketed his phone unseen and went to make the coffee. He found Ian in the kitchen frying eggs, and he got busy filling the filter with grounds and adding water to the machine.

Once that was done, he opened the sliding glass door and let Jane and Jasper, Tam and Blaine's dogs, out into the back yard. He stood at the glass and watched them, feeling the weight of his phone in his back pocket intensify by the second.

The scent of sausage and eggs made his stomach grumble. He ignored the buzz in his pocket and instead called out the door for Jasper to come back. He liked to wander, but Conrad would never forgive himself if something happened to the dog on his watch.

"Breakfast," Ian said, studying his phone. "Is your phone dead?" He glanced up. "Cayden's in a tizzy about using Lamborghini in the Summer Smash."

"I thought we weren't going to enter a horse from Bluegrass." Conrad stayed by the door as the corgis hopped up the steps to the porch and trotted inside.

"Now he wants to. Apparently, he's sent you a bunch of texts, and you haven't responded."

"Not yet," Conrad said, as if he'd read his brother's texts and had just chosen not to answer. "I don't see how we can have Lambo ready for the Smash. He can barely pick up his gait." Sometimes the horse still didn't make the switch, and while Conrad wouldn't ride him in a real race, the last time he'd been in the saddle, Lambo had been way too far from the rail.

"He doesn't have a jockey or anything." Conrad sat down at the table just as Ian slid three eggs onto his plate. "Isn't Trey running Perfect Strike in the Smash?"

"He is, yes," Ian said, putting the sausage links on the table and sitting too. "But Trey doesn't enter on behalf of Bluegrass."

"We can just host," Conrad said. "If Cay wants us to enter every year, he should give us enough time to train a horse properly. We can't put up a subpar horse, not as a training facility running a race where the horses are sold."

The idea made him cringe and his heart thrum in a weird way. He set his phone on the table and swiped it on. Cayden had texted several times, and Conrad read through those quickly. He tapped out a response that wasn't too happy about the idea of having a horse race-ready in only six or seven weeks.

He had two texts from Ry, and one was her address, and it had come in last night. This morning, she'd said she might have to cancel, but she'd keep him updated. A sigh filled him, and he checked the timestamp. That message had come in only a few minutes ago, while he'd been standing at the sliding glass door.

Anything I can do to help? he sent to Ry, when really his throat had tightened to the point that he couldn't swallow.

He looked at Ian, who didn't seem to care who Conrad was texting. He wanted to ask his brother for advice, but Ian wouldn't give it anyway. He never talked about women, and Conrad knew he didn't trust himself to know what to do about women. His ex-wife hadn't loved him, and he hadn't seen it.

Conrad hadn't either, and he'd liked Minnie.

I'm sewing today, Ry said. *Sometimes I get lost behind the machine.*

Conrad smiled, imagining the beautiful redhead behind a sewing machine, the hours slipping by. *I could stop by the store*, he offered. *Bring dinner there.*

That's a great idea, she said. *Let's plan on that instead.*

Conrad smiled, because at least he'd get to see her.

"Date tonight?" Ian asked, and Conrad quickly flipped over his phone, as if he'd been caught sending naughty things by his mother.

"Yes, yeah," he said. "I just hope she doesn't cancel." He got up and poured a cup of coffee. He took it to the table, and then returned to the pot to pour one for himself.

"You think she will?"

"I think...I think I make her very nervous," Conrad admitted. "She makes me nervous too, like I did something wrong, but I don't know what, and I have to make up for it."

Ian frowned at him. "What could you have done to upset her?"

"I think I hurt her when we were teenagers," he said. "She said something about how she left our New Year's Eve party early, because she didn't want to watch me kiss someone else."

"Huh." Ian furrowed his brow. "Did you date her?"

"I took her to the prom," Conrad said as he sat across from Ian again. "We kissed a couple of times." He shrugged. "I don't know. I guess she thought it was more serious than I did." The moment the words left his mouth, he realized what he'd said.

He met Ian's eyes. "She thought it was more serious than I did," he said in tandem with his brother. Conrad groaned and ran his hand through his hair. "What if she thinks that's what I'm doing again? That I'm not serious?"

"I mean..." Ian shrugged. "Up until now, you haven't been."

"*She* doesn't know that, though." Conrad felt a new kind of desperation he didn't know how to deal with. "I *am* serious about her. I can't think about anything or anyone else. It takes me forever to fall asleep at night. I couldn't even check my phone, because I'm terrified it'll be her, canceling on me."

His chest heaved, and he regretted every word that had just come out of his mouth. He jumped to his feet, though he hadn't eaten more than three bites of breakfast.

"Forget it. I have to get to work."

"Con," Ian said after him, but Conrad reached for his cowboy hat and stuffed it on his head.

"Come on, guys," he said to the dogs, and the trio went out the door despite Ian calling his name again.

* * *

"That's a good boy." Conrad ran the brush down the horse's flank, the rhythmic motion soothing him. He'd taken a ride on his personal horse immediately following breakfast, and that had helped too. He couldn't take back what he'd said to his brother, and Ian wouldn't tell anyone.

Humiliation doused him again, and he leaned his head against Powerplay's long nose. Bluegrass and the Chappells didn't own this horse, but Glenn Marks Stables had bought him for three quarters of a million dollars at the spring fling auction.

His father had won the Belmont Stakes and the Derby, and his mother had won the Derby just last year. Powerplay didn't have an official name yet, not one he'd race under, but he had the long-legged look of a racehorse that had been born and bred to run.

"Sir?"

He turned at the sound of a woman's voice, and Anita Powell's face changed from confusion to relief and then disdain. "Conrad," she said. "You're not allowed in here."

Conrad looked around. "I'm not 'in' anywhere." The road went right past the Marks Stables, and he'd been walking by when Powerplay had nickered at him. Conrad always carried a few butterscotch candies in his pocket, and this horse had brains to match his long legs.

"Step away from the horse, please," Anita said, folding her arms. She wore a long-sleeved button-down shirt in dark blue, and she must be sweltering hot in that thing at this time in the afternoon. If she was, Conrad couldn't tell.

"Sorry," he said, dropping his hands from Powerplay's face and stepping away from the horse.

"You haven't been loitering here in the afternoons, have you?" she asked, cocking one eyebrow so high, it disappeared under her cowgirl hat. Her stained blonde hair spilled over her shoulders today, while she sometimes wore it in braids or a ponytail that came out the back of her hat near the nape of her neck.

"No," Conrad said quickly. "Just walkin' by today, that's all."

"Mm hm." She didn't trust him at all. "Because I've seen one of you Chappells loitering."

"There's a lot of us," Conrad said quickly. "I'm hardly ever over this way. I'm just over here today, because I had to talk to Cayden." Why he was even still here explaining himself to her, he didn't know. She didn't own Glenn Marks Stables. She was just an hourly trainer, and he doubted she had the authority to touch Powerplay.

She said nothing, and Conrad backed up a few more steps, the weight of her glare too heavy for him. "Anyway... see you."

"Mm hm," she said again, and Conrad got out of there. His phone rang as he strode away, and he swiped on the call from Ginny, thinking Cayden had asked her to call him and sweeten him up about the Summer Smash.

"Howdy, Ginny," he said.

"You've got some mail here," she said, her voice chipper. "It looks like an invitation or something."

"You can open it," he said. "I'm about five minutes from the homestead."

"I'm ripping it open right now," she said, a loud rip coming through the line. "It's an invitation to your fifteen-year high school reunion."

"Blergh," Conrad said. "You can toss that."

"You don't want to see it? It looks fun," Ginny said. "I can't believe you've only been out of high school for fifteen years. My goodness, I'm *old*."

Conrad picked up his pace. He didn't want to cause any trauma for Ginny, and he knew that she and Cayden had been trying to adopt. Their case worker had said their age might make a difference. A birth mom had chosen their profile a few months ago, and as far as Conrad knew, things were still going well there.

"Let me guess: it has balloons on it."

"It does," Ginny said. "How did you know that?"

"Because my class president was Nicola Snowson, and that girl loved balloons."

Ginny giggled and said, "I'll toss it, but I do have million dollar bars if you want one of those."

"I'm sixty seconds out." Conrad laughed and hung up, and less than sixty seconds later, he joined Ginny in the kitchen at the homestead. A whole tray of million dollar bars sat on the counter. The dining room table held neatly stacked rows of baby clothes, and Conrad smiled at them. They were shades of orange, blue, green, and white; no pink, purple, or mauve in any capacity.

"Are those for Boone?" he asked, indicating a pair of pajamas striped like a tiger.

"Yes." Ginny grinned at the clothes and sighed. "Only a few more weeks now. I swear time is moving backward."

"Feels like that sometimes, doesn't it?" Conrad faced her, and she held up the invitation to the reunion. Teal and magenta balloons screamed at him with foil, and he smiled. "You didn't throw it away." He took it from her and read the details quickly. "Things like this make it feel like time is racing forward, flowing through my fingers, and I can't stop it."

"I know that feeling," Ginny said, glancing away.

Conrad wished once again that he hadn't said anything. Perhaps he should cancel on Ry tonight. With the way this day was going, his mouth was going to ruin his second chance before he even got it.

"Will you go?" Ginny asked.

Conrad looked away from the balloons and the posh country club address where the event would be held, and focused on Ginny. "Would you go?"

"If I had a reason," she said with a smile. "I would." Her phone rang, distracting her, and she picked it up. "It's my mother. Excuse me." She answered the phone as she went into the living room, and Conrad heard her say, "I'll come get you, Mother. Or should I call the ambulance?"

Conrad swung her way, hearing the front door close a moment later. He hurried after her, but by the time he made it to the front porch, Ginny was behind the wheel of her SUV, backing up. He stood there and watched her talk into her phone as she turned and then drove away.

Feeling helpless, he went back inside the homestead. He packed up a couple of million dollar bars and headed back to the house in the corner of the ranch to get ready for his own trip to town.

A couple of hours later, he pulled up to the boutique, the million dollar bars on the seat next to him, as well as a bag of chicken sandwiches and coleslaw from Kentucky Kings, one of his favorite chicken restaurants in Dreamsville. He hoped Ry would like it too, and he collected everything and headed for the entrance.

The boutique stayed open until eight o'clock that night, and he wasn't expecting to see Ry on the floor. She'd told him to just go through the door behind the register, but he'd only taken a couple of steps when he saw her off to the left, standing with another woman.

Her eyes met his, and he immediately saw the plea in hers. He changed strides as she smiled and nodded. "...I just don't know if I'll have time to go, that's all," she said as he approached.

The other woman turned toward him, and Conrad stopped short. He recognized her, and "Annette," came out of his mouth.

"Conrad Chappell," Annette Lansing said, and she giggled like he was her high school boyfriend. She leapt at him, and he almost dropped the food he'd brought for Ry. She laughed like a hyena and stepped back. "You'll come to the reunion, won't you? You got your invite, right?"

He looked at Ry, who shook her head quite violently.

Annette spun back to her, and she plastered a smile on her face. "You don't have to have a significant other to come. It's just a party."

"She has a significant other," Conrad blurted out, drawing Annette's attention back to him. Her dark green eyes glittered with curiosity, and Conrad knew he shouldn't, that his mouth had already gotten him into trouble today.

But he still said, "Ry and I are dating, and of course we're going to be at the reunion together."

Chapter 7

Ry blinked her long lashes, feeling them get stuck to one another. She wanted to grab Conrad by the arm and drag him away from the floral skirts and into her office. Then she'd demand to know what in the name of all that was holy he'd been thinking.

She kept her smile on her face as Annette Lansing said, "Oh." She turned back to Ry, her eyelids fluttering like hummingbird wings too. "Why didn't you just say that?"

"I...well, you were just saying you hoped Conrad would be there, as there were so many single ladies in our class who'd like to reconnect with him, and..." She let her voice trail off, because Annette *had* indicated that she'd like to "meet up" with Conrad and find out what he was up to.

Annette's face flushed, and heat dove through Ry too. This conversation needed to end. Never mind that she'd been fielding calls and texts from her friends about the reunion all day long. It seemed like the entire town of

Dreamsville and Lexington had been papered with that blasted invitation Max had given her last night.

"I've got dinner, baby," Conrad said, laying on the drawl and the honey real thick. "Are we done here?"

"Yes," Ry said, flashing a smile in Annette's direction. She'd just embarrassed her, and regret lanced through her. "Sorry, Annette," she mumbled.

"It's fine," the other woman trilled out. "I'm just glad y'all will be there."

Ry turned away from her, sliding right into Conrad's side as he met her in the aisle. "She's lasering me with her eyes right now. I'm going to be ashes by the time we get to the doorway."

"Just keep walking," Conrad said, his hand landing on Ry's hip and shooting fireworks through her bloodstream. "I've got you, honey." He even bent his head down, and Ry caught sight of his smile.

They did make it through the doorway, and every muscle in Ry's body sagged. "We made it." She led the way into the sewing studio, because there was more room and bigger tables in there.

Conrad sighed as he set the paper bags of food on the nearest one. "My sister-in-law made these million dollar bars. The chicken is from Kings."

"I love Kings," Ry said, and so much joy filled her as she beamed up at Conrad. "Thank you, Conrad." She too hugged him, and she hoped it didn't come across as her throwing herself at him the way Annette had.

She held him tightly around his shoulders while his

hands landed on her waist. She took a deep breath of his cologne, committing the woodsy, clean, almost water-like elements of it to her memory, and then she stepped back. She cleared her throat and turned toward the bag of food.

"Did, uh, Annette really say she wanted to reconnect with me?" he asked.

"She really did," Ry said, a giggle starting in the back of her throat as she set the first fried chicken sandwich on the table. "She was going on about Josie, and Lindsey, and oh did you know, Shelley Burns is back in town? She's recently divorced, and she is single-looking-to-mingle."

She looked up and into Conrad's face, finding his smile so handsome and so kind. "Are we, uh, really dating?"

He removed the coleslaw from the bag. "This is a date."

"This is a meal in my sewing room, because I don't know when to quit," Ry corrected.

Conrad paused, his eyes hooking into hers as hard as Annette's laser-eyes had been firing at her. "It's a date, Ry. I've asked you out several times. We've eaten at restaurants before." He faced her fully, and he looked so strong and so confident in that blue and white plaid shirt, those jeans, and that sexy, leather cowboy belt with a blinged-out buckle.

"Listen, I know you think I'm going to screw this up again. You think I'm not serious about us, but you're wrong." He didn't touch her, and Ry found she wished he would. She reached up and ran one fingertip down the front of his shirt, bumping along the buttons.

"You looked me up online, right?" she asked, not quite sure why this was what they were talking about.

"Just for a few seconds," he said.

"Okay," she said, drawing the word out into one with Southern syllables. "I might have looked through your social media feed for longer than a few seconds today, and it seems like...it seems like you've had a lot of girlfriends over the years." She hadn't come right out and said that he couldn't commit to a woman, but the words vibrated right there between what she had said.

"I can't deny that," he said. "Because I wasn't serious about any of them. You're not them, Ry."

"Do you really want to go to the reunion with me?" Ry asked.

"Do you want to go?" he asked.

"You know, it would really help me out," she said, sighing as she sank into her chair. "I've got all my friends on my back, telling me I have to move on. I've got Annette Lansing coming into my store to badger me about it. Even my mother asked if I was going to go and see if I could reconnect with someone from high school so I can get married and start a family." She rolled her eyes and couldn't meet Conrad's.

"Then let's go," he said, unwrapping a chicken sandwich.

Ry nodded, more teeming beneath her tongue. "Look, I'm just going to say this, so it's out."

Conrad's gaze landed on the side of her face, but Ry couldn't look at him. "Go on."

"I wouldn't say you're my boyfriend," she said. "Yet. We just started to date, and—ahem—the kiss was a fluke thing at a wedding, and I wouldn't necessarily say we're exclusive yet. Unless you want to be, and then okay, I'm fine with that. I'm not seeing anyone else, and no one's asking or anything..."

She trailed off, mostly because she'd run out of breath. She stuffed her mouth full of chicken so she wouldn't say anything else idiotic.

Conrad cleared his throat, and she caught the tail end of him ducking his head and lifting his sandwich to his lips. "How long does it take for a man to become your boyfriend?"

She quickly swallowed and reached for her soda. "Depends," she said. "On how often we see each other."

"Let's say this man in question sees you every day from now until the reunion. Then would you introduce him around to all your classmates as your boyfriend?"

"The reunion is just over a month away, so I would say yes, if I saw this man every day for over a month, and he brought me all my favorite foods, and flowers, and maybe held my hand, and let me pat his two cute little dogs, then yes, that cowboy—uh, man—would be my boyfriend." Ry had spoken so much she'd run out of breath *again*. She needed to pull back and give one or two word answers.

"What would your favorite foods be?" he asked.

"I like the pig tails from Cowboy Kitchen," she said. "Extra pulled pork, with the regular barbecue sauce." She smiled at him and reached for her soda again. "I *love* the chile verde breakfast burrito from Mama Ruth's. I drive through The Gray Leaf every morning, because they have this amazing earl grey tea."

"Slow down. A man can't type so fast with just his thumbs."

Ry laughed, but Conrad kept typing furiously. He finally looked up. "Do you work Sundays? What if this man wanted to take you to the Guitar Festival in Louisville in a couple of weeks? That sounds very boyfriend-ly, doesn't it?"

"A Sunday trip to Louisville?" Ry teased. "That's *very* boyfriend-ly. I'm not sure I can answer that right now. I think this man should take it one day at a time." Ry *had* to live her life one day at a time. She couldn't commit to a date in a couple of weeks. Her warehouse could burn down the night before, or she could suddenly get a hundred orders she couldn't fill.

She once again wondered if starting something with Conrad was as wise as it sounded in her head. In the quiet moments of her life, when her phone stayed silent, and she wasn't focused on anything to do with Andy and Ryan, having Conrad as a boyfriend sounded like pure bliss.

But Ry wasn't seventeen anymore, and she had real responsibilities and real people depending on her. Sometimes the weight of what Andy and Ryan did and was could smash the oxygen from her lungs.

Somehow, she kept breathing, and she even glanced at Conrad to find his brows furrowed. "What?" she asked as she picked up a French fry. Her phone went off, and she glanced at it. "My word," she said just from the quick notification that flashed at the top of the screen. "Even my brother is asking about the reunion."

She swiped on her phone to read the whole text.

Just heard about your 15-year reunion. Are you going to go?

Mom put you up to this, didn't she? Ry asked him.

No, Tyler said.

How else do you know about this? You live in Atlanta.

I heard from Baylor, Tyler said. *His sister is excited about it, and he asked me if you'd be there. He's single again, you know...*

Ry stared at the last part of his message. "He has to be kidding," she whispered to herself.

"Who?" Conrad asked.

Before she could answer him, Ry got another message from Wendall. He'd been messaging her about "getting out there" again. Her chest caught, because she'd told him that Conrad was just a friend, and Wendell had apparently been too busy instructing his servers to see the kiss at the wedding a few days ago.

Ry had declined to tell him much, other than Conrad needed to talk to her. The conversation had lasted less than five minutes, and her ability to serve expensive food to fancy guests hadn't been compromised, though her knees had been quite weak after that kiss.

"My brother," she said, turning the phone toward Conrad. "Even he's telling me to go to the reunion. Everyone and their mother's colt is pestering me right now."

Conrad barely glanced at the phone. "Who else is badgering you?"

"Remember Winifred Halson? We used to be pretty good friends."

"Sure, the Halson's have one of the better hay farms."

Of course he would know the family's involvement in the ranching industry. He probably had to buy hay from time to time.

"She's one of the few people I reconnected with when I returned from Savannah. She's already planning our outfits for the reunion. She wasn't thrilled when I said I might not go." Ry sighed and finished her chicken sandwich. "I'm pretty sure she's the one who sicced Annette on me tonight."

She silenced her phone and turned it over. "I'm tired of everyone telling me what to do."

"What do they tell you?"

"That Andy's been dead for five years now, as if I don't know how long it's been. That five years is a long time, and I can move on. She won't be upset with me for living my own life." She sighed and leaned back in her chair, feeling more and more distant from Conrad—from everyone—as she expressed her frustrations.

"I'm doing just fine. There's nothing I hate more than people asking me how I'm doing." She leaned forward again and put her elbows on the table.

"Noted," he said. "I will not ask you how you're doing. I will not tell you what you should do. I will bring earl grey tea in the mornings and chile verde burritos for lunch. We're not kissing every time we're together, but we are dating and we're going to go to the reunion together."

He met her eyes. "Do I have it right so far?"

"About," she said, her voice rusty.

He reached across the table and covered one of her hands with his. "What about this? Holding hands? Is that allowed?" He slowly slid his under hers and put his fingers in the spaces between hers. "This? Because I have to admit, I kinda like this."

He gave her one of those sly, sexy grins, and Ry had zero defenses for that. "This is okay," she said, her traitorous fingers tightening in his. Squeezing, as if telling him that she thought holding his hand was far better than okay, which of course, it was.

"You're smooth with the ladies, aren't you?"

Conrad ducked his head. "I don't try to be," he said.

Ry took a deep breath, her brain feeling addled, especially when she asked, "What does a cowboy's Monday about lunchtime look like?"

"Let's see, on Mondays, we take naps in the hayloft during lunchtime," he said, his wit quick and sharp. He grinned at her. "But I could be convinced to forgo the nap in favor of a good turkey sandwich or two."

Chapter 8

Conrad couldn't help checking the clock on his phone every ten minutes. The numbers seemed to move slower and slower the closer to lunchtime it got, and when he dang near got knocked down by a group of trainers leaving the track, he shoved his phone in his pocket and focused on the task at hand: walking.

It felt hard at the moment, and not only because Ry hadn't texted to say when she'd be at the ranch for lunch. His guilt stung at his lungs, and he quickly navigated off the path so others could get by him while he texted.

Instead of doing that, though, he called Ry.

"Hey," she said breathlessly after the first ring. "I'm on my way, I swear."

"You shouldn't come," he said, hating the words as they left his mouth. The scent of something roasted met his nose, and he turned toward the grandstands. There was a restaurant inside, and they were open every day for lunch and dinner in the summertime. He could eat there, get a dose of air conditioning, and get back to work with Lamborghini, the horse he'd been working with for the past several weeks.

The horse had a delicate schedule, as he seemed to know he could win millions one day. He liked to sleep late, eat a casual breakfast in his private pasture, and only get to work once Conrad forced him onto the track in the afternoon. They'd run easy yesterday, which had followed another fairly light training day. So today, Conrad would be running the horse, and running him hard.

It was time to see what Lambo could do, and if he'd remember all of the things he'd been taught about corners, rails, and his stride. Conrad has his doubts, because the jet black horse seemed to be a particularly ADHD type of toddler-equine. That was why Conrad had him in the first place. Ian couldn't handle the horses that forgot their lessons, and he was much better suited for the more serious equine personalities, like the blue roan he had on his rotation right now. Stars For Eyes was a great horse, and Conrad had no doubt she'd pull in some wins in her career. Even Trey had his eye on her, and he'd said he and Beth could enter the horse in the Sweetheart Classic next year.

"Why shouldn't I come?" Ry asked, and Conrad blinked into the clear, blue Kentucky sky. "I've already got the sandwiches ordered."

He sighed. "I just feel bad. You're so busy, and the last thing you need to be doin' is ordering me a sandwich and then driving it all the way out here."

"I'm a big girl, Conrad. I'll do what I want."

He turned away from the dirt track, though the mere sight of it usually calmed him. "Okay," he said, plenty of doubt in his voice. Duke and Lawrence had a little office in one of the row houses, and Ian and Conrad had a corner of one of the barns where they kept their training notes, schedules, breeding papers, and other things. It wasn't exactly conducive to lunching with a gorgeous woman. For one, it had no air conditioning and for two, no table.

"Do you want to come to my house?" he asked.

"I thought you said there would be a hayloft involved," Ry said, her voice set on teasing. "I even wore my khaki shorts today, expecting to get a little dirty."

His eyebrows went up. "You thought...we'd be rolling in the hay?"

She sucked in a breath. "No," shot across the line. "No, of course not."

"I think that goes against your no-kissing rule," he said, hoping his tone came across as teasing and flirtatious too.

"Your house is fine," she said, not wasting any time now. "Where do you live?"

"On the ranch," he said. "Way back in the northeast corner." He continued to tell her how to get there, and he started the walk himself. Sometimes he drove his truck over, and he'd even been known to pull one of Spur's tricks and ride a horse. His eldest brother did that more than anything, but Conrad felt like he spent enough time in the saddle some days. Walking rejuvenated him, and when he felt like singing along with the radio, he drove.

"I'll see you in a bit," she said. "I swear I'll be leaving in less than fifteen minutes."

Conrad simply agreed with her and let her hang up. The sun beat down on him, and he enjoyed the heat and sound of silence surrounding him. Only his footsteps could be heard on this lonely stretch of road, with all the activity from the ranch, the horses, and the trainers behind him.

Sweat ran down his face by the time he crested the front steps and arrived on the porch. He was just reaching for the doorknob when the front door burst open. "...mind your own business, Ian," a woman yelled, brushing right by Conrad as if she didn't see him there.

His eyes landed on Anita Powell for half a heartbeat, but she kept right on going. Surprise darted through Conrad as he turned to watch her fly down the steps and across the front lawn. She got on an ATV he hadn't seen, and the growl of the engine filled the country silence with even more tension.

As she swung the vehicle around, one final glare toward the house, Ian stepped beside Conrad. "She's an impossible woman."

"What was that about?" Conrad asked, still watching Anita as she drove away. The quiet returned to the world, and Conrad looked at his brother.

Ian shifted his feet, his face definitely turning a shade redder than normal. "She thinks I'm interferin' in the training of their stupid yearling." He rolled his eyes and went back inside.

Conrad's pulse tapped out a few additional beats. "Are you?"

"Of course I'm not," Ian said. "It's Glenn Marks. Why would I even look at his horse?" He threw Conrad a death glare too. "What are you doin' here? You never come home for lunch."

Instant worry cut through Conrad. "Uh, Ry's bringing sandwiches." He pulled out his phone. "I'll tell her you're here too." Somewhere in the back of his mind, he heard her say she'd already ordered the food, but he started to swipe anyway.

"I already ate," Ian said. "Don't worry about it." He picked up his cowboy hat from the table and put it back on his head. "Have fun on your lunch date."

"It's not a date," Conrad said automatically, removing his hat with one hand as his phone dropped to his side in the other. Ian brushed by him too, and Conrad got the distinct feeling there was more going on than he knew.

He watched Ian leave through the side door that went into the garage, and Conrad sighed as he hung his hat on the hook beside that door. Could there be something going on with Anita Powell? She probably just pushed all the wrong buttons for Ian.

Conrad had felt a little attacked by her yesterday too, so he understood that. He moved over to the fridge and opened it, bending down to stick his face right into the coolest part of it. A sigh moved through his body, and he took out a big bottle of water.

Ian was right; Conrad rarely came home for lunch. He

hardly knew what to do with himself, but he knew he was thirsty. So he guzzled the water on the way to the couch, where he collapsed with a sigh and a groan.

He recapped the bottle and closed his eyes.

The next thing he knew, he was being startled awake by loud knocking and someone calling, "Conrad? Are you still here?"

His adrenaline pumping—he never *actually* took a nap on Mondays during lunchtime—he jumped to his feet. He hurried to the front door and nearly pulled it off its track when he opened it.

"Stupid," Ry muttered to herself. "You're so—late." She looked up on the last word, those pretty brown eyes wide and filled with anxiety. "I'm so sorry." She held up a white plastic sack. "I brought turkey sandwiches."

"Are you going to stay to eat?" he asked, taking the bag from her. It sure seemed like she'd just drop the food and go. He stepped back out of the doorway. "C'mon in."

She edged past him, and then he went through the living room toward the dining room table. "Water or anything?" he asked, not really sure what the "anything" would be. He could make coffee, he supposed.

"Water's great," she said.

He went by her, feeling like they'd entered junior high all over again and needed to perform a delicate dance around the opposite sex. After collecting water bottles for both of them, he joined her at the table.

"Sorry I didn't text," she said, unpacking the sandwiches.

He noted there were four, so Ian could've stayed easily. "I kinda fell asleep," he admitted. "So I wouldn't have seen it anyway."

Their eyes met, and a smile curved Ry's face. "You fell asleep?" She started to laugh, and the sound of it infused so much joy into Conrad's soul. It had been a very long time since he'd wanted to impress a woman.

"Why's that so funny?" he asked. She plagued him, and he hadn't been sleeping well.

"I guess I thought the naptime comment was a joke," she said, still grinning at him.

"It was," he said. "I sat down on the couch, though, and that's a game-changer." He unwrapped his sandwich, the scent of fresh lettuce and turkey hitting him in the nose. His mouth watered, and he took a big bite. A groan pulled through his stomach, and he couldn't have stopped it even if he'd wanted to.

"Aren't you training Lamborghini this afternoon?" she asked, and she took a much smaller bite than he had.

He nodded while he finished chewing and swallowing. "Yeah, later. After lunch." He glanced around for his phone. "What time is it?"

"Almost two," she said, that panic re-entering her eyes.

It streamed through him too. "Two? Like two o'clock?"

"Yes." She smiled again. "I'm sorry I was late. I honestly didn't think you'd even be here still. I thought your text silence meant you were angry."

He got to his feet to double-check the time on the microwave. It read one-fifty-seven. His stomach clenched, and he shoved another huge bite of food into his mouth while he pivoted toward the couch in the living room.

His half-empty bottle of water sat there, with his phone wedged between the armrest and the couch cushion. He retrieved it, unsurprised to find the lights flashing. He'd missed texts and a call, most of them from Ian, but one from Spur.

Just text them, he thought. *It's fine.*

Their schedule around Bluegrass wasn't etched in stone. Besides the covering, which had already been done for the year, Duke monitored the pregnancies and paying the stud-fee bills, balancing his notebooks, and setting things up for the fall sale.

I'm going to need another... He paused, trying to decide how long of a lunch he could take. He'd already slept on the couch for over an hour. *Forty minutes*, he tacked onto his text and sent it. *Sorry. Ry just got here.*

Ry? Spur texted immediately. The phone rang in the next moment, and Conrad rolled his eyes.

"I can go," Ry said behind him, and he spun toward her as he swiped on Spur's call.

"No," he said to her. He lifted the phone to his mouth. "I'm with people."

"Who's Ry?" Spur asked anyway. "It better not be that fertilizer sales guy. I told him no, Conrad, and that's final."

"It's not a fertilizer sales guy," Conrad said, smiling at Ry. "It's a personal lunch. Can I have my forty minutes or not?"

Spur stayed silent for a minute, then blurted, "Personal?" as if he had no idea what the word meant.

"I'll be saddling Lambo in forty minutes," he promised, and he hung up before Spur could say anything else.

He returned to the table, noting that Ian had simply texted in, *Fine*, and looked at Ry. "I have about thirty minutes to eat."

She nodded, those eyes still round as the moon that hung in the sky. "I'm sorry," she said again. "It took so long to get out of the store today."

Conrad didn't tell her that he'd have to work late to make up for the nap and the delayed start to the training. It wouldn't help her guilt, and it didn't matter anyway. The sun wouldn't set for hours.

"It's fine," he drawled instead. "What are you working on right now?"

Ry's face lit up, and Conrad sure did like that. She wore very little makeup today, and he liked the freshness of her face. She always wore something unique and beautifully sewn, and today was no different. Besides the khaki shorts, she wore a blouse that looked like a butterfly garden. Greens, blues, purples, and pinks splashed across her torso and chest, with a frilly little sleeve that barely capped her shoulders.

"I've decided to do a blouse bar for my spring collection," she said, obviously excited about this prospect. "Max and I are also talking about expanding into athleisure and plus-sizes."

"Sounds amazing," he said, and he meant it. They'd texted about her education at SCAD, a design college in

Savannah. He'd told her about the horses he trained, and she'd recently been asking him one-liner questions about himself during their nightly text-chats.

"Do you like to hike?" he asked her.

Her face scrunched up. "The outdoors don't really please me," she said.

Conrad burst out laughing, because he couldn't imagine being cooped up inside all day.

"Do you?" she asked.

"Yeah, sure," he said. "Don't worry, though. I won't take you on a hiking date." He finished his sandwich and reached for his bottle of water.

"Favorite late-night snack?" she asked.

"Ranch veggie straws," he said without thinking too hard about it.

Surprise entered her eyes, and he could just picture her lounging in bed, reading his answer on her phone and being just as shocked. His eyes drifted down to her mouth, and all he could think about then was kissing her.

"Interesting," that mouth said, and wow, he wanted to touch his lips there. "The no-kissing rule is still in effect."

That got him to pull his eyes back to hers. "Why is that?" he asked, slipping into that smooth persona who always knew exactly what to say. He watched as Ry shuttered herself off, and he hated the voice he'd used.

"I mean, I just told you about my embarrassing addiction to veggie straws. You know I like turkey sandwiches." His stupid mouth was getting him in trouble again. "You know I only own jeans, and my favorite color is blue. Heck, you know I'd like to go to Spain over England, and that I've been to eight US states."

He crumpled up his sandwich wrapper. "I know you're smart and talented. I know you love silk and trying to get it to do things no one else has succeeded with. I know you miss your sister, but you're doing fine. I know you hate people asking you how you are. I know you're a hot mess when it comes to baking—your words, not mine. I'd need personal proof of the baking disasters before I'll believe it. I know your driver's license is near suspension because you like to speed."

He tried to take the bite out of his voice, especially when she leaned away from him. He sighed. "I'm just saying. We talk every day, even if it is through a text. We know stuff about each other. Kissing is you know, natural. It's the natural next step."

He cleaned up their garbage and took it into the kitchen. "It's okay. I'm not going to rush you. I'm not even asking to kiss you. *You* brought it up."

"You were staring at my mouth."

"It's a pretty mouth."

"I hate your one-liners," she said, her chair scraping as she stood too. "You're almost too smooth. I feel like you might be playing me."

Conrad shook his head and kept his eyes down. Their breakfast dishes sat in the sink, and while his normal life rule was to do dishes once a day—and it wasn't at two o'clock in the afternoon—he opened the dishwasher and started loading in the plates and mugs he and Ian had dirtied that morning.

"I'm not playing you," he said, his voice barely reaching above the clatter of the ceramic. "I explained this already." With that done, he faced her. "I don't know how else to say it."

If he could kiss her, surely she'd *feel* how he felt about her.

"I just...because of some things that have happened in the past..." Ry stepped closer to him, and Conrad turned off the sink. She pressed in close to him, taking one of his hands in both of hers.

He couldn't back up, because the dishwasher was still open, and he'd trip. He kept his head down though, his mouth already doing too much damage as it was.

"I need to go slow," she whispered. "I want to know you; the *real* you. The Conrad Chappell who's thirty-three years old, not the one I thought I knew at seventeen."

"I'm thirty-four," he murmured. "My birthday was in April."

"See? I didn't even know that," she said, her voice half-playful and half-kind.

He chanced a glance at her. "When's your birthday?"

"September," she said. "I'll be thirty-four then too."

"What happened in the past?" he asked.

Fear filled her eyes and then blipped away in the next moment. "It's far too long of a story to tell right now," she said. "Your forty minutes are almost up." She actually tilted her head back, and all he'd have to do was move six inches to kiss her. Surely she knew that and was tempting him, teasing him, and driving him mad.

He wasn't going to break her rule, though. If she wanted to kiss him, she'd have to do exactly that: Kiss him.

He wasn't going to kiss her.

He brushed his lips along her temple, thinking, *Not on the mouth. You won't kiss her on the mouth*, and twisted to close the dishwasher. "You're right. I better go."

Ry moved away from him, and Conrad wondered what a man had to do to get in her good graces. He wondered what had happened that had caused her to think she needed to move so slowly.

It's not slow, he told himself. He'd run into her—literally—at the family-style soup restaurant only six or seven weeks ago. They hadn't been able to get together much for the first few weeks, but he'd seen her every day since the wedding.

"Tomorrow," he said, his mind firing. "I'll bring you tea. What time do you usually go into the store?"

"Nine or so," she said, her voice quiet. "You don't need to bring me tea, though. It's so far out of your way."

"Nine or so," he repeated. "Okay. Can I walk you out?" He indicated for her to go in front of him, which she did. He went with her all the way across the porch and down the steps to her car. "Thanks for lunch, Ry. That sure was fun."

He dared to slip one arm along her waist and pull her into his body. She hugged him back, and then he put the proper distance between them, watching her. She seemed tense now, and something flashed in her eyes he didn't like. Something that told him he might need to go slower than he thought he had been. Something that made his stomach tighten and his lungs constrict.

Ry erased the emotion quickly and got in her car, saying, "See you soon."

He just nodded and waved while she backed out of the driveway. Then he went back inside to get his cowboy hat, because he'd need it to dodge the questions from his brothers that afternoon.

Chapter 9

Ian Chappell refused to walk down the main road leading through Bluegrass's boarding stables. The last thing he needed was another confrontation with Anita Powell.

Scruffy ran through his mind, and his hand went quickly to his face. No, he hadn't shaved in a couple of days. He also wasn't "scruffy" because of it. His hair *was* on the long side, and he'd actually considered cutting it after Nita's comment.

"She needs to lighten up," he muttered to himself, glancing down the road and toward the Glenn Marks Stables row. She worked with the horses there, and Ian could admit Nita was beautiful. He had no problem working with women. He just didn't want them in other areas—the more private areas—of his life.

Determined not to shave for another week, Ian turned away from the stables without seeing Nita. That was just fine by him. He didn't need a woman to keep him company. He didn't need the pressure of trying to keep her happy. Already, the tension inside of Conrad was enough for Ian to sense, and he'd only started to really see Ryanne Moon a week or so ago, at Lawrence's wedding.

Brother number six that was now married. So much had changed in the past couple of years, and Ian felt like he was still stuck in time from a decade ago. He never aged, he only felt older. He never moved, the world just spun around him. He never progressed, he just kept doing the same thing day after day.

It wasn't a terrible life, but he had a feeling it wasn't the happiest one either.

Conrad had been spending a little bit of time every day with Ryanne, which was fine with Ian. It was. Somewhere in the back of his mind, about the time Trey had announced he and Beth were actually married, he'd known that Conrad would advance from the bachelor life sooner or later.

He'd simply been hoping it would be later.

His phone rang out the special ringtone for his mother, and Ian's mood darkened in an instant. He couldn't ignore the call, though, so he determined to get it over with as quickly as possible. Spur's plea to all the brothers to go make things right with their mother echoed through his mind as he said, "Hey, Ma."

She hated being called *Ma*, and he regretted doing it the moment the word left his mouth. He thought of Ginny, and how she was always so formal with her mother. She even called her Mother, and though they didn't get along, her mom had been having a few health problems here and there, and guess who'd been there for her?

Ginny.

Ian could learn a lot from that, and he employed his patience and determined to be on his best behavior during the call.

"Your daddy wants to talk about Stars For Eyes," Mom said. "Do you have time to come to dinner tonight?"

"Sure," Ian said, already ready to hit the sack. He'd been going back to the corner house in the middle of the day lately, just to get out of the heat and get away from everyone. "Daddy can call me himself, you know."

"You know how he is," Mom said with a sigh. "He thinks if he just wants you to come, you'll just show up. As if you can read his mind or something."

Ian grinned, because Daddy was a little bit like that. "All right. Six-thirty?" His mother had been serving dinner at six-thirty for the past fifty years, and she saw no good reason to change now.

"Yes," Mom said. "You can bring a friend, or—"

"Who would I bring, Mom?" Ian barked into the phone, forgetting entirely the example of Ginny. "Conrad? He's about my only friend these days."

"That's not true," Mom argued, as if she knew anything about Ian's life at all. "You've got all those trainers you work with. Spur's your friend. Duke. Any of your brothers."

"If you want someone else to come, Mom, invite them," Ian said. "I'm not going to."

"Fine," she huffed.

"Fine," he said back. "I'll be there at six-thirty." He'd have to be in off the ranch by five-forty-five to shower, as Mom wouldn't tolerate a horsey-smelling man showing up for dinner. Not at her table.

He hung up and shoved his phone in his back pocket, realizing how fast he'd started walking. He forced himself to move slower and reduce the tension in his muscles. He had been divorced for a while now, and while he didn't want to start dating anytime soon—or ever again—he could admit that his life would be really lonely once Conrad got married and moved out of the corner house.

The sound of yelling drew his attention, and he jogged forward as the anger in the voice registered in his mind. He knew that voice...

Around the corner, he found Nita Powell faced off with two other trainers. They all had clenched fists, and one of them—a man named Judd Rake—said, "You have *no* idea what you're doing with that horse, and I'm going to tell the boss." He took a menacing step forward.

"I know ten times what you do," Nita said, her voice just as powerful as Judd's. "Tell Glenn whatever you want. He knows what I can do." She didn't move a single inch as Judd took another step.

"Hey," Ian barked, actually afraid the man might take a swing at the much smaller woman in front of him. He arrived on the scene, his chest heaving and the scent of moldy straw thick in the air. "What's goin' on here?"

"Nothing," Anita said, but she did shrink behind him slightly. "Judd here was just cleaning out a stall." She glared at him with the power of gravity, and Ian thought he'd actually be withered if she'd looked at him like that. She *had* looked at him like that, and he had wilted on the spot.

Anita wasn't one to be trifled with, that was for sure.

"It's your stall," the man said gruffly, stepping past Ian. He knocked his shoulder into him, and Ian's fury roared. "You clean it out."

"I am *not* cleaning it," Nita called after him, but Judd kept right on going.

Ian looked back to the other man. "Rafe?" he asked.

"She's not our boss," he said, and he too started to leave. At least he didn't ram into Ian in some macho show of masculinity. The tension decreased, at least for Ian. When he looked at Nita, she still had her hands cinched tightly and lasers shooting from her eyes.

"What happened?" he asked.

"Look at that straw," she said as a demand more than anything. "Would you put that straw in your horse's stable?" She indicated the straw on the ground. It looked like it had been thrown or spilled in a somewhat violent manner. "It's moldy, and we paid three quarters of a million dollars for this horse. He doesn't lay in moldy straw."

Disgusted, she picked up the pitchfork leaning against the stable wall and started cleaning it up.

"So you said something to them," Ian said, looking around for a wheelbarrow. One stood down at the end of the row, and he went to get it.

"Of course I did," Nita said. "Just because I don't own

the stables doesn't mean I want anything but the best for our animals."

Ian parked the wheelbarrow where she could pitch the straw into it, and he started helping her clear it all out of the stall too. He hesitated to say something to her, but in the end, he decided he should. "You know, sawdust is better than this."

"Glenn wants straw for now," Nita said. "He said Powerplay doesn't get sawdust until he learns to stop gnawing on his bandages."

Ian smiled, because he could appreciate tough equine love. He had to give it all the time to the horses he worked with. "Smart."

"Whatever," Nita said, so much sarcasm in her voice that it punched Ian in the gut.

"I didn't do anything to you, you know," he said.

"You literally just stuck your nose in my business again," she said, straightening and challenging him with a cocked eyebrow.

Dang, she was beautiful. All that white-blonde hair spilling over her shoulders and under that cowgirl hat. The muscles in her arms and shoulders. The fire in those blue eyes...a man could get burned by that blue fire.

Ian knew. He'd been charred, crisped, and left for dead by a woman with blue, fiery eyes.

"He looked like he was going to hit you," Ian said, pausing in his work too.

"I don't need your help," she said. "In fact, they *already* think I'm weak and stupid because I'm a woman. You showing up like some caped diffuser just proved them right."

"I did not," he said, confused about "caped diffuser." Was that some reference to him being a superhero? The idea of that was purely laughable. "I asked a question. You handled it fine."

"That's right," she snapped at him. "I *did* handle it fine. I don't need you to fight my battles."

"I wasn't," Ian said. "Just like I wasn't interfering with your training last week either, Nita. I said he needed work picking up his cross, which he does. That's it."

"I already knew that."

"I know you knew it!" Ian said, instantly regretting raising his voice. This woman drove him to the brink of insanity, that was for dang sure. He drew in a deep breath. "It was mere conversation between trainers. Nothing more. It wasn't a commentary on you, your methods, or what you should do that you weren't. Nothing."

He'd tried to explain all of this last week when she'd ambushed him in his own home. When Nita got going, though...watch out. She could talk and talk, and he hadn't been able to mount his defense very well.

Nita said nothing now, and they finished cleaning out the stall and restocking it with proper straw. He didn't need to be doing this at all, but she didn't tell him to leave.

"Thank you," she said, and it sounded like it took great effort for her to get the words out. She looked up at him, the moment between them suddenly like his favorite piece of steak. Tender and warm. She ducked her head and tucked her hair, and Ian had no idea what was happening.

"You're welcome," he said, his statement almost a question. Then, because it was so dang hot, and she was so super pretty, he added, "Have you had lunch? I was just on my way home to get something to eat."

Chapter 10

Anita Powell could only stare at Ian Chappell. Lunch? At his place? With him?

His phone rang, and he practically dove into his pocket to get it. "Hey, Con," he said, turning his back and walking away. "What? No, that's not right."

He glanced over his shoulder and lifted one hand in a wave, and Nita did the same thing. Now she didn't have to answer his invitation to lunch. She wasn't even sure that was what he'd done, as she hadn't been asked out in quite a while.

"There's no way he asked you out," she muttered to herself. She got the rotten straw put in the bin where it belonged, wheeled the barrow back to the supply room, and went to retrieve Powerplay from the holding stall where Judd had put him.

The blue roan wasn't very happy to have been there so long, but Nita wanted to tell him to join the club. She should've been done with her work here at Bluegrass, and now she'd have to head to her job at the Parks Department without going home to shower first.

She told herself she didn't need to shower to move from one outdoor, horse-related job to another outdoor, grass-related job. She'd end up just as sweaty, just as dirty, and just as annoyed as she was right now, no shower needed.

Nita reminded herself she needed the money, and she wouldn't have to work two jobs forever. She just needed to get out from under this slight bubble of debt, keep her focus on her savings account for her own training stable, and make things happen.

She was a good trainer. She was, and she repeated that fact to herself as she stalked away from the Glenn Marks Stables and toward her beat-up pick-up truck.

Anita had always been overlooked in the horse training industry. She'd *wanted* it that way in the beginning, so she could make her own name in her own way. Now, though, she wanted to scream from the rooftops of this blasted ranch that she was as good as anyone else there, including the men and women who'd trained champions.

"This year," she told herself as she turned onto the highway and started back toward Dreamsville. Her phone rang before she'd gone a mile, and she was surprised Glenn had waited that long to get a call off.

Rather, it was *Judd* who'd showed some sort of restraint in tattling on her to their boss. She pulled to the side of the road, because her conscience didn't allow her to talk on the phone while she drove. She'd be distracted, and then she'd miss her turn. Nita knew her strengths and weaknesses and having a stressful conversation didn't mix well with navigating for her.

"Hey, Glenn," she said.

He sighed, which she'd expected. "I wish you wouldn't call me by my first name," he said. "You have to be alone by now. Probably on the way to the Parks Department."

Nita didn't confirm or deny what he'd said, which in and of itself was a confirmation.

Glenn sighed again. "Judd said there was some trouble with Powerplay."

"No," Nita practically spit out, quickly reminding herself that she didn't need to get riled up again. The situation was over. "There was no trouble with Powerplay... Dad." She cleared her throat, as if that word had suddenly hooked her flesh together inside her mouth. "The trouble is with Judd, as always. He doesn't respect me, and he doesn't listen to me, and he was trying to put moldy straw in the stall."

Her father said nothing, and Nita told herself to remain silent too. If Judd hadn't found out that Nita was Glenn's daughter, there wouldn't be any trouble at all, and they'd have cleaned up the moldy straw and done up the stall together, the way she had with Ian.

She lost a few seconds thinking about the handsome Chappell, only able to remind herself of his extreme saltiness just before she lost herself to those deep, nearly black eyes. He held secrets in those orbs, and Nita had never wanted to know more about a person than she did Ian Chappell.

She'd heard rumors, obviously. There was nowhere faster that rumors ran than small towns and ranches. She was entrenched in both, and she knew he'd been married and divorced. Years had passed though, and all of the details were really murky. She wondered what he knew about her, and the thought made her stomach tighten considerably.

"I'll talk to Judd," Glenn said.

"Don't do that." Nita sighed. Everyone thought talking helped, but in Nita's experience, it didn't. "He doesn't like me; it's fine."

"I didn't know he was standing outside my office."

"I know." She really didn't want to have this conversation again. Judd had overheard her father on the phone with her mother and his ex-wife. They'd been talking about her, obviously, and it was the first time anyone at Glenn Marks Stables knew that Anita was actually Glenn's daughter.

"I would've thought he'd respect you *more* once he knew who you really were, sugarbaby," he drawled. "Not less."

"He's just jealous," Nita said, suddenly feeling so tired. Perhaps she could call off on mowing the lawns at the town parks today. She immediately rejected the idea, because what would she do instead? Go home and feel sorry for herself?

"How long you gonna work at the Parks Department?" Glenn asked.

"Just through the summer," she said, though they'd had this conversation too. "Then, I'll be ready to buy a stable of my own."

"I saw the email with the logo," he said, a hint of pride creeping into his voice. "I thought it looked real good, Nita."

"Thanks," she said, looking out the window at the blue, blue sky. It calmed her for some reason, and the very next image in her head became Ian. "Do you think...?" She couldn't even say the words.

"Do I think what?" Glenn prompted.

"Do you think they'd respect me more if I was a man?" she whispered. "Or had a boyfriend, maybe?"

Her dad stayed quiet again, which meant he was thinking hard about what she'd said. "I don't know, sugarbaby," he said. "I want to say no, of course not. You're who you are, and you're an amazing woman and an amazing trainer. It doesn't matter what your gender is."

She nodded, because she believed that too. She wanted to, at least.

She couldn't help wondering if she got one of the really good horse trainers to go out with her, she'd find less resistance to her presence in the stables. Reaching up, she fingered her bleached hair, feeling how fried the ends were. If she fixed those, maybe she could get someone to ask her out.

She never wore anything but cowgirl boots or steel-toed boots, and she supposed she could switch out her usual boots for something cute—like ankle boots. Other women wore those. She could put some makeup on—and not the kind with sunscreen in it.

In the back of her closet somewhere, she had a little black dress just waiting for her to go on a dinner date. Right now, she only met up with her microwave every evening, and usually for only three to five minutes.

Then she remembered the last boyfriend she'd had, and her desire to go out with anyone, ever again, vanished.

"I have to get going," she said, and Glenn said, "Yep. Love you, sugarbaby. I'm sorry about Judd."

"It's fine," Nita said. "I can handle Judd."

"Let me know if you can't."

"I will." She said good-bye and hung up the phone before easing back onto the highway. She didn't drive nearly as fast now, because the horrible, almost-snapping tension in her body had fled. *She* wasn't the one who'd called her father, though she also wasn't the one who'd done anything wrong.

Twenty minutes later, she pulled into the parking lot at the Parks Department, and she took her phone from her cup holder. She'd signed up for a dating app several months ago, at her sister's insistence, but she'd only ever logged in again once. She did so now, and a flood of notifications streamed at her.

Overwhelmed, she quickly closed the app and sighed. She didn't want to meet a man online.

"You don't want a man at all." She said the words, but there was no power behind them. Deep down, she did want someone to share her life with. She just wanted to run into someone at work or in the grocery store, have a spark of attraction, tuck her hair, and exchange a shy, interested glance.

She thought of her exchange with Ian from only a half-hour ago. She touched her hair, her mind whirring. Had she done that when she'd thanked him? She had—holy horses, she *had*.

She made the same motion now, her chest coiling and releasing as her breathing increased.

She'd looked at the ground.

She'd spoken softly.

She'd exchanged a glance with him.

A shy, interested glance?

She couldn't think about this right now. Her second job waited, and even if she somehow came to the conclusion that she was interested in Ian Chappell, there was no way he'd be interested in her.

Then why did he ask you to lunch at his house? The thought barreled through her head like a runaway freight train coming closer, growing and gathering and growling at her until she couldn't think about anything but Ian's invitation to lunch.

Chapter 11

Ry stirred the now-warm caramel into the popcorn, the nerves in her hands snapping and jumping the way the kernels had in the microwave. "Is this a good idea?"

She'd once had a brown bulldog named Bells, but she'd had to rehome him when she'd taken on both sides of Andy and Ryan. It wasn't fair to the animal for her to work fifteen hours a day and then be miserable when she did make it home.

Because she didn't have Bells, no one answered her question. At least the bulldog would growl or bark when her voice pitched up, and he always knew when she needed an answer.

She finished the caramel popcorn and poured it out of the bowl and onto the parchment paper. The whole house smelled like salt and sugar now, and at least she had that going for her. She'd been pulling out her most unique garments in the past two weeks, because she knew she'd be seeing Conrad at some point during the day.

He'd brought her tea twice now in the morning, and he'd stopped by with lunch a couple of times. Most often, she found him parked in the lot beside her when she finally left the boutique. He'd be on his phone or asleep with his head back against the rest, just waiting to take her to dinner or drive around town with her for a few minutes.

He wasn't giving up, that much was certain, and Ry had invited him to her house for dinner, a movie, and snacks. It felt like a huge leap in the relationship for her, like she'd decided to enter the long jump in the eleventh hour and hadn't prepped properly.

"It makes no sense to be nervous," she told herself. She'd been out with him plenty of times now. They'd argued a little bit even. She'd been getting to know him more and more with every plaid shirt she saw. He had them in blue, navy, azure, robin's egg, slate, and cobalt.

He loved bright colors, and he owned polos in yellow, butter, and canary. She found herself wondering what he'd have covering his torso when she left the house each morning, and then when she'd get to see it.

Tonight, she wore a black denim dress where she'd added pleats to the neckline and made the skirt much fuller. She'd bought the garment and glitzed it up a little bit by sewing in bright, floral panels that lightened the load on her shoulders and added personality.

She never wore shoes around the house, but she'd reconsidered that tonight. In the end, she'd decided to stay barefoot, but as the doorbell pealed, she panicked and flew down the hall toward her master suite.

The rack in her closet overflowed with shoes, but she suddenly didn't have a single pair that would work with this dress. Perhaps she should change real quick. Her heart raced forward and then back, clogging her throat and making her choke.

The doorbell rang again, and that propelled her out of the closet. "Coming!" she called, striding out of the bedroom again and commanding herself to calm the heck down. She slowed her step as she returned to the living room, and she was practically crawling when she reached the door.

Knocking sounded on the wood, and she jumped away from the sound. "Ry?" Conrad called.

She steadied her hand and opened the door. "Sorry." The word exploded from her mouth as if she'd been holding it in all day. "I was back in the bedroom."

Conrad stood there and gave her a look that told her how beautiful she was without saying a single thing. The shimmery quality of his gaze made her feel skinny and sexy, when she rarely felt that way.

"I thought you weren't going to start every one of our conversations with some form of apology," he said. He lifted the flowers he carried almost like a peace offering for calling her on saying sorry before hello.

She did have a tendency to lead with apologies, because she was always late. When he'd told her he'd been waiting in the parking lot for over an hour, her guilt had nearly gutted her. He didn't just have time to waste. He had things to do at the ranch and around his house. He didn't need to be waiting for her in parking lots.

He didn't need to bring her lunch, tea, or flowers.

He wants to, she told herself, even if the concept of that still made her furrow her brow as if she was trying to solve a complex calculus problem.

"They're just roses, Ry," he said, giving the blooms a little shake.

She took them and said, "Thank you." She bent down and inhaled the scent of the deep, rich, red roses, and her pulse finally settled into her chest properly. When she looked up, his smile accelerated her pulse right back to speeding, but she reminded herself that he couldn't see her cardiogram.

"C'mon in," she said. "You sure look nice tonight." He wore a plaid shirt in orange and white, with pinstripe black stripes along the boxes. "What color is that?"

"I think I decided on sunset," he said with a grin that told her he had actually been thinking about a modification of orange. They'd laughed together over the weekend as she'd gone over the many different names for colors like blue and yellow, and yes, orange.

He looked down at his shirt. "It looks a little bit like the goldeny-orange you see in the sunset." He met her eyes, a clear question in his eyes. "What do you think?"

"I think it's fantastic," she said, her voice trembling a little bit, the way a new puppy might when going for a car ride for the first time. "I hope you're ready to not be impressed. I picked up dinner, and the snack tonight comes from bags and bottles."

"It smells...tantalizing," he said, following her into the kitchen. His hand landed on her hip, burning straight through the denim there in a way that made her question her no-kissing rule. Perhaps tonight, she'd be breaking that rule.

"You are amazing." His tone reminded her of a slow, summer night. Deep, rich, full of delight. "I'm sure whatever you have will be wonderful."

She pulled herself back to the present. She wasn't outside with the magic of the fireflies, and she needed all of her wits about her to keep herself from turning right now and pressing her lips to Conrad's.

"It's just steak fajitas from Borrowed Barley." She looked up at him, hoping his handsomeness wouldn't blind her. "Don't get too excited."

"How do you feel about havin' that popcorn first?" he asked. His gaze hadn't left the parchment paper with all the sticky-sweet stuff, and Ry may have fallen in love with him all the way right then and there.

Pushing against that feeling, she stepped out of his arm and collected a couple of bowls from the cupboard. "I love having dessert first." She handed him one of them and then picked up a glob of the popcorn. "I've got a swing out back if you'd like to sit back there for a few minutes."

"Lead on, lady." He filled his bowl too, and then Ry went out onto her back deck. The swing only held two, and she sat down. She held perfectly still until he took the left side, and then she let him toe them back and forth. "How long have you been in this place?" he asked, popping a couple of kernels into his mouth.

"Four years," she said, her mind flying backward to moving day. It had been one of the worst days of her life, returning to Dreamsville, and not because she didn't want to be coming back to where she'd grown up. She hadn't wanted to leave Savannah, because it felt like she'd closed a door on the part of her life with Andy in it.

Her eyes moved to the shed in the back corner of the sprawling yard. "I chose this place, because it had the storage I needed to keep running Andy and Ryan."

"Ah." He nodded and kept them moving on the swing. They swayed back and forth, and Ry thought it was a pretty good way to describe the last five years of her life. She'd move forward a few feet, then get tugged backward into her grief. She'd claw her way out and make some strides with the clothing company, only to be sucked back into the realization that her sister would never see the storefront she'd opened a few weeks ago.

She filled her mouth with the caramel popcorn, wishing she could stuff the holes in her soul the same way.

"Are we going to talk about the past tonight?" he asked, the movement in the swing almost coming to a halt.

Ry drew in a long breath through her nose, her mouth still sticky with caramel. "I don't know," she said.

"I could look a few things up online."

Ry turned to look at him, horror racing through her with a sharp, stinging snap. "What?"

"You told me you had a long story about the past," he said. "You, Andy, Savannah, why you need to go slow. I thought tonight…" He lifted one shoulder into a shrug, which didn't really fit with the intensity in his expression. Those eyes could pull a woman beneath their surface and never let her go.

"My sister died in a car accident," Ry said.

"You could've moved onto your parents' property," he said, and it felt like he was pushing to her. "They have plenty of sheds and whatnot."

The caramel popcorn turned to cardboard in her mouth. "I couldn't have moved in with them." Her voice gave away too much—too much pain, too much history, too much vulnerability.

His gaze landed on the side of her face, heavy and like a drape over windows meant to keep out light. "Why not?"

Ry bent down and put her bowl of popcorn on the ground. She curled into his side, because she didn't want to look him in the face during this story. He dutifully lifted his arm and cradled her against his chest, and the moment should've been tender, sweet, and pure perfection. The tension riding beneath the surface, though, kept the smile from her face and the sigh submerged in her chest.

"My mother wishes I was the one who died in the car accident."

"Ryanne Moon," Conrad said, his Southern twang nearly gone. "That is *not* true. I'm sure that's not true."

"It's true." The squeaking of the swing could've drowned out her voice if she hadn't oiled it last week. "Not only that, but when Andy died, part of Momma did too. Part of me did. My life in Savannah did. I was engaged to someone, and that died. Everything just...died."

For a terrible, screaming moment, Ry existed back in the hospital where she'd been when she'd first been told Andy had passed away. Everything in her life hinged on that moment, and she'd had to figure out who she was all over again.

She drew another deep breath, her splintering insides stitching themselves back together with pure oxygen. "I've been taking one step at a time ever since. It's slow."

"I'm so sorry," he said. "Your fiancé couldn't move, or...?"

Ry didn't want to talk about her fiancé—she hadn't even thought that word for years now—and she knew inviting Conrad to her house for dinner and snacks had been a mistake. She slipped out from underneath his arm and stood. "I'll go check on the fajitas."

She made it into the house, the sound of his cowboy boots on the boards behind her. "Can you not talk about him?" he asked.

"I can," Ry said. "I just don't want to."

"Why not?"

She threw him a glance she hoped would cut through him like a serrated knife. Couldn't the man take a hint? She supposed he hadn't been particularly great at picking up her cues in the past, so she shouldn't be surprised he wasn't doing a great job tonight.

He didn't back down, but he did lift one palm up as if in surrender.

"How about you tell me something that's really hard for you to talk about?" She turned away from him, hoping her back would give him an idea of how she felt about this. The scent of beef met her nose as she opened the oven, and she breathed in the salty, spiciness of it.

"Some women have called me a player," he said. "I suppose for a long time, I was. I wasn't serious about women. I liked having a girlfriend, but I didn't want to make her my wife."

Ry put the food on the stovetop and faced him, her heart banging like one of those battery-powered monkeys with a bass drum.

"I'm not that man anymore," he said, the vein in his neck throbbing in tandem with her pulse.

"What changed for you?" she asked.

"I saw my brothers starting to meet good women—real good women—and fall in love with them. They have this best friend at their side all the time. They love each other; they trust each other; they confide in each other—all their hopes and dreams." Again with the indifferent shrug that didn't match the stoic look on his face or the shimmery quality of his gaze. "I want that."

"It does sound nice," she said, reaching for the door handle on the fridge to get out the sour cream and guacamole.

"Do you think you can do that?"

She paused, the fridge door between them like a shield.

"Never mind," he said. "It's fine." He turned and started for the back door again. He swept the cowboy hat off his head and hung it on the hat rack beside the door. She hadn't even realized she owned a hat rack until that moment.

You don't, a voice in her head said. *That was Andy's.*

Conrad turned to face her again. "I guess I just need to know if you think you can get to that point. If we can."

"What point?" She felt like she'd taken a step and cracked through the surface of the Earth. She was dropping down, spiraling down, hurtling down, and she couldn't stop herself.

"The point where we trust each other enough to confide in each other. The point where you can talk to me about your feelings about your sister and your ex-fiancé and your mother."

"I just told you about two of those." All three, if she wanted to be technical.

Conrad scoffed, the heat coming from his eyes now enough to warm the fajitas without an oven. "You did not."

"I did," she said.

"You literally walked away from the conversation when I asked you about him."

"You're pushing me into a corner I don't want to be in." The walls started closing around her, and Ry had the sudden urge to flee. *Get out. Get out now.*

"That's exactly what I'm saying, Ry. I want you to talk to me about things; you don't want to. So I'm asking you: Do you think we can get to that point, or should I just put my hat back on and head home?"

Chapter 12

Conrad wasn't sure why he'd picked this fight with Ry. At the same time, it felt like something important. Something he needed to know to keep trying so dang hard to be in her life.

He sure did like this woman, and if he were being really honest and he didn't have to tell anyone else, he'd started to fall in love with her. When something exciting happened on the ranch, Ry was the first one he wanted to tell. When he saw a cute cat meme on social media, he wanted to send it to her first. When he thought about going to talk to his mother, he first wanted to run everything by Ry to learn what he should change in his speech.

She couldn't even tell him about a man she'd been engaged to five years ago. Was she even over him? Was she even ready for a relationship like the type he wanted?

"His name was Tobias Marsh," Ry said. She spoke in a smooth, even tone that sounded nothing like the marble-like quality of her eyes. "And no, he couldn't relocate from Savannah. He taught interior design at the SCAD." She turned away from Conrad, who now felt like a jerk for making that flicker of hurt flash across her face. "Last I heard, he's married to someone else, and they have a couple of kids now."

Conrad wanted to ask her if she wanted kids, but his internal filter shrieked at him to *stay silent! For the love of all that's holy, do not ask her that!*

"Are you over him?" Conrad asked, and that was ten times worse than asking her if she wanted kids.

Her head flew up, the shock in her eyes enough to bowl a man backward. "Yes," she clipped out.

He nodded, feeling very much like he'd left his body somewhere on the side of the highway between the ranch and this rambler in a quiet part of Dreamsville.

"I'm not the same person I was in Savannah at all," she said, putting two plates on the counter. "I've had to rebuild one square at a time. New friends. New house. New job responsibilities." She sighed as if the weight of all jobs across the globe rested on her shoulders and her shoulders alone. She rounded the counter, stepping away from him and making the flowers in her skirt wave at him as they went over to a barstool.

She sure did love floral prints, and he rarely saw her without one somewhere on her body. That fact made him smile, and it felt like the very first natural smile he'd had in quite a long time.

"It's embarrassing," she said, shooting him that daggered

look again. "Losing everything and coming back to where you grew up."

"I never even left where I grew up," he said, stepping over to join her at the bar. They sat side-by-side, and Conrad took a moment to just breathe. He never did that, and it sure felt nice to do it in the silence of Ry's house, with her.

"I'm just trying to do right by Andy." Ry pulled the plate of tortillas closer. "Sometimes I feel like one giant failure."

Conrad looked at her, finding the anguish, the agony, and the hope. "You are not a failure," he said. "You are the opposite of that word. You have a storefront now. Weren't you bragging to me last week how your recurring subscribers had just topped two hundred?" He infused all his adoration for her into a single smile, and he hoped she could feel it beaming from his very person.

"That was called *celebrating*," she said, tapping him with her elbow. "Bragging. Jeez, you make me sound terrible."

He chuckled, the anxiety of the moment trickling away with every *ha* he uttered. He leaned his head down, his lips getting dangerously close to that tantalizing ear. "I want to celebrate with you too, Ry. Everything that happens on the ranch. Everything in my personal life." With his pulse everywhere in his body now, he touched his lips to the side of her neck. His body screamed with want, with desire, with joy that it wanted more of her. More, more, and more.

"I'm real serious about us." His mouth barely moved, hardly giving the words a chance to grow wings and fly. "Just so you know. I'm not the same person I was five years ago either, and I'm real serious about us."

She turned toward him, her mouth oh-so-dangerously close to his now. "Wife-and-family-serious about us?"

"Mm hm." He let his eyes drift closed, so he had to rely on his sense of touch and smell and hearing to experience her. If only he could taste her too...

"Good to know," she said, and she turned her head, the softness of her dark hair brushing against his nose.

"You're killing me quietly," he said, opening his eyes and reaching for a tortilla too. "I think you're enjoying it a little too much."

She grinned at him, and it was the kind that said *I-know-just-what-you're-talking-about-but-I'm-going-to-pretend-I-don't*.

Conrad could bide his time. Maybe five years ago, he wouldn't have had the patience for Ry's slow progress toward kissing him again. But now...with her...he could wait, because he knew the next time he kissed her would change his life.

* * *

"Hey, hey," Duke said the moment Conrad entered the homestead. "There he is." He looked over his shoulder. "He's here."

Conrad wanted to turn around and walk back out. He hated it when everyone made a big deal out of his arrival. He kept going, though, and loosened his tie as he entered the enormous kitchen. The scent of browning ground beef met his nose, and he sure did like the pile of tortillas with the little bowls of lettuce, cheese, tomato, and olives surrounding it.

"Did you get lost on the way home from church?" Spur grinned at him and handed him a plastic container of ice. "The glasses need to be filled." His older brother knew Conrad liked having a job to do. Then he didn't have to shoulder the staring quite so much.

He didn't answer Spur's question as he continued past the end of the peninsula and rounded toward the table. Mariah was busy setting down knives and forks, with Lawrence going behind her with a stack of plates.

"You're back," Conrad said as the other conversations picked up around the kitchen and dining room. Ginny and Cayden had invited everyone to eat a Sabbath Day lunch with them at the homestead, and Conrad never passed up free food if at all possible. With as many people as would be there today, he figured he could fade into the background.

"Yep." Lawrence flicked him a grin and set another plate down. "We got back late last night."

"How were the mountains?"

"Spectacular," Mariah said, her tone brightening the whole house. "You should go."

"Maybe I will." Conrad returned her smile, his as real as any he'd put on his face in a while.

"Cayden's got us right back in the action," Lawrence grumbled. "All he's talked about since we got back is the Smash."

"It's coming up," Conrad said by way of explanation. Organizing a huge racing event took hours and hours, days and weeks and months.

"Are you going to race Lamborghini?" he asked.

"No," Conrad said for at least the sixth time. "He's not ready, and it'll just be an embarrassment." He tossed his brother a glare, and because Lawrence was astute and could read looks better than books, he didn't pursue the topic.

Mariah said, "I heard you were going out with someone." She set down her last knife and fork pairing, and her statement spurred Conrad into getting the ice in the glasses someone else had already put on the table.

"Yes," he said.

The conversations around them dried up, and the only sound became Lawrence delicately putting a plate on the table, and the clink of ice in the glasses as Conrad dropped them.

"So it's official-official?" Duke asked.

"I don't even know what that means," Conrad said.

"Why didn't you invite her to lunch?" Ginny asked.

"To this crazy?" Conrad shook his head, kept his eyes down, and his feet moving around the table. "No, thanks."

"I like this crazy," Lisa said, and he caught her moving to Duke's side and wrapping her arms around him. "Our house is so quiet."

"Some of us crave the quiet." Cayden's voice would've sucked up every available drop of water and still been thirsty.

"Oh, come on," Ginny said. "You like the family lunches."

A baby started to fuss, and Olli rose from the couch just as Conrad faced her. She looked exhausted, as did baby Gus. He wanted to drop the ice container and take the baby. Instead of making that big of a commotion, he handed the ice to Lawrence, saying, "Will you finish?" before he moved toward his sister-in-law. "Let me take him."

Gratitude flashed in her eyes, and she passed the six-month-old to Conrad.

"You don't look good, bud," he whispered to the boy. Behind him, Spur said he liked the crazy for a while, and then he liked going home with his family too.

"There's a time and place for both," he said, and it seemed like most people agreed with him. Conrad certainly did, though he didn't need to add his voice to the fray. Olli went down the hall and into the bathroom, and Conrad settled into the rocking chair with her son.

"Are you hungry, Gussy? I think Aunt Ginny made tacos, and I know you like those."

The little boy perched on his lap and looked up at him with wide, brown eyes. He looked so much like Spur, and Conrad's heart expanded ten sizes simply looking at the child. He'd always liked kids, and the pure, unadulterated desire to be a dad did a lot more than tug through him.

His lungs laced tight with the pull, and he closed his eyes and started rocking the two of them. He hummed in the back of his throat, and Gus molded himself into Conrad's chest a moment later. He clung to one of Conrad's fingers with his whole fist, and that made Conrad feel perfectly needed and completely necessary when he normally didn't.

He hadn't gotten lost on the way back to the ranch from church. He'd followed Ry to the boutique and helped her carry in a huge shipment of garments that were supposed to arrive last night and hadn't. When her phone had dinged a notification at her that they'd been delivered that morning, she'd texted him and asked for help loading them inside.

At this point, Conrad felt confident that she could ask him to rope the moon, and he'd try to do it for her. He'd never fallen so fast and so completely for a woman before, and he wondered if the slow physical approach had anything to do with it.

A fist of fear reached right into his chest, gripped his heart, and squeezed. What if when he finally kissed her again, the novelty of the relationship wore off, just as it had with all of his other girlfriends?

As voices flowed around him like liquid, getting into all the crevices and cracks, he thought back through the list of women he'd been out with. Who had he liked best?

That was easy—Hilde. He'd dated her for a while, and when she'd ended things with him, he'd been past upset. He'd tried to get her back into his life a couple of times, and it had taken a while to get over her.

She'd consumed him too. Maybe Ry wasn't special.

She is, he told himself, and he knew down deep in his heart that he was right. They went so well together, and everything felt so easy with her. Maybe not getting together, but Conrad had found a system that was working for both of them.

"We're here," Blaine called, cutting through the

cacophony in the kitchen, as well as in Conrad's brain. "Shoot. He already has Gus."

He opened his eyes to find Blaine standing in the doorway that led from the front door, Tam coming to his side. She looked equally as exhausted as Olli had, and the baby in her arms was already crying.

"I'll take her anyway," Conrad said, because he had his whole left side for Caroline. He grinned at Tam as she brought him the newborn, and he settled her into the crook of his left arm. Gus looked at the baby as if she were an alien, but he didn't fuss or even move.

"There you go," he said to the little girl, who quieted with the movement. Tam tucked her in tightly with the blanket, and Gus lifted his chubby foot to get his out from underneath the fabric. He looked up at Conrad, who gave him a smile. "It's okay, buddy. Cousin Caroline is just going to join us for a pre-lunch nap."

"Nope," Ginny called. "It's ready right now. Get your hats off and your arms folded. Trey's going to say grace."

Conrad found Trey easily, because he held his step-son, TJ, in his arms, making them a big, obvious target. His wife, Beth, stood next to him, their baby girl in her arms. Fern was a beautiful child, with dark, wispy hair and huge eyes that seemed to soak up all the wonder in the world. She needed them, because Fern had registered very low on the auditory scale. She was legally deaf, though she could hear some sounds.

Trey and Beth had already been taking sign language classes, and they spoke to her and signed to her simultaneously. They did the same for TJ, and Conrad even knew some things now just by observing them.

"Dear Lord," Trey said, and Conrad hastened to close his eyes and bow his head. He didn't do much praying these days, but Trey had a powerful, strong cadence that touched Conrad's heart in a way no one else in the family could.

He prayed for good health for the lot of them. He prayed that they'd have access to the things they needed and wanted. He prayed for comfort and security in the family. He thanked God for their bounteous blessings, and said, "Amen."

"Amen," Conrad repeated, and while he might have surged forward in the past to get his plate loaded with tacos, today he stayed in the recliner with his niece and nephew.

Blaine put a car seat next to him and said, "Can I leave George here? If he makes a noise, just rock him with your foot."

"I can do that." Conrad met Beth's eyes, and his eyebrows went up. He nodded as hers did too, and she brought Fern to him. "Just settle her right there," he said, tucking Caroline further to the left. "She'll fit just fine."

The little four-month-old let her mama tuck her between Gus and Caroline, and Beth pushed her pacifier in Fern's mouth. "You be good for Uncle Conrad." She made a sign, and Conrad got the rocking chair going again, his eyes drifting closed. He could so wait to eat if he got to help his family and hold babies at the same time.

"Smile," Ian said, and Conrad opened his eyes and did

what his brother said. Ian snapped a picture on his phone and added, "I'll send that to you."

Conrad looked down at the precious cargo on his lap, once again wondering if Ry wanted children. She'd said "wife and family," not him, and he simply kept the question on his list of things he wanted to talk to her about.

Chapter 13

Ginny Chappell could not stem the flow of tears steaming down her face. She'd promised herself and Cayden she wouldn't cry once they reached the hospital, but she could not stop. She didn't know how to feel all of the things streaming through her body and mind and heart. The only way she could keep walking was because the tears let some of the emotions out, and Cayden's hand in hers was so incredibly strong.

He had been her rock in a stormy sea for so long, and she loved him so deeply. That thought got her tear ducts to dry slightly, and she used her free hand to wipe her face. She'd put makeup on this morning, just as she always did, as if today would be another easy, normal day for her.

Today, though, was anything but normal. She hadn't left the homestead to go to Sweet Rose Whiskey, and she hadn't kissed her husband good-bye when it was barely light so he could go to his office on the ranch. They'd stayed in bed even after they were both awake, and though she'd been ready to get up and shower and get going, they'd had hours before they needed to be at the hospital.

She'd stayed in Cay's arms, and they'd eventually made love. Ginny adored the sweet, tender way he took care of her, and she knew a baby wouldn't change that. The infant they were meeting today would change so many other things, though, and she felt as if she stood on the pinnacle of a precipice, the slightest wind able to blow her left or right to her certain death.

"It's room four-twelve," she whispered, sure Cay wouldn't hear her past the talking at the nurse's station, the beeping coming from open-doored rooms, and the general activity at the hospital.

"Four-twelve," he repeated, because he seemed attuned to her very core. A few seconds later, they reached the door, which sat closed. They both stopped, and Ginny surprised herself by being the one to lift her fist and knock.

"Erin?" she said into the seam of the door. "It's Ginny and Cayden." She tried the door handle and found the door unlocked—she wasn't even sure hospital doors locked at all—and opened it a few inches.

Erin sat up in bed, her smile exactly the type a woman would wear on the day she gave her baby boy to someone else to raise.

Thanking every star in heaven, Ginny managed to keep her tears at bay. Erin had been crying too, but she was dry-eyed at the moment as well. "Come in," she said, her eyes moving from Ginny's to the baby in the plastic bassinet at the side of the bed. She wasn't holding him, and Ginny wondered if she had at all.

The baby had been born last night, and their case worker had called about ten o'clock and told Ginny and Cayden they'd been invited to the hospital today, just after lunch. If all went well with Erin, she'd be leaving the hospital the next morning, and she wanted Ginny and Cayden to meet their son.

With great difficulty, Ginny kept her eyes on Erin as she released Cayden's hand and hurried to her side. "How are you? Feeling okay? We brought that mango cheesecake you love, because I know they don't feed you well in here."

She embraced the other woman, pressing her eyes closed as Erin's shoulders vibrated slightly. She clung tightly to Ginny as if she alone could rescue her from this storm. Ginny couldn't rescue anyone, as she often felt so adrift herself, but she held onto Erin as if she could. If she willed it to be so, maybe she could be strong enough to save them both.

"I'll put it right here," Cay said, and the rustling of the plastic bag filled the room.

"Thank you." Erin's voice pinched along the outer edges, and she wiped her eyes quickly. She grinned at Cayden, who did have a calming influence on every man, woman, child, and beast who came in contact with him. The only person Ginny knew who'd been able to resist his charms for a while had been Mother. Even she'd come around eventually, and she adored Cayden more than anyone, it seemed.

"They just brought him in," she said, looking at the sleeping infant again. "He should be good for a while. They fed him and changed him, they said."

Ginny noted that Erin herself had not done those things. Ginny couldn't wait to do them, and she watched with fresh tears blurring her vision as Cay stepped over to the bassinet and gently picked up the baby.

He cradled the boy in his arms, his head down and his eyes almost closed. He murmured something to the child, who grunted and squirmed, and then Cay lifted his eyes to hers. She moved toward him hungrily, and he passed the little boy to her.

Every fiber of her heart sang, and they multiplied as they moved through her body, replacing her regular cells with the kind that knew how to love endlessly. The baby smelled like powder and cotton, dryer sheets and milk, and Ginny took the longest, deepest breath of him that she could manage.

"Oh, I love you so much," she whispered, and she hoped Cay had told the child something similar. Her eyes met Erin's, and they wept together for a few seconds.

"You're going to be so good for him," she said, immediately clearing her throat. "What are you going to name him? The nurses said they'd stop by while you were here to find out. Then they can get the birth certificate application done."

Cay and Ginny exchanged a glance. "We'd like to name him Boone," Cay said in that poised voice he used on buyers and people with a lot of money. "It means 'a blessing,' and that's what he is to us. A pure blessing. You both are." His voice broke on the last word, and he ducked his head.

Erin's smile filled the room now, and she nodded. "That's perfect, you guys."

Ginny rocked back and forth, shifting her weight from one foot to the other, a soft song coming from her throat as she enjoyed this blessing straight from heaven. "We're going to give him Cay's daddy's name as a middle name." She glanced at her husband again, admiring him for his emotions and his strength. "It's Jefferson."

Julie and Jefferson had met Erin, as Julie wanted to be involved in everything her sons did. They did a good job at telling her what she could and couldn't do, and when she'd asked to meet Erin, Cay had asked Erin. They'd gone to lunch together, and it had turned out fine. Erin hadn't decided to choose someone else, at least.

"That's perfect," Erin said, keeping her eyes down as she opened the Styrofoam container of cheesecake. "Boone Jefferson Chappell."

Ginny hadn't said all three names in a row like that, and they struck a chord deep inside her. Love and appreciation reverberated through her, Erin's tone warbling as it faded into silence. That reigned for a few minutes, wherein Ginny moved with Boone over to the only chair in the room. She balanced Boone on her lap so they were facing one another, but the brand-new baby didn't open his eyes.

Then Cay said, "You can see him any time you want, Erin. We're not going anywhere."

Erin broke down into sobs then, and as she nodded,

Ginny and Cayden converged on her. The four of them made a huddle-hug, and after a few moments, Erin said, "I know this is right. I know he's your son. I know I can't take care of him. Thank you for taking him, and I hope I can be a very small part of his life."

"You can," Ginny promised her.

"We will take good care of him," Cay said.

Behind them, the door opened, and that broke their moment. "Ah, Momma and Daddy are here," the nurse drawled, smiling as if she dealt with awkward, emotion-charged adoptions every single day. Perhaps she did. She moved over to Erin's side. "How you doin', honey?"

Erin took a big breath, and Ginny felt the air move right into her lungs too. "Good," she said. "Real good."

"You ready to let him go? You gave him his last hug and all that?" The nurse looked at Ginny holding the baby and back to Erin. A moment of panic struck Ginny behind every single rib, sliding toward her gut in painful steps.

"Yes," Erin said firmly. "I'm ready to give him the life he deserves."

Chapter 14

Aw, he is the most adorable baby I've ever seen!

Ry didn't know a person alive who wouldn't smile at the picture she'd just gotten from Conrad. His brother and sister-in-law had just adopted a little baby boy, and he was the cutest little human being currently on the planet.

Conrad, she'd learned, adored children, and some of the hours he hadn't been spending with her over the past couple of weeks had been devoted to "Little Booney," as he called his new nephew.

He'd sent her a picture of him with each of his nieces or nephews, and one where he held three of them on his lap in a rocking chair, with a fourth in a seat at his feet. He hadn't come right out and asked her if she wanted kids, but it was clear he did.

A lot of them, she suspected.

I'm on my way to you, his next message read, and Ry

reached for the flat iron again. Bees nipped at her stomach lining, and it had everything to do with this stupid flat iron. She couldn't believe she'd thought it would be a good idea to curl her hair. The humidity would only pull on it and straighten it all out again, and she wished—not for the first time—that she was one of those girls whose hair frizzed in the humidity. Not her, though.

She hadn't curled her hair in ages as it was, and an increased measure of stupidity ran through her as she waited for the flat iron to do its job.

Honestly, the things she'd done for this high school reunion should be illegal. Three hundred dollars for a dress she'd spent far too long modifying. She could've designed and sewn one herself for the amount of time and money she'd poured into this thing.

Three hours at the salon to get her hair cut and colored, and her nails done—hands and feet. Since the reunion was in the summertime, there wouldn't be a single toe inside boots or shoes. No, every woman there would be wearing peep-toe heels or strappy sandals or wedges they could barely walk in.

Her shoes were of the peep-toe variety, and she did enjoy the way they shone as if their maker had sewn a battery-powered light just beneath the surface of the ivory leather. Just enough to make them seem special.

She also knew no one else at the reunion would have shoes like them, because she'd gotten them from a designer friend down in Savannah who hadn't released them into the market yet.

With her hair as good as it was going to get, Ry left the

bathroom and picked up her clutch from the top of the dresser. Carrying such a purse was a waste of good hand strength, in Ry's opinion, and she plucked her phone from it and left it behind in the bedroom.

"Should've sewn pockets into this thing," she muttered to herself. A quick glance at the digital clock on the stove told her that she didn't have time to take the garment off and do exactly that. She'd done a ton of other work on the skirt of this dress, and she hoped she had the legs to pull it off.

She'd chosen a dark purple dress, because she looked good in dark shades like navy and eggplant. It made her auburn hair shine like red gold, and she needed very little jewelry as accents if she could get her clothes, eyes, and hair to play together right.

She'd then taken nearly translucent ivory panels with Japanese cherry blossoms and branches embroidered into them and sewn them in horizontal circles from mid-thigh to calf. Three of them ran down the length of her legs, with the purple fabric in strips between them, and the original ruffle on the bottom.

Her doorbell rang, and Ry wondered how much time she'd lost curling her hair. Hadn't Conrad texted only a few minutes ago?

She hurried to get the door, her breath whooshing right out of her body at the sight of the sexiest cowboy alive standing on her front porch. He whistled between his teeth as his eyes raked down her body. "My, my," he said, that player grin on his face. His eyes locked onto hers, and every bit of heat in his gaze flew into her body. "Don't you look like a million bucks?"

"You're wearing my vest," she said, a touch of surprise in her voice. Why, she wasn't sure. He'd asked her to make him something "unique" for tonight. As if the man needed any more reasons to make him stand out in a crowd. Half the single women who would be at the reunion tonight were probably coming just to have a chance at the mighty Conrad Chappell.

She held his full attention, and Ry suddenly knew it, felt it, and...wanted it.

He looked down at the black paisley vest, just a hint of color in the thread—purple like her dress. "I sure am. I love this thing. Fits like a glove, and I'm dressed up without wearing a jacket." He grinned at her in a casual yet meaningful way. "Just don't tell my mother I'm not wearing a sportscoat. She'll lose her mind." He chuckled, the sound driving right into Ry's heart and making her wonder why she'd waited for five weeks to kiss him again.

She wanted to throw herself at him and seal the deal, but he cocked his elbow and said, "Ready, ma'am? I do believe we have a high school reunion to get to."

Ry laced her arm through his, grinning at the overdramatic Southern drawl. "Am I going to be with Kentucky Pete all night?"

Conrad burst out laughing, the sound spilling up into the sky and infusing the world with happiness. "Kentucky Pete."

She laughed with him as he led her down her front steps

and to the passenger side of his fancy pick-up truck. He wore navy slacks with a white shirt and that vest, a pair of almost red shoes on his feet. They sparkled in the evening sunlight they were so polished, and he himself looked like *two* million dollars—especially with that matching cowboy hat perched so delectably on his head.

The drive to the country club happened in ease and the company of country music. Dozens of other cars and trucks had already arrived, and Ry's nerves stung at her a little bit more. Conrad came to her door; Conrad escorted her down the pristine sidewalks; Conrad didn't seem to notice everyone staring at them.

Ry felt the eyes. She saw all the exchanged glances. She noticed every head that swiveled and every gaze that narrowed.

She'd carried this weight only one other time, and that was at Andy's funeral. She'd hated the whispers then as much as she did now. The worst part was, she wasn't sure if her former classmates were talking about her sister's death or her arrival on Conrad Chappell's arm.

She told herself it didn't matter. They could stare for all they were worth. She accepted the glass of champagne Conrad handed her, and they faced the wide, open floor that usually hosted grooms and brides for their first dance.

A slow, country ballad came over the speakers, and a voice came over the loudspeaker. "All right, Class of 2006, get out there on the dance floor! Cut a rug. Find someone you haven't talked to in a while and find out what they've been doing!"

Conrad looked at Ry; Ry looked at Conrad. "May I have this dance?" He swept his cowboy hat off his head and actually bowed at the waist. His mother would be so proud.

Her grin couldn't be contained on her face, and she even allowed a giggle to pass her lips. She put her hand in his, and that may have been the moment she got out of her own way and fell a little more in love with the handsome cowboy.

He moved them out onto the dance floor, his grip along her waist strong and sure. She would never trip with Conrad at her side. He'd hold her up, he'd steady her, he'd take good care of her.

Her heart throbbed against the box she'd put it in, because she'd been trying to keep it safe. She didn't want to make it easy for this man to reach into her chest and smash her heart again. It didn't seem to mind, though.

"Ry," Conrad said, dancing them around the floor with ease. "There's something I wanted to talk to you about."

"All right." A flicker of something nervous flashed across his face, like a stab of lightning that didn't quite come out of the clouds. She'd seen them before, and she'd never really been sure she'd seen them at all. His fear or anxiety or whatever it had been disappeared so fast, she wondered if it had been there at all.

"I hope it doesn't matter to you, but it's something I've had on my mind."

"All right," she said again, her own anxiety now poking at her a lot harder than his flicker had done.

"It's just...my brother said I might want to mention it to

you and see if it's a big deal. Something you need to get used to. Whatever."

"Maybe just spit it out then," she said. "You're making me nervous." She glanced around to see who was watching them. There had to be someone out on the fringes of the dance floor, but that area existed in shadows now, and she couldn't see them. Everyone on the dance floor seemed to be focused on their dance partner, and Ry moved her attention back to Conrad.

He ducked his head slightly, creating a small vortex where only they existed. They breathed in together, and he said, "I've got a lot of money. All us boys inherited quite a bit from my daddy, and our ranch does real well."

"Oh." She blinked, a money discussion not one she'd even considered.

"Does that bother you?"

"I...don't think so?" She studied his face. "Should it bother me?"

He chuckled, a flush working its way across his face to the tips of his ears. "I don't know either."

"Which brother said you might want to mention it?"

"Spur," Conrad said. "Cayden said it would probably be a good idea too. He's dated some women who had a hard time coming to terms with it." Conrad let a sigh slip past his lips, and it sounded like air leaking from a balloon. "I don't know. Ian had a wife who only wanted to be Mrs. Chappell for his money. I was just...I thought I should mention it."

His eyes flitted around the room, almost like he was looking for an escape route. A fast escape route.

"How much money are we talking about?" Ry asked, and that brought Conrad's gaze back to hers. "I mean, if it's a lot of money..."

His face had turned to wood, and wow, wood didn't move. He didn't blink.

"Conrad," she said, putting a smile on her face. "I'm teasing. I don't care about your money." She nestled her way deeper into his arms, glad when he tightened them and held her close. She let her eyes drift closed and let herself go to the safety and whisper-close quality of Conrad's touch.

She'd never known dancing with a man could be so exciting and so intimate. She breathed in the musky, outdoorsy scent of his cologne, those smells mixing with the cotton and warmth of his skin, and Ry thought she'd passed straight into heaven. Everything around her felt light, delicate, and soulful, and she never wanted this dance to end.

The lighting around them dimmed, causing Ry to open her eyes. Conrad had taken them to the edge of the dance floor, and when she pulled back and looked up into his face, she saw him with new eyes. Without a second thought, she tipped up in her peep-toed heels, her gaze fixed solidly on his mouth.

He moved toward her too, hesitating at the very last moment, the final nanosecond before he'd kiss her. "I don't want to break the rules." His voice held every quality of her ideal dessert—sexy, rough, and downright sinful.

"I do," she whispered, and then...she did.

She'd kissed this man before, but he'd been a boy or she'd

been in a strange state of mind at a wedding with her sister's once-boyfriend.

Perhaps a boy with some experience with girls. Perhaps a boy who knew how to kiss a girl. Perhaps a boy with plenty of older brothers to give him advice.

He was no boy now.

This was a man she was kissing, and he was kissing her back the way only a man as wonderful, tender, and warm as he could do. He was all cowboy in his stroke, and all heartthrob in the way he let her lead the way, and all wow in every sense of the word.

Ry had no more defenses against Conrad Chappell, and just as she'd suspected, on their very next kiss, she'd opened the door to her heart. Wide.

Chapter 15

Conrad had known his patience would pay off, and boy did it ever. He'd never kissed a woman the way he was kissing Ry. He'd never been kissed the way she kissed him. There was so much more to it than the physicality of the touching of two mouths, and Conrad wasn't sure he'd ever experienced a kiss that meant more emotionally than it did physically.

He also knew very keenly where they stood, and how many people were watching. He wanted to keep kissing her and kissing her, but a tinny, growing voice in the back of his mind told him to *stop!*

So he stopped.

He pulled back and drew in a long, deep breath through his nose, trying to make his brain work amidst all the hormones, the pleasure, and the scent of Ry's skin in his nose. The taste of her in his mouth.

"Do we have to stay?" he asked, keeping her right against him so she'd know he wanted her close.

"Here?" she asked.

"Yes, here," he said. "Do we have to stay? The food looks dry, and I don't care about any of these people." The unsaid words implied he only cared about her, but he couldn't get his voice to say them.

"I hear the food at Six Stars is amazing," she said. "They have dancing on the weekends." She stepped back, both of his hands still in hers. He could hold this woman all day and all night and never grow tired of her. He felt like someone had taken off all the old Conrad skin in the past five or six weeks, and with every text and every tea he brought her, every meal they shared and every mile he drove to be with her, a new skin had been stitched together for him.

He felt whole when he was with Ry, and he hadn't felt that way about anyone or anything in so long.

"Yeah," he said, his smile dragging out the word. "Let's go to Six Stars." Spur loved Six Stars, and he took all of his first dates there. He'd taken Olli there, and they still went often.

Conrad had never been a fan, as the restaurant was loud, and sometimes the food came out slowly. Tonight, he didn't care. Tonight, he just wanted to be with Ry, and they could sit on the same side of the booth, and he could kiss her again and there'd be so much going on around them, no one would even care.

He released one of her hands and kept the other in his as they faced the exit. A whole slew of people stood between them and freedom, but Conrad would knock them over if he had to. Not really, but he felt like he would.

They started along the edge of the dance floor, and after several steps Conrad thought they might actually be able to make a break for it. Then Wyatt Gray stepped out of the crowd and said, "Conrad Chappell?" His smile filled his whole face and overflowed the way water did to a shallow riverbank.

"Howdy, Wyatt." He did not release Ry's hand to shake Wyatt's. "We're just headin' out."

"Out?" Wyatt glanced at Ry as if he hadn't even seen her at Conrad's side. "The party just started." His confusion annoyed Conrad, but his mother had taught him to be polite, especially in a crowd.

"Right, I know." He knew how to placate angry, confused horses. He could handle Wyatt Gray, who'd been somewhat of a class clown in high school. "It's just that I'm not feeling super well, and Ry said she'd drive me home. Make sure I got there all right and all that." He smiled at Wyatt and shook his hand. "It's really great to see you, though. I just don't want to get anyone sick."

"Maybe you shouldn't be makin' out with Ryanne then," a woman said, and Conrad sucked in a breath.

Her fingers in his tightened as the middle-aged woman came out of the shadows. Conrad had placed Annette by the sound of her voice, and she looked a couple of steps above good tonight. Though the invitation had said "dressy casual," Annette wore a gown that almost looked like something she'd have worn to the prom decades ago.

"Wow, you look amazing," Conrad said, stepping into her. He'd dated her for a few months in their senior year, and he'd been learning in the past few weeks that a lot of the girls he'd been out with back then had thought their relationships with him had been more serious than he had.

Ry was just one of them, and regret lanced through him stronger than it ever had before.

"Thank you, Conrad," Annette said, her playful, party voice making a return. "Too bad you have to go. I was hoping to dance with you tonight."

"I'm with Ry," Conrad said, needing Annette to understand what that meant. "I'm fairly sure she would've dominated my dance card." He glanced past Annette, hoping he'd gotten his point across. "So great to see everyone. Really, I'm sorry I have to go."

"Maybe Ryanne could stay," Annette said, stepping to Ry's side and hooking her arm through hers. Ry wore a look like Conrad was about to push her out of an airplane at ten thousand feet.

For a moment, his voice went on vacation, and while he tried to find it, Ry said, "Thanks, Annette, but Conrad lives so far out in the country, and he's afraid he might faint at the wheel."

"Yeah," he said. "I'm feelin' all weak in the knees." He put his best smile on his face and guided Ry around the group, his hand securely on the small of her back. "They're watching, aren't they?"

"Burning a hole in my back," she muttered.

"Just make it to the door." He kept his plastic grin in

place until they reached the hallway. He felt like breaking into a run, the sight of daylight through the glass doors up ahead a place of safe haven for a man desperate to get out of the building.

They finally made it onto the sidewalk, only to be faced with Winifred Halson, one of Ry's better friends in Dreamsville. She shrieked and danced over to Ry, who laughed and hugged the other woman.

Conrad suppressed his sigh, because turning it loose would only make him look like a jerk. His gaze found the man Winifred had arrived with, and they shrugged simultaneously. "Howdy," Conrad said. "I'm Conrad Chappell. I'm not sure I know you."

"Nope, I'm out of New Orleans," the man said, his voice one that should be on jazz records as the lead singer. "I'm Jackson LeFave."

"Great to meet you." He nodded to Winifred and Ry, who had each other clutched by the shoulders. "Are you seeing Winifred?"

Jackson's features softened as a smile touched them. "For about six months now. You and Ry?"

Conrad nodded, not sure how long to put on their relationship. He'd just kissed her—really kissed her—for the first time fifteen minutes ago. He had seen her every day for the past month, and he had gone out with her in high school for a little bit. He definitely felt like he was hitting home runs lately, but he also knew he could strike out at any time.

Winifred pulled away and said, "Wait. You're not leaving, are you? I just got here." She looked from Ry to Conrad. "Conrad," she whined. "You can't go."

"Come to Six Stars with us," he said. "The music in there is too loud. The food is garbage." He leaned closer and grinned, sure he could win over Winifred. "Plus, not sure if you knew, but there's all these people from high school we haven't talked to in fifteen years...for a reason."

"Stop it," Ry said, but her tone didn't chastise. "You really could come with us." She looked at Winifred hopefully. Conrad knew how powerful and how devastating hope could be, and he just wanted Ry to be happy.

"I'm just shocked you came, and now you're leaving so early," Winifred said.

"Think about that for a second," Ry said, taking hold of Conrad's hand again. "We'll be at Six Stars." She waved to her friend and started walking toward the parking lot. Conrad went with her, the evening turning to dusk as they stepped.

"It's a beautiful night." He gazed up in the sunset-sky made of gold, pink, and navy. The colors deepened with every passing moment. He spotted a sidewalk that veered off the main path and between two tall hedges, and he tugged her in that direction. "Let's see what's out here. Are you starving? Do we have a minute?"

"We have a minute," Ry confirmed.

Conrad had been to this country club dozens upon dozens of times. Mom ran charity organizations that met here and which held luncheons here. He knew this path went out to a fountain of a jockey and a horse, the water coming from the man's outstretched hand.

He'd never kissed a woman out in these gardens or under a sky so stunningly gorgeous, and he wanted to.

He barely made it around the first hedge, where rows and rows of flowers took up the beds, before he twisted back toward Ry and slid his hand along the side of her neck. "Ry, I think you're the most beautiful woman in the world."

"Mm, the whole world? Have you seen every woman in the whole world?"

"Yes." He grinned at her. "Yes, I have." He brought her mouth to his and kissed her again, beyond thrilled that the rules for their relationship had changed.

* * *

A week later, Conrad sat on the tiny couch on the landing, no novel in sight. He stared at his phone, sure a zombie apocalypse was about to strike, because he was about to do something even more shocking.

Cancel on Ry.

She was usually the one to postpone their get-togethers. She hadn't outright canceled anything for weeks now, since he'd first run into her at the soup restaurant, and she'd been in the throes of opening her physical storefront.

Hey, can we reschedule dinner tonight?

His thumbs hovered above his keyboard, trying to think of a reason why without lying to her and without telling the truth. "Impossible," he mumbled to himself, looking up from the device and out the windows that faced north. "What do I say here?"

"Con?"

"Coming," he called down the steps to Ian. The last thing he needed was to show any emotion over canceling on Ry to spend time with his brother. Ian needed him, Conrad reasoned, and he should be able to take some of his time and dedicate it to his family.

I'll explain later, he added to the text and sent it. He'd still have to come up with a reason why he needed to cancel, but he'd bought himself a few hours at least. Probably all the way until morning.

He didn't wait for her to answer. He got to his feet and shoved his phone in his back pocket, his heart dipping lower and lower in his chest until it beat somewhere behind his stomach. It was one night. He'd be fine; Ry would be fine; they'd be fine.

"Ready," he said, arriving in the kitchen.

"You don't have to come with me." Ian smashed his huge hat onto his head, and Conrad knew he'd chosen this extra-wide brim as a defense mechanism.

"You asked me to."

"I know, but now I feel stupid." Ian swiped his keys from the kitchen counter. "Just forget it. I can go to the equipment sale myself. I've done it before."

"I've gone loads of times," Conrad said as his phone vibrated in his back pocket. "Besides, you promised me bison sliders. Don't think I don't know you're trying to get out of *that*."

"Right." Ian rolled his eyes, his tone like a desert. "Because I need to save the ten bucks. Come on. Let's go. We're already gonna have to stand in the back."

Conrad smiled at his brother's saltiness. "You said six-fifteen. It's six-sixteen. We're barely late."

"I'll drive fast."

"You gotta be careful on the highway into town," Conrad said, following him out of the house through the side exit. "Ry says there's a cop there every time she comes out to the ranch."

Ian made a noise somewhere between a grunt, a growl, and a grumble. It certainly wasn't a talk-more-about-Ry sound. Conrad shut his mouth, determined not to say anything else about his girlfriend. He didn't need to hurt Ian's feelings on purpose.

On the way to the equipment sale—something the local IFA did several times a year—Lawrence texted to ask if Conrad and Ry would like to double with him and Mariah. That kept his thumbs busy arranging something with Ry, who was still as busy as Old Mother Hubbard with her boot full of children, and Lawrence, who was putting on the Smash in under two weeks.

Blaine texted to ask if Conrad and Ry would come sit with the twins and the dogs so he and Tam could have a real date night, and that caused another flurry of texting.

By the time Ian pulled into the parking lot, the steam practically rose from his head and flowed from his ears. "You should've just gone out with Ry," he spat.

"It was Lawrence, if you must know," Conrad said. "And

then Blaine." He didn't mention that they'd of course included Ry in things, because everyone knew he and Ry were seeing each other. They had a real relationship now, and Conrad wasn't sure how to appease Ian, stay close to him, and do what he wanted too.

Another impossibility.

He had the distinct thought that he should put his phone away for the night and just be with Ian. So he tossed the phone in the center console and got out of the truck. "Conrad," Ian said, but Conrad closed the door against his protest.

Ian got out of the truck, scowling as if Conrad had just taken *his* phone and told him he couldn't use it for the rest of the night. "You're being ridiculous."

"*I'm* being ridiculous?" Conrad grinned and shook his head. He slung his arm around Ian's shoulders and since he stood an inch—a whole inch—taller than his older brother and added, "Come on, *Ee-yan*. Don't be so grumpy. Maybe there will be a huge pile of those ropes you love, and you'll need your A-game to get them."

"Stop it," Ian said, shoving Conrad off of him. "You're the one who loves those stupid ropes."

"So true," Conrad said. "And I need you on your A-game to get them for me."

Chapter 16

Where are you? Ian read the first part of the text as it came in, Nita's name attached to it. Instant annoyance rang in his ears. Why did she care where he was?

He let Conrad get ahead of him a little, and he swiped to read the rest of the message. *They're going through some new lunge saddles that have your name all over them. If you're not coming to the demo and sale today, I could get a couple for you.*

As he finished reading, his heart spit out three extra beats and another text from Nita came in. *You could just pay me back.*

I'm walking in right now. Sorry, we were running late.

He sent the text, immediate regret running across cyberspace with it. He didn't need to apologize to Nita Powell. He didn't work for her; if anything, she worked for him, as Glenn Marks Stables, her employer, rented their stable space and track time from Bluegrass Ranch.

So not him, but his family. Trey ran all the track scheduling, and Ian was one step away from Trey. Lawrence handled all the billing for the stable rentals, and Ian had spoken to him that morning.

He stuffed his phone in his pocket, wondering when his heart had started filling like a stupid balloon. What it had filled with was worse than anything Ian could imagine—hope. He told himself not to look for Nita, but his eyes betrayed him and started scanning the crowd surrounding the arena at the back of the IFA, where they did live animal demos for products, feed, and obedience trainings.

Right now, a beautiful black and white horse stood like a king in the ring. The chairs in the half circle surrounding the circle that sat down in the floor were almost full to capacity, and Conrad managed to snag a couple on the end of a back row, way over on the side.

That meant Ian had to really crane his neck to see everyone, but it wasn't hard to find Nita. She sat in the front row, dead center, looking straight at him too. She even lifted her hand in a very auction-style movement that he supposed was meant to be a wave.

To his complete horror and shock, he returned the gesture.

"What in the world is happening here?" Conrad asked, his eyes as big as a wide-eyed frog.

"Lunging saddles," Ian said, though he knew dang well Conrad hadn't even looked at the horse in the ring. Not yet, anyway.

"You're waving to Anita Powell? I thought you two

didn't get along." He blink-blinked, as if the half-wave where Ian's hand didn't even go up to his shoulder was a national disaster that needed to be called into the President of the United States. Military deployed to question Ian about his feelings for Anita Powell.

He wouldn't be able to answer the questions.

He gave Conrad his phone to get him to look at something else, and he shifted in his seat. The demonstrator kept talking about the lunging saddles, and Ian did like the look of them. He'd had plenty of horses that needed the extra weight on their backs to learn to run the rail right, and some that needed a saddle in order to tire themselves out appropriately.

Heck, he used them just to remind his horses that he was their guide, and that if they'd just listen to him and do what he taught them to do, they'd never be led astray.

"So it was a business wave," Conrad said.

"Mm." Ian wasn't even going to give a full word to Conrad's inquiries. He loved his brother with the fierceness of the sun, but he didn't have to talk about how he felt. He couldn't even believe he felt anything.

He hadn't for so long.

His heart had been so hard, it was as if he'd injected liquid cement into his veins, let it run through his whole system, and then flipped a switch to solidify all of it. He'd kept himself safe that way. He kept his assets safe. He didn't have to hurt, and he didn't have to think about why his first marriage had failed.

It wasn't a marriage at all, he told himself as the demo

ended and the polite clapping started. He definitely wanted to try a couple of the lunging saddles in different weights, but he wasn't much interested in the whips that were brought out next.

Nita liked the whips though, a thought that both surprised and irritated him. He knew her. It didn't mean he wanted to take her to dinner, hold her hand, or make her his girlfriend. In fact, Ian didn't want any of those things.

He still had no idea why he'd asked her to the house for lunch a few weeks ago, but he'd barely seen her since then, and he hadn't planned on bringing it up again. Surely she wouldn't either.

The demo ended, and Ian got to his feet. He knew almost every man and woman here, because he'd been in the horse training industry for over twenty years. His first wife's daddy had owned another training facility, this one closer to Louisville, and Ian ran in all the training circuits. They all knew one another, so him getting a text from Nita about the lunge saddles wasn't that big of a deal.

"Why did you apologize to her about being late?" Conrad asked, drawing Ian's attention back to where he still sat on the back row.

"What?"

"You could've just said we'd just gotten here. You *apologized*. Were you supposed to meet her?"

"No," Ian said, rolling his eyes. "I don't know why I said it." He walked away from Conrad, more frustrated with himself than with his brother. He went down a couple of steps to the front row, his radar honed in on Nita. Even as he walked toward her, he realized he shouldn't. Not if he wanted to avoid Conrad's suggestions and questions.

He couldn't stop himself, though, and he arrived at her side a few seconds later. "How many are you going to get?" he asked.

Nita took a long second to study the laminated sheet in her hand before she focused on him. She had a gorgeous pair of eyes, and man, Ian was a sucker for blue that deep. Did she even know what eyes like that did to a man? Was she seeing anyone? How could he find out?

He felt himself hit the brakes, because his thoughts were seriously out of control.

"Probably one of each," she said. "They come in different weights, and he's got three of them." She spoke in a completely controlled tone, the same way she always did—at least when she wasn't chewing him out. There was no way she even knew he was male.

"I'll probably do that too," he said, tucking his hands in his pockets. He had no idea how to talk to a woman, least of all Nita Powell.

"I heard you were going to enter Stars For Eyes in the Smash," she said. "Last minute throw-in. Sneaky."

"It's not sneaky," he said, cutting her a look out of the corner of his eye. He quickly looked away as she raised one hand to brush her hair out of her face. Her fingernails were clean and immaculate, as if she'd just been to the salon. Ian couldn't picture her there at all, and she was the polar opposite of his ex-wife.

That's what you want, right? part of himself asked.

The other part, the part that housed his heart and didn't want to deal with that carnage again, answered, *No, we don't want a woman at all.*

"Okay," Nita said, her voice pitching up in a way that said she didn't believe him. He wasn't going to argue with her.

Bart looked away from the man in front of him, and Ian caught his eye and lifted that hand in the same exact wave he'd given to Nita earlier. He hoped Conrad saw that.

"Hey, Ian." Bart grinned and shook Ian's hand, who smiled at him with all the professionalism of a horse trainer who knew he was only as good as his tools. "Did you see the demo?"

"I was a tad late," he said. "But I saw enough to know I want a saddle in each of the three weights."

Bart's eyes could've turned to stars, just like his horse's name, and he signaled for one of his boys to come take Ian's order.

* * *

The night before the Summer Smash, Ian walked around the side of Spur's house, where he'd tethered his horse beside his oldest brother's. He kept his head down against the setting sun, though the heat was brutal in the middle of the summer in Dreamsville. No cowboy hat could keep it out, though at least the extra-wide brim he liked kept the UV rays from his face. He already looked like tanned leather in the middle of the winter, and he sometimes wished his skin didn't soak up the sunlight so readily.

At the same time, Ian loved being outside in the open air, the wide sky overhead and the scent of horses, hay, and home hanging in the air.

He knocked on the door, only to have Olli call, "It's open!"

Ian entered the house, which smelled more like flowers than anything else. He didn't hate the scent, because Olli was a genius when it came to what pleased the nose. She'd been working on candles and colognes for about as many years as Ian had been getting horses to obey him. She owned a now-massive perfumery that sat right there on the property where she and Spur lived.

She bent over the baby swing in the living room, lifting her son from it. "I'm leaving, I swear."

"It's fine," Ian said, guilt and a keen sense of self-consciousness hitting him square in the gut. "You don't have to go."

"Ginny's ordered my favorite Chinese food, and my darling husband refuses to eat it." She gave Ian a grin and passed him Gus. "Hold him for a second, would you? I just need to grab my shoes."

Ian didn't quite know how to hold a baby, but Gus was basically a sack of potatoes, and he did think the child was the cutest little lump ever. He grinned at Gus, who immediately reached for his cowboy hat. He knocked it hard enough to dislodge it, and Ian chuckled as he went ahead and took his hat all the way off. He should've done that the moment he walked inside anyway.

He walked over to the back door and hung his hat next to Spur's, turning as he asked, "Where's Spur?"

"Right here," his brother said, appearing at the mouth of the hallway, a giant smile on his face. "Hey, buddy. Come see Papa." He looked and sounded like a completely different man than he'd been a year or two ago, and Ian wondered if he could endure the same transformation.

Did he even want to? Change was hard, and Ian was comfortable right where he was.

"'Bye, baby," Olli said, moving right into Spur's personal space. An invisible barrier popped up between Ian and Spur with his family.

They existed on a plane Ian had never been on, even when he'd been married to Minnie. They'd never been this happy. This content with one another. This in sync. Spur kissed Olli really quick, the peck intimate but not at the same time.

Olli took Gus, and the bubble broke.

Ian cleared his throat and backed up, too close to the two of them for Olli to get by with the baby. "Thanks, Olli."

"Anytime, Ian." She gave him a friendly smile, and strode right past him and out the front door.

"Pizza's on the way," Spur said, turning toward the living room. "What have we got tonight? Baseball?"

"I don't care," Ian said, because he didn't. There weren't any good sports on in the middle of the summer, and he never took time to sit down and follow a team anyway. He followed Spur into the living room, which held two comfortable couches that nearly swallowed a man when he sat down.

Ian took one end of the largest one, a long groan coming from his mouth. With anyone else, it would've been a mistake. With Spur, it was why he came to sit on his brother's couch and eat pizza while a baseball game neither of them cared about played in the background.

"Sounds bad," Spur said, finally locating the remote among the other items on the coffee table in front of the couch. He flicked a glance in Ian's direction as he sat down on the other end of the couch.

Ian simply stared at the silent TV. "It's not bad, actually. It's..." He reached up and ran his hand down his face. "Confusing. I'm confused."

"About what?"

Ian didn't know how to order the words. "I think... There's this horse trainer..." He blew out his exhale, frustrated with his lack of eloquence.

"A problem with a horse trainer?" Spur guessed.

"No. Yes. Maybe?" Ian didn't think he was having a problem with Nita, but she *had* shown up at the house and chewed him out. Then they'd worked together to get her prize horse's stall all fixed up. He'd asked her to lunch. She'd texted him about the lunging saddles.

You're an idiot, he thought. She'd done nothing to indicate that she thought of him as anything but an annoyance.

The doorbell rang as Spur puzzled over what Ian had said, and Spur got to his feet to get the pizza. With the box perched precariously on top of a couple of candles, he flipped open the lid and put a couple of slices on a paper plate.

"Here you go, Ian. Start at the beginning."

Ian watched his brother take three slices for himself and settle back into the couch. He didn't need to censor anything with Spur. He'd been married too, and he'd gone through a divorce as well. He and Ian had been having these private meals for years, and they'd helped Ian immensely. Just knowing he wasn't alone helped him so much.

"I think I've been having feelings for Anita Powell," Ian said, the words flowing from him as smooth as cream from the container.

Spur choked, his head whipping toward Ian at the same time. He dropped his pizza slice, which had one enormous bite taken out of the pointed end of it. "What?" He coughed around the word, and he dang near went into a fit before he got the food chewed and swallowed.

Ian simply stared at him. "Really?"

"You should've warned me," Spur said, getting up to get a drink from the fridge. "Water? Coke?"

"Always Coke," Ian called over his shoulder. Mom would have something to say about that, as usual, but she wasn't here tonight.

Spur handed him a can of Coke and looked at him again. "You're having feelings for Anita Powell?"

"I think so?" Ian sounded like he was guessing now. "I don't know. Like I said, I'm very confused."

"This is…" Spur retook his seat on the couch and twisted

the lid on his soda water. How he drank that stuff, Ian would never understand. It was so *bitter*. "Listen, brother. You know I would never tell you how you feel. Or say that it's wrong, or that how you feel should be different, or that you should change it. How you feel is how you feel. It's fine, and it's authentic, and you have to make sense of it."

"I'm not furious anymore." Ian reached for his pizza. "That's something."

"That's something *huge*," Spur said.

"I've been thinking about Nita," Ian said. "I just don't know what that means." He looked to Spur for help, because Spur was the oldest and always knew what to do.

"I have no idea either," Spur said. "What have you been thinking?"

Heat filled Ian's face, and he filled his mouth with pizza so he wouldn't have to talk right away.

Spur chuckled and said, "Ah, I see. You're *thinking* about Nita Powell."

Ian cleared his throat. "Right. What do I do about it?"

"I have no idea," Spur said, another chuckle accompanying the words. "I'd say run with it and see what happens, but you won't like that answer."

He was right; Ian didn't like that answer. He wanted to try it, though...

Chapter 17

Ry wished she'd worn a dress to this horse race. Conrad had whistled when he'd picked her up, and he'd backed her straight back into her house, closed the door, and kissed her breathless before they'd come to the ranch for the Summer Smash.

He didn't mind her knee-length, dark-wash denim or the bright, splashy blouse of green, mustard, violet, and azure on a black silk. She hadn't been able to pass up the gorgeous fabric, and she'd made a simple drape tank top a couple of afternoons ago.

But other women carried an air of sophistication the way they carried purses, and Ry simply didn't have that.

Conrad waited for the elevator, and when they got on, there was an attendant there. A real person making sure people went to the right floors. "Afternoon, Mister Chappell," the man said, smiling at Conrad. "Family suite?"

"Yes, please, Rich." Conrad probably had butlers and maids fawning over him and his dirty laundry day and night.

Ry knew that wasn't true, but she still cut him a look while he was focused on his phone. A sigh leaked from his mouth, and he rolled his whole head as he put his phone away in his back pocket.

"What?" she asked.

"Just my mom," he said. "She's...intense. You'll see."

Nerves hit her right behind her pulse. "Maybe I should be warned before I have to see."

He waited while the elevator dinged and the couple that had gotten on with them vacated the car. "The Smash doesn't start for another forty minutes, right? She just texted me that I should've been here ten minutes ago, and that I better have Daddy's lucky hat."

Ry glanced at his hands, but she already knew he didn't have anything. "You don't have a hat."

"No, because I forgot it. I'm a horrible son, in case you're wondering. I called Ian, and he's bringing it. He's usually on time, so I'm surprised Mom doesn't already have it for Daddy." He spoke with a level of frustration and annoyance that Ry hadn't heard him use before. It surprised her to find out that the Chappells had cracks among their ranks.

The elevator reached the top floor of the racetrack stands, and Conrad tipped his hat to Rich as they walked out. He pulled in a deep breath and pushed it all out as they walked toward the door at the end of the hall.

"You're making me nervous," she said.

"I don't get along that well with my mom," he said. "That's all. There's enough people here to avoid her." He reached for the door handle and opened the door for her. She looked at him, her eyebrows raised.

"Why don't you get along with her?"

"It's a long story," he said, leaning closer as his playful smile took over his face. Ry liked it when they were text-flirting or enjoying a casual meal on the strip of lawn behind her boutique. In a serious conversation, though, she didn't appreciate him frosting over it as if the situation would resolve itself if he wanted it to.

"Then you'll tell me when we go to the motorcycle rally next weekend." She folded her arms and waited for him to confirm.

The smile slipped. "Okay," he drawled. "Can you go in now? If I enter before you, Mom will be all over my poor Southern manners, and she's probably about to start yelling about why the door is open and if we were raised in a barn."

"Whatever—"

"Who's holding that door?" a woman yelled, and Ry's eyes widened.

She burst into giggles while Conrad quirked one eyebrow in a way that said, *See? Now you've gotten us in trouble.*

A woman appeared in the doorway, and Ry tamed her giggles in a single blink. "Oh."

"Mom," Conrad said, sweeping into his mother's arms. "Ian has Daddy's hat. I sent it with him. Isn't he here yet?"

"Of course he's not here," she said. "He's racing Stars For Eyes."

"Not until the end," Conrad said. "He said he'd bring it." He stepped back. "Don't worry, Mom. I'll make sure Daddy has it before y'all head for home."

"You better." His mother looked past him, but he did have shoulders that spanned an impressive width, and she couldn't quite see Ry.

Conrad turned and stepped to his mom's side, putting his arm around her shoulders. He had that flawless smile on his face, and boy, he was good at putting on a front that wasn't real. Ry wasn't sure if she liked that or not.

"Momma," he said. "This here is Ryanne Moon. Ry, this is my mom, Julie Chappell."

"It's so great to meet you," Ry said, extending her hand toward Julie. "Conrad said you had gorgeous hair, and he wasn't wrong."

Julie blinked, her smile appearing a moment later. She was clearly flattered, and she stepped forward and hugged Ry. "You come sit by me," she said. "I want to make sure Conrad is treating you right."

"Mom," Conrad said, letting her go by him. He caught Ry's hand in his, though. "She's sitting by me today. Plus, I'm not making her go in there alone. That would be like throwing fresh meat to wolves."

"We're not that bad," Julie said as she walked back into the suite.

Conrad gave her some distance before saying, "Yes, we are." He gave Ry an apologetic look. "I apologize for whatever is about to happen." He then led her into the suite, and Ry had a hard time figuring out where to look.

The opulence of the suite could steal a person's attention for a good long while. So could all the tall, handsome cowboys, of which Conrad blended right into. He was the best looking, in her opinion, but plenty of dark eyes and long-nosed cowboys looked her way.

His sisters-in-law made Ry feel like a slug, and she stayed one step behind Conrad as he led her into the fray. She hadn't met anyone in his family officially yet. She'd been at the house a time or two when Ian had been home, and she'd met him. He wasn't there right now, and neither was Cayden, Spur, or Lawrence.

Their wives were, though, and Ry kept her smile in place and catalogued all of their names. She knew them already, though, because Dreamsville wasn't that big of a town, and the Chappells were a prominent family.

Mariah, Lawrence's wife, carried a baby girl named Fern that Ry recognized from a picture Conrad had sent her once. She knew the baby wasn't Mariah's, and when a brunette bustled over with a little boy in tow, she remembered that Beth was Fern's mother.

"Thanks, Mariah." She passed the little boy to her and added, "You stay by her while I go talk to your daddy. Ya'hear?"

"Yes, ma'am," Mariah whispered in a voice that everyone could hear, and the boy repeated it. Ry couldn't help smiling at him, and her heart positively melted when he spied Conrad and leapt toward him.

"Uncle Conrad," the child said. "Can I sit with you? Mama? Can I go with Uncle Conrad?"

"It's fine, Beth," Conrad said, but Olli protested.

"No, I called Conrad half an hour ago, if y'all will remember right. Gus has been teething, and I just need twenty minutes slobber-free." She passed the child on her hip to Conrad, who held him like he'd done so countless times in the past.

Ginny—Southern whiskey royalty Ginny Winters—looked at Ry. "I called Conrad second." She cradled her baby in her arms, and Conrad had told her all about the adoption and the naming of this miracle baby.

"I'll take him," she offered, and Ginny's face lit up.

"I just want to gossip with Olli while she's slobber-free," Ginny said, grinning at Olli. It was clear the two women were close friends, but Beth had a place among them, as did Mariah.

"The party is here," another man bellowed, and Ry sucked in a breath as her adrenaline flowed through her in waves. "Where's Conrad?"

"Taken," Olli said, linking arms with Ginny and striding away with the words, "Come on, Gin. We better get out of here before they give us those babies back."

Mariah grinned at Ry. "Yes, they're always this loud."

"Hey, brother." The man who'd just started the party grinned at Conrad. "You're busy already."

"I have a free hand," Mariah said. "I can take one of the twins."

"You get the spitty one then," Blaine said. "And that's

Caroline. Tam has her." He glanced over his shoulder, but his white-blonde wife was handing the little girl to Julie. Blaine turned back to Mariah. "You should take George. He's an angel, but don't let Tam hear you say that. She gets mad when I say the girl baby is a bit of a fussy-fuss."

"I can hear you," Tam said, and Blaine startled.

Ry smiled at the entire situation, at the energy all of these people had. They loved each other, and their kids, and she hadn't felt this level of acceptance in a long time. A few friends had stayed in touch with her, and she'd let them into her life and her worries and doubts. But her family had grown distant.

She didn't like that and wanted to do something about it. What, she wasn't sure, but as she waited for Mariah to get the angel baby boy named George and listened as Blaine said, "He'll make you want a baby of your own," she knew she needed to do something to bring her family back together.

It was time. Andy had been gone for five years now, and there was no reason to suffer alone.

They moved down to the huge front wall of windows, and Ry took a seat between Conrad and Mariah. "Will Lawrence come up here at all?" she asked.

"Nope." Mariah settled the infant on her lap. "He's crazy-busy with all the sponsors and the races. Spur will probably come up, but Cayden and Lawrence won't."

"Ian should," Conrad said. "Right before his horse races. This is the best view for racing."

Ry nodded along like she understood everything they were talking about, but horse racing hadn't really been on her radar until Conrad had mentioned that his family was running this race event. She'd said she'd come, of course. This was what Conrad did for a living. It was in his blood. It was who he was.

Horse training had pulled them apart before, but Ry was determined it wouldn't do that again.

"What do you think?" Conrad asked, his head lowering closer to hers so he didn't have to speak so loud. He had TJ on his right and Gus on his lap, perfectly at ease with attending to both of their needs. "You've got a pretty angelic baby too. Do you want one of your own?"

Ry's gaze moved down to the baby in her arms. He was asleep, and the purest moment of peace moved through her watching him. He brought warmth into her chest, and part of her heart that had died when Andy did rejuvenated in a way she hadn't known needed to happen.

"Yeah," she said, her tone the type she'd use in church. "I'd like an angel-baby like this."

"Sometimes they're devils," Conrad said. "I'm pretty sure my mom wondered why she'd decided to have another baby by the time she had me."

"You're number seven?"

"Yes, ma'am."

"She had eight, so you must not have broken her too badly." Ry put all the energy of her heart behind her smile, and Conrad leaned over and pressed his lips to her forehead.

"I want more than one baby," he said. "I love kids, in case you haven't figured that out."

"They love you too," Ry said.

"Uncle Conrad," TJ said, and he diverted his attention away from her and over to the little boy. Below, the first horses started to come out onto the track, and a new kind of energy filled the room.

"Here they come," someone said, and the older gentleman turned around. He caught sight of Ry, and his whole face lit up. He got to his feet with a wobble and a limp and leaned toward her. "You must be Conrad's Ryanne."

"My daddy, Jefferson," Conrad said, grinning at him. He stood and kept a tight grip on Gus as he hugged his father. "And yes, this is my Ry." He beamed at her, and Ry sure did like the rhyming sound of his voice when he called her his.

"So great to meet you," Jefferson said just as an announcer came over the loudspeaker, and he spun back to the track. "That's Cay. Let's show 'im we're here, boys."

Whistles filled the air instantly, along with the loudest whoops and applause Ry had ever heard. The baby on her lap startled and started to cry, as did the one on Conrad's lap. He didn't mind a bit and just kept cheering and yowling the way only a cowboy can.

"Wow," she said as they started to calm down. "I definitely needed a better warning for this family race."

Conrad just grinned at her, and he was *so* charming and he didn't even know it.

Chapter 18

Conrad caught sight of Ian veering off the path up ahead, moving to the right—toward the Glenn Marks Stables. His heart frowned and rejoiced at the same time, and he didn't know how to process the dual emotions. He did understand wanting to spend time with a horse who would listen and not give advice. He often felt like he just needed a sounding board for a few minutes.

He and Ry were going to Louisville in a few weeks, and things between them had been amazing since the high school reunion they'd attended a few weeks ago. He still did his best to see her every single day, even if it only happened for a few minutes while she left work or arrived at the boutique.

Today, though, he'd run into a snag with Lambo, and he'd just texted Ry to let her know he needed the evening with his horse. She'd replied with one word—*okay*—and Conrad had put his phone away.

He approached the Glenn Marks Stables, his step

slowing without him telling it to. He didn't see Ian standing in the open walkway in front of the stalls, where the horses were. Several of them stood in their stalls, workers moving about checking water and feed and clipboards.

Powerplay lifted his head over the half-tall stall door and nickered at Conrad, obviously recognizing him. "Hey, you," Conrad said back to the horse, who'd clearly called to him. He glanced around to see if Nita or any other Marks trainers were around, and he didn't see anyone.

Feeling a little bit sneaky, he walked over to the horse and dug in his pocket for a treat. "How you doin'?" he asked, running one hand along the horse's neck. The power from the animal moved from him and into Conrad, and he knew this horse was going to win, and win big. "Who's training you, huh? Have you started doing much yet?"

The horse was just over a year old, and the big money races were all for three-year-olds. The Kentucky Derby, the Belmont Stakes, and the Preakness. Surely Glenn would have Powerplay ready for those races, and that meant he'd likely not started yet—at least if Marks was worth his salt, and he was.

Conrad had started training horses as early as eighteen months, but their skeletons weren't fully developed until almost three years of age, and too much too soon could do more damage than good. It made zero sense to cause injuries in a horse they'd already invested hundreds of thousands of dollars into.

For a horse as young as Powerplay, he probably got plenty of time in the pasture, and he'd likely have been assigned a trainer and a jockey already, so the three of them could get to know one another. They'd walk around together, and just be pals.

Once he started his training, he'd be broken first. Then he'd start to learn how to use the long, lean legs the Lord had given him.

"You're a real beauty, aren't you?" Conrad asked the horse. "I'm dating a woman who's gorgeous. All this shiny, red hair." He could almost feel the silkiness of Ry's hair between his fingers right now, and a twinge of guilt came with thoughts and talk of her.

"I didn't lie to her," he whispered to Powerplay. "I do need to work with Lambo tonight." His stomach still wouldn't settle, and his fingers twitched as they moved up and down Powerplay's neck. If the horse could purr like a cat, Conrad felt certain he would be. "It was just an omission. It doesn't hurt her."

Ian had asked Conrad if they could do an evening riding session with Stars For Eyes and Lamborghini, as someone had purchased Stars For Eyes after his impressive performance in the Summer Smash a week or two ago. Hammerson was coming to pick up Stars For Eyes tomorrow morning, and Ian wanted just a few more hours with his horse.

He loved every horse he'd ever trained, and while selling them to someone else to run and race was part of the business—and a big part, as that was how Conrad and Ian contributed to making money for their family ranch—it was still hard for Ian every single time.

For Conrad too, who'd texted Spur last night if he might consider letting Bluegrass keep Lambo and race him as their own. Trey was doing more and more of that with his own horses, and Conrad wanted to talk to him too. Conrad could take a wild, rambunctious horse and teach him how to hone in on his natural instinct to run. He could teach him how to corner and how to pick up his stride.

He wasn't great at working with a jockey, who was the one out on the track during the race. Trey was, though. Trey had been working with one for a couple of years now, and together, they'd won the Sweetheart Classic twice in a row, with two different horses.

Trey hadn't tried to do any training besides his own horses at Bluegrass. He lived on his own farm now, and he had plenty there to keep him busy. He still managed their track time and all the various trainer personalities that came and went at Bluegrass, because he was a Chappell and he didn't want to be omitted from the family.

Powerplay huffed at him, his treat now gone. "No more," Conrad said. "I shouldn't have even given you that one." He smiled at the horse. "What do you think? Do you think I should ask Ry to come riding with me and Ian?"

He wanted to ride with his girlfriend, and they'd talked about her coming out to Bluegrass to meet his horses. She hadn't done it yet, though, because the end of a month and the beginning of a new one found her packing hundreds of items for her monthly subscribers. She'd recently hired someone to manage the subscriptions on a full-time basis, and she seemed happy with Chelsea's quick pick-up of how it ran.

"She'll be so busy tonight," he rationalized to the horse. "It's better this way anyway."

His phone chimed in his back pocket, and he stepped away from Powerplay to check it. Ian had asked, *Where are you? I thought you were right behind me.*

I am, Conrad said, already walking away from Powerplay. *I got caught up talking to someone along the way.*

He sent the text and looked back at Powerplay, who seemed reticent to see him go. Something. Some horse. He'd gotten stuck talking to himself was the real truth.

"I'll see you later, bud."

Powerplay nickered at him again, but Conrad just chuckled and shook his head as he walked away.

In the family stables, he found Ian brushing down a couple of horses that Blaine and Duke had likely been working from that day. "What's left?" he asked, because he didn't mind the soothing, rhythmic motion of taking care of a horse either.

"Just hay for these two," Ian said, glancing over at Conrad with plenty of interest in his flickering gaze. "Who'd you run into?"

Conrad cleared his throat and turned to get a pair of gloves. "Oh, you know. Just a trainer on the path."

"You stopped at Glenn Marks," he said.

"So what if I did?" Conrad shot a glare at Ian. "You do too, by the way. I saw you veer through their stables. Is Nita here tonight?"

"I have no idea," Ian said coolly, going back to his brushing. He moved further around Featherweight, Blaine's horse, and out of sight. Yeah, he had *no* idea. "I know she won't like you talkin' to that horse."

"She doesn't know."

"She knows," Ian said, his voice echoing slightly against the stall walls.

Conrad didn't argue back with him. He pitched hay into the feed bag and hung it for a horse named Florence Nightingale. The work came as easy as breathing, and Conrad had always liked being in the stables, the pastures, and out on the ranch. As the seventh son, he'd hated watching all of his older brothers go out for chores while he stayed home with his mom and Duke, the youngest brother.

Daddy started taking the little boys out when they were five or six, though Conrad had started riding a horse when he was three years old. He'd always felt something for horses, and if he wanted to stop and chat with Powerplay for a few minutes, he was allowed.

"Is Ry bringin' you dinner tonight?" Ian's voice sounded like he had to push it really hard to get it out of his throat.

Conrad didn't want to talk about his girlfriend. He'd done that very little with Ian over the past two or three months since Ry had come back into his life, and he'd done that to spare Ian the strained, tense feeling in his voice.

"No," he said. "She's busy with her subscriber boxes."

Ian said nothing, and they finished the chores in the family stable and headed over to the rowhouse where they kept their racers. Conrad was working with three right now, and he had three more coming up in age in the next several months.

Ian typically only worked with one or two, in a more intense fashion, and losing Stars For Eyes would definitely be hard for him. It wasn't really a loss. It was a graduation for the horse, and when Conrad saw it like that, some of the melancholy erased from his soul.

"Hey, Stars," Ian said, pure fondness in his voice. He ran his hand along the horse's neck in the exact same way Conrad had for Powerplay just a few minutes ago.

He turned away and saddled Lambo while Ian did the same for Stars For Eyes. They swung into the saddle, and Conrad let Ian take them where he wanted to go. He headed away from the track, away from the main epicenter of the ranch, and out to the north, where the rolling hills and green pastures spoke comfort to Conrad's soul.

They didn't say much, because they didn't need to. Conrad let Ian have his thoughts, and he allowed his to wander wherever they wanted to go. Out here, anything was fair game, and he thought about his relationship with Ry and where he'd like it to go. He thought about what that might do to Ian, and where they might live.

She had a house fairly close to downtown Dreamsville, though the suburb was quiet and he didn't feel like the pulse of the town was only a block away. It was about thirty minutes from Bluegrass Ranch, and Conrad didn't want to live in a house that sat thirty feet from another one.

Out here on the ranch, there was nowhere else for anyone to live. Spur had moved in with Olli once they'd gotten married, but she lived right next door to the ranch. Blaine had moved into Tam's house, but she owned it outright, as she'd inherited it from her grandmother. It also wasn't in town, but just down the road a mile or two.

Trey lived on a border parcel of land, just across the highway, as that was where Beth Dixon's farm had been. They'd known Beth for years, but Trey's attention had been drawn to her because her son, TJ, kept wandering onto Bluegrass property, and Trey would take him home.

Cayden and Ginny had taken over the homestead, which made a lot of sense considering how much Cayden did on the administrative side of the ranching operation. Lawrence and Mariah were building a house on a piece of land they'd found on the other side of Olli's place. Right now, they were living in her house, which was quite the distance from the ranch for Lawrence to drive.

Duke, who'd married Lisa Harvey, who ran a stud farm about a half-hour away from Bluegrass. Since her father had died and she'd taken over the operation, she needed to be there—and she had a great big house to herself. Duke lived there with her, naturally.

The house where Mom and Daddy lived on the ranch had been built about forty years ago, specifically for the retired generation to live in. They wouldn't be moving. And then there was the corner house where Ian and Conrad currently lived. He couldn't kick Ian out of the house because he wanted it for his wife and family, but he had nowhere else to go.

He needed to talk to Spur about that too, and he hoped

his brother might have a solution for him. He closed his eyes and let the motion of Lambo's steps push him left and right. *Where will I live?* he prayed. *Give me an idea, or bless Spur to have one.*

He was that serious about Ry, he knew that. Serious enough to pray, something Conrad didn't really do all that often, despite going to church most weeks. He didn't even want to think about what Mom would say if he stopped going completely.

"I thought you said Ry wasn't bringing dinner," Ian said, interrupting the wandering, looping thoughts in Conrad's mind.

His eyes snapped open, and it took him a moment to focus. "She isn't."

"Why's she standin' right there against that fence then?" Ian nod-pointed to his left, where a fence ran along the dirt road that ran north all the way to the edge of the ranch. "With pizza?"

"I don't know," Conrad said even as Ry lifted the box of pizza as if to say *hey, baby. I brought dinner. Got a minute?*

His heartbeat went into a frenzy, like those fish in those big tanks that didn't get fed very often. When the food got dropped, they darted left and right, up and down, zoom-zooming all over to get to the food.

His pulse did that same zig-zag through his chest and up into his head now. Mostly because he was excited to see her —and he'd never say no to pizza—but also, every other zing seemed to scream at him that he hadn't quite told her the truth…and she knew it.

Chapter 19

"I didn't mean to interrupt," Ry said as Conrad dismounted. "Honest. I thought you'd be on the track. You said you were behind in training."

"I know." Conrad looped the reins on his horse around the top rung of the fence and came toward her. His smile put off just as much wattage as it usually did, and his touch along her waist felt just as electric as it always had.

He lowered his head to kiss her, and something seemed... off. Sure enough, he pulled away real fast, and he didn't laugh afterward. There was no mention of how great she looked or how happy he was to see her.

She'd made a mistake in coming here tonight. She'd wanted to see him, though, and keep their daily streak alive. Chelsea, her new subscription manager, had learned everything with lightning-fast speed, and she didn't need to be babysat as she printed labels and packed bags with garments.

Ry had left her to finish that night, and she'd called in an order at Sauced. She'd hoped to find Conrad on the track, sit with him for a few minutes, and then watch him work.

Her chest pinched as he opened the pizza box and said, "I love this barbecue chicken pizza. Thank you, baby." He barely met her gaze though, and Ry simply knew something was going on she didn't know about.

She'd given him nearly all of her heart at this point, and the tiny piece she had left felt like a stone in her chest. Had she done the wrong thing? Had she been stupid and blind *again*?

He settled down onto the grass along the side of the road, obviously quite content to take a break right here out in the middle of the ranch. She sat beside him, her mind storming with things she could say. She wasn't sure she should, though.

"Are you going to eat?" he asked after he finished his first piece.

Ry reached for a piece of pizza but didn't take a bite. "Conrad," she said, taking slow, Southern time to get the two syllables out of her mouth. "I feel like something's going on."

"What do you mean?"

She looked up into the sky. While it was definitely evening, and the sun arced down in the west, it would be light for at least a couple more hours still. "Remember when we dated in high school?" she asked, not quite sure why the story started there.

"Yeah," he said.

Her mind brought it all together.

"We went out for a few months," she said. "You took me to the prom. We even kissed a few times. Then summer came, and you left."

"Yeah." A sigh came with the word this time.

"You weren't serious about us then, which I get. We were kids. But I...I told you this at the very beginning. I loved you. Like, I thought you were so amazing, and I thought we'd have this fantastic senior year together, and maybe after we graduated, we'd get married and have kids and life was just so full of, I don't know, shininess."

"Ry." That was all he said, but the word carried enough sadness for her to know he hadn't meant to make her fall in love with him when they were seventeen years old.

"Then you came back from Louisville, and it was like we hadn't even talked before. You went out with someone else. Then someone else. Then someone else..." She knew all of their names too, but she didn't need to put the full display of her pathetic-ness on parade for him.

"I feel like...I feel like that right now. Like, we've reached critical mass. We get two or three amazing months together, and then you're...done."

"That's not true," he said. "At all."

He'd told her that before, and she'd believed him. She bent her head and studied the Kentucky grass beside her thigh as if she'd never seen the stuff before. "You told me you had to work late, but I found you horseback riding with your brother."

Conrad exhaled, and it was a strong, hissing sound that was so much more than a sigh. "Ian sold Stars For Eyes, and he wanted to spend a few more hours with him before the new owner comes tomorrow morning. That's all. It really has nothing to do with you."

She lifted her eyes to his and studied his face, trying to find the truth or the lie. "Then why couldn't you tell me?"

"He's...sensitive about women."

"You've told me that before," she said. "Six of your brothers have managed to get married without worrying about how Ian will take it."

"They don't live with Ian."

"Neither will you if you get married."

"Are you saying you want to get married?" New hope lit his face, and Ry had no idea what to do with it. Confusion ran through her, and she shook her head.

"We're not talking about marriage right now," she said. "We're talking about why you have to protect Ian from me, and why you can't tell me the truth."

"I didn't lie," he said. "It *was* work-related."

Ry rolled her eyes and looked up into that brilliant sky again. It felt wrong to be having this conversation under such a gorgeous sky. The breeze bustled by, cooling some of her frustration. "I bet you told your horse."

"No," he said, far too much punch in his tone for it to be true.

"Sounds really defensive," she said. She wasn't going to make concessions with Conrad again. With any man. She had a vision of what she wanted in a husband and father, and it wasn't someone who told half-truths to spare his brother's feelings over his wife's. It wasn't someone who whispered his secrets to horses instead of her.

"It...he wasn't *my* horse." The words tripped over themselves as Conrad uttered them, and Ry turned to look at him again.

"But you did tell a horse."

"Just one."

"That you don't even own."

"You make it sound like I committed a crime."

"I want you to talk to me."

Conrad blinked, obviously surprised at the statement. "I do talk to you."

"You do not." She stood up and brushed off her shorts. "I'm sorry I interrupted your *training*. I'll let you get back to it."

"Ryanne," Conrad said, pulling out her whole name as he scrambled to his feet too. "Come on. Don't go mad."

"I don't want to stay here and be mad." She looked over his shoulder, emotions piling on top of emotions, enough to make her start to tear up. She definitely would not cry in front of him. "I think I just need a couple of days to think."

"About what?" he asked, putting his hand on her arm and sliding it down toward her fingers.

"You...you know what?" She met his eyes for half a breath before she couldn't hold his gaze. "You expect me to tell you how I'm feeling. I've told you about Andy, about my mom and how she blames me, about the stress behind Andy and Ryan. All of it. I didn't even know you didn't get along with your mom until the Smash. You think you talk to me, because you tell me all the good things. But I want more than that. I want the secrets your horses get, and I want to talk about the bad things too. The things you struggle with. The things you hope to overcome."

She drew in a long breath while he stood there, his head hanging down. She hated talking to the top of a cowboy hat, but she kept going. "Maybe you're already perfect, but—"

"I'm not perfect," he said, plenty of power behind the words.

"Then there's real things to talk about," she said. "Instead of you sharing that part of your life with me, you hide it behind vague texts and promises of a long story I never get to hear."

He lifted his eyes to hers, the dark depths of them blazing with fire. "I don't like talking about my mother."

"I don't like talking about my dead sister, but I did it. You *made* me do it."

"I did not *make* you."

Everything inside Ry shook, and she pulled her hand away from Conrad before he could feel the tremors. "I don't want to talk about kids and marriage and happy-happy-shiny-shiny unless you're willing to talk about why Ian is more important than me, or why you don't get along with your mom."

"Ian is *not* more important than you."

"Okay, whatever." Ry turned and headed for the driver's side door. "I have to go. I have inventory to pack."

"Ryanne," he said again. "Please don't go like this."

She hesitated, the desperation in his voice stinging her

heart. She turned back to him from the safety of the back bumper of her SUV. "I like the cranberry walnut muffins from Baker's for breakfast."

"You get to the boutique about nine."

She nodded, and then she got in her car and left. She had no idea how he'd get the pizza box back to civilization, but right now, she didn't care. She'd stood up for herself, and she'd laid it all out on the line for him.

When she finally reached a paved road instead of a dirt one, a switch flipped in her head. She expected him to talk about his troubles with his mother and how he could resolve them. She had to do the same.

Instead of making the turns required to get back to Andy and Ryan or her house, she headed for her childhood home.

When she pulled up to the house, she took a moment to just look at it. Everything about it seemed a hair older than the last time she'd been here, which was admittedly, a couple of months. Her shoulders hunched up toward her ears with tension, and she had to exhale and force them back down.

The last light of the day faded into twilight, and Ry got out of the SUV and headed for the front door. Her parents were getting older now, and they wouldn't be up for much longer. She knocked and then opened the door, feeling foolish for some reason. She shouldn't have to knock on her parents' front door.

"Mama?" she called. "Dad?"

Her father appeared in the doorway that led into the kitchen, their house one of the older ones in Dreamsville that didn't have the open floor plan. Surprise had etched its way onto his face, and it shouted from his mouth when he said, "Ry."

"Hey." She smiled at him. "I thought I'd stop by for a few minutes. See how you guys are. Are you busy?"

"It's Ry," Dad said, turning and facing the kitchen. He then gestured for her to come in. "Come in, baby. Of course we're not too busy to see you."

Ry tucked her hands in her back pockets and walked into the kitchen. Mama was putting something away in the fridge, and then she faced Ry. Her smile didn't appear as quickly or take up as much space on her face. Pain flickered in her eyes like the power trying to decide if it was going to stay on or turn off.

"Hey, Mama," Ry said. She stepped into her father first, because he was closer, and she held him tightly while her eyes drifted closed. "I've missed you guys."

Her dad said nothing, letting his vice-grip on her say it all. His emotion streamed from him, and while he'd never been a hugely talkative father, Ry had always known he loved her. She could feel it now too.

"How are things? How's Danny-Boy?"

As if on cue, the dog barked, and Dad released her to go let him out of his kennel. "He's a rascal," he said, and the dog's claws slid on the wood floor as he tried to race toward Ry. She laughed and crouched down to give the beagle a good scrub along his face. He was so playful, he nipped at her hands and arms, knowing she was prolonging the moment that she'd have to hug her mother.

She told herself that she'd just laid everything out for Conrad, and she could do the same thing here. None of them would truly heal until she did.

Ry finally stood while Danny-Boy continued to jump up on her. Dad chastised him and drew his attention away with a toy rope.

"Mama," Ry said, her voice breaking slightly on the last part of the word. She rushed into her mother's arms and held her tight. "I'm sorry I haven't come by. Things have been crazy at Andy and Ryan."

Her mom pulled in a tight breath, and that gave Ry the spark of irritation or guilt or something to keep the conversation going. "Do you blame me for her death?"

Mama pulled away and wiped her eyes. "No," she said, but it sounded false.

"You do," Ry said. "I wasn't even in the car, Mama. I don't know why you can't even look me in the face." She turned to her father. "What have I done wrong? I'll fix it. I *want* to fix it." Her chest heaved, because she felt like she might cleave in two at any moment, and her chest would be open from throat to pelvis, and all of her organs would come falling out.

"I've met a man," she said, her voice pitching up. "You know him. It's one of the Chappell men. I went to junior prom with Conrad. We started seeing each other again, and I so want to bring him here to meet y'all. I just know you'll love him as much as I do."

She stopped talking then, not even sure why she'd brought up Conrad. Heck, she might not even have a chance with him after all she'd said tonight. She wasn't sure she loved him, but she knew she was dang close—and hanging on to that last shred of her heart with an iron fist.

Her mother and father both stared at her, waiting for her to say more. Ry decided she better just get it all out tonight.

"I don't...feel welcome here, though." There, she'd said it. "I feel like you both don't want me around, whether that's because you think Andy and I shouldn't have been in Savannah in the first place, or if it's too painful of a reminder to see me and not be able to see Andy." Tears flowed down her face now. "I miss her so, *so* much. I loved her with my whole heart, and it hasn't been whole since the day she was taken from us. I want to talk to her, and I can't. But I lost you too, and I just...I'm so tired of trying to figure out what I did wrong. Just tell me, and I'll do my very best to fix it."

She hated the horrible hotness that came with crying. The tight tension in her whole chest. The crumpled feeling on her face. She drew a breath, wiped her tears, and sniffed everything back where it was supposed to be.

"Please," she added. "I just need someone to talk to me." Conrad wouldn't; Mama hadn't; Dad followed Mama's lead.

"I don't blame you for Andy's death," Mama said, her tone jagged and barely hers. "I just miss her." She started to cry. "I can only think of her when I see you, Ry, but that's not your fault. It's mine. You don't need to do anything different."

Dad stepped over to Mama and put his arm around her shoulders. She leaned into him and cried for a few seconds. "I'm sorry I've pushed you away. She adored you; she worshipped the ground you walk on; she would've done anything you wanted."

Ry didn't know what any of that meant. Why did that hurt Mama? She hadn't been cruel to Andy; she hadn't done anything her sister didn't want to do. "She believed in me," Ry said. "I know that. She pushed me to be better. She still does. It's because of her that I opened the brick-and-mortar store. It was *her* dream to do that, not mine."

Mama nodded, her tears as fresh as ever. "We're so proud of you."

Ry looked back and forth between her parents, willing them to say more. What Mama had just said had not translated to Ry's understanding.

"I think we were all just hurting for a long time," Dad said, his voice even and calm. "Mama didn't know how to reach out to you. You didn't know what to say to her or me. Everyone knows I'm no good at saying what needs to be said."

"Let's have pie." Mama started to get out plates.

"I don't want pie, Mama." Ry just wanted to go home and forget this night had happened. "You can't just serve cherry pie and expect everything to be okay." She'd tried that tactic in the past, and Ry had just left the house feeling as frustrated and guilty as ever.

"It helps, though." Mama got the pie out of the cupboard and put it on the table. She added plates and forks, and Ry saw no other option than to sit down. The three of them did, and she took the pie her mom put in front of her.

"What happened was an accident," Dad said. "No one blames you."

"I feel like you do, though," Ry said, pushing a mushy cherry around on her plate.

"I will do better at that," Mama promised. "I just don't know what to do instead. What would you like me to do?"

"I want to talk about her," Ry said. "She's gone, yes. We all loved her, though. I don't get why we can't talk about her." She looked at her parents. "She inspires me to this day. Max and I are developing a new line of athleisure, and we're naming our inaugural designs after her. The Andrea Collection." Ry smiled then, because the past month of designing work had been so much fun. "They're bright colors and tanks that don't show the midriff. Andy hated stuff like that. She wanted classy and bright in the same garment, and her whole line is going to be just that."

"That's wonderful," Mama said, her smile one of the most genuine Ry had seen her wear in a long time. Perhaps five years.

"Will you come when we unveil the line?" Ry asked. "You came to the grand opening at the store, but you stayed for maybe ten minutes." She hadn't said much to them then, because the grand opening had been so crazy. Conrad had come too, and she'd barely spoken to him.

A bright light strobed in her head. "I'm sorry I let my work consume me. I need to learn how to turn it off at five or six and be more present in your lives. In my own life."

"You've done right by Andy," Dad said in almost a whisper. He looked up and met her eye, pure power and determination in his. "You've been working like a dog for five years to make sure her legacy doesn't die, and it's enough."

Every muscle in Ry's body sagged, because no one had ever told her what she'd done was enough. She began to cry again, and she took a bite of the cherry pie. It was delicious—tart and sweet, with a flaky crust. After swallowing, she said, "Thank you, Dad. I've tried."

"You've done more than try," Mama said. "You've *done* it, Ry. It's time to let her go."

Ry shook her head and looked at the pie. It made her sick now, and her stomach cramped. "I don't know how to do that."

"We didn't either, for a long time," Mama said. "I think it was another thing I let come between us. I loved her—I still do. But I let her go. You haven't, and I don't know how to talk to you about…anything really. I want to. But I don't know how. You're so wrapped up in Andy." She reached over and covered Ry's hand with hers. "It's time to let her go."

Ry nodded, because she knew Mama was right. "I'll try," she said, because she had people in her life currently she didn't want to lose as a result of the sister who wasn't.

Chapter 20

Conrad drove away from Andy and Ryan, praying with his whole soul that Ry would understand. He hadn't been able to wait to see her that morning, but he had just left her cranberry walnut muffin in front of the back door of her shop.

The other five he'd purchased that morning rode in the truck with him, all of them on the way to Mom's.

His fingers automatically tightened around the steering wheel. He had to tell himself to relax, that this was just breakfast with his parents. Deep down, though, he knew it was more. Mom had said she'd brew plenty of the dark roast, so she sensed there was something more than this weekday breakfast too.

He never did anything like this. The only time he went to see his mother was when the other brothers were going too. Now that there were so many women in the family, and more and more kids all the time, Conrad could easily avoid

Mom at the family gatherings, whether at her house, the homestead, or the pavilion.

Today, he'd be the only one there. He almost turned around right then, the wheel even jerking a little bit to the left. He righted the vehicle and kept going. "It's time," he told himself, his voice nearly deafening him in the cab where he drove alone.

Spur had been encouraging everyone to make amends with Mom for a while now. Conrad knew a lot of them had done it too. They still argued from time to time, because there were ten of them in the core family, and they all had strong, loud opinions. They were Chappells at their very core, and Conrad didn't know how to change that about himself.

Ry deserved more, and he'd stayed out in the pastures with Lambo until nearly dark, thinking about what she'd said. No, he hadn't shared a whole lot of his troubles with her. Conrad didn't want to be the whiny cowboy billionaire, complaining that his mother had said cruel things to him in the past. He didn't want to hurt Ian's feelings; he'd been sparing his brother...at Ry's cost.

He shook his head, his mouth so tight it ached. He hadn't seen things that way, and he wasn't sure he did now. If he wanted to go riding with Ian, he should be able to. He didn't want to be so chained down by a wife and family that he couldn't do what he considered the basics of life. Horseback riding with Ian was one of those things. Working with his horses was another. Family dinners any day of the week counted.

He wanted to read his fantasy novels on the tiny couch on the landing too, and stay up too late making blondies with roasted almonds and marshmallows. He didn't want to compromise on every single thing that made Conrad into Conrad.

At the same time, he could've been more honest with Ry, and he figured that was her point. He should've told her he needed some brother-time with Ian and the racehorse he'd sold instead of telling her he had to work late.

He swallowed against the pinch in his throat. He *had* lied to her. He shook his head and muttered, "Idiot."

She already had a hard time believing he was interested in her. He wasn't sure why, because he could kiss that woman until he died and still not get enough of her. His eyes widened as he made the turn onto the dirt road that would take him toward his parents' house.

"Am I in love with her?" he asked, begging God to give him a sign straight from heaven. Nothing happened, and Conrad made a left to go around the homestead and gardens where Cayden and Ginny lived and along a frontage road that led to his destination that morning.

He had to love her completely, because Conrad had been physically attracted to a lot of people. Love had to be more than that, but he'd never known it, so he wasn't sure if he'd achieved that in his relationship with Ry yet or not.

"You like talking to her," he thought out loud. "You can't wait to see her. You want to help her be successful. You want her to be happy. You know what would make her feel successful and happy."

He liked kissing her, laughing with her, and talking to her. When he had something good to say, he wanted to tell her first.

"What about the bad?" he asked himself. Deep in his heart, he already knew the answer. The first person he wanted to talk about the bad things with was...Ian. Or Lambo. Or Powerplay.

Shoot, Ry was right *again*.

Not only did that need to change, which would require pretty hefty modifications in Conrad's behavior, he'd also need to talk to Ian about this. The very last thing he wanted was to hurt Ian, even if they hadn't always gotten along. They'd bonded over the past couple of years, especially once the other brothers started peeling off and creating their own lives and families away from Bluegrass.

"No," he muttered as he parked in his parents' driveway. "The *very* last thing you want is to lose Ry." That woman could not walk out of his life. He'd never be whole again— and he wondered if that was love.

He collected the muffins and got out of the truck. The summer morning sky above him seemed to cheer for him, telling him he could do this. He'd be happier in the long run, even if the right-now was hard.

Conrad could be unhappy for a few minutes to have more peace in the future. At least he hoped he could.

He didn't bother knocking and went right up the front steps and through the door. "Mom," he said, finding her standing in the kitchen. "Daddy."

"He's getting dressed," Mom said, and Conrad could

not imagine being married to her. Daddy had been a powerful force growing up, in Conrad's opinion, and he'd definitely never held back his opinion when it came to ranch business. On the personal side, though, Daddy was a marshmallow. Whatever the boys wanted to be happy, Daddy was fine with. Mom had been the cruel taskmaster around the house, and with eight boys, Conrad supposed he couldn't blame her.

For that, he didn't. It was the other things she'd said and done over the years that had cut him to the core. He swallowed just thinking about bringing them up on such a beautiful morning.

"It's gorgeous outside," he said, though he'd already made a vow with himself not to talk about the weather. He cringed as he set the muffins on the kitchen counter.

Mom gave him a smile that looked frosted on her face. "It is," she said. She looked at him, her bright blue eyes so piercing. Hardly any of the boys had gotten those eyes from her, though Conrad's features were definitely some of the lightest. His eyes shone with more gray than blue, though, and his hair had a hint of red in it in the bright sunlight. That all came from Mom.

"How are you, son?" she asked.

"Good," he said, the word clipping from his mouth. He shoved his hands in his pockets. "You?"

"Just fine," she drawled. She reached for a washrag on the counter and began moving it in big circles across something she'd likely already cleaned.

Seconds ticked by, and Conrad looked toward the

hallway that led down toward the master suite. As if he'd gotten a telegram from heaven, he knew Daddy wouldn't come out until Conrad had finished saying what needed to be said to his mother.

"Mom," he said, clearing his throat. "I wanted to…" He had no idea what he wanted. He knew what he didn't want to happen—he couldn't allow Ry to break-up with him. "Things with Ry are gettin' pretty serious."

Mom nodded, her jaw locking in place. She turned away from him and tossed the rag into the sink. "Is she pregnant?"

Conrad blinked double-time, then triple. "What?"

"That's why you called last night, right? You need a quick wedding, and you need my help to pull it off." She turned toward him, her eyes burning and cold at the same time.

Conrad shook his head before she even finished the first sentence. Irritation combined with pure anger and spiraled through him. "No," he barked. "Though it shouldn't surprise me that that's what you thought. You *never* give me the benefit of the doubt."

Mom opened her mouth to speak, but Conrad put both hands against the counter and leaned into them. "You've been talking at me for thirty-four years, Mom. It's my turn."

She snapped her mouth shut, some of the fire in her eyes dying out. She folded her arms and gestured for him to go on.

"You have never believed in me. When Ian and I would go to the horse trainings, who did you make the cake for when we got back with the certifications? Ian. When the ranch enters big races, whose horse do you involve yourself with naming, with going out to the track to watch them run, to renting whole houses in Louisville for the Derby? Ian's. Never mine. Never *once* mine, Mom."

She swallowed, but she didn't try to deny it.

"I already know Ian has more natural talent than I do," Conrad said. "I already know everything I do disappoints you. But to hear you ask me if my girlfriend is pregnant? Wow, you must think I'm the biggest loser in the world."

"I don't," she said.

"I don't believe you," he said evenly. "You've said cruel things to me over the years, Mom. You've told me I'm going to have to work harder than Ian to be as good as him. Fine, I can accept that we all have different strengths. You've never once acknowledged any of mine, though."

"I have," she said.

"Name one." He straightened and folded his arms. While he knew sometimes things were never as black and white as they felt, in this instance, they were.

"Do you know who made more for the ranch last year with the horses they trained?"

Mom's mouth fished, opening and closing like she was a water creature on land, trying to find air.

"*I* did," Conrad said. "Besides what Cayden did for the Smash last year, *I* trained the most horses we sold—for big money too, Mom. About twice what Ian brought to us."

His mother's face cracked then, but Conrad was having a hard time feeling bad for her. "I'm sorry," she said.

"I don't know what I did or said when I was fourteen or

fifteen," he said. "But you've been on me since then, always telling me how I wasn't good enough. Heck, the first time I went to Louisville over the summer between my junior and senior years, when we got back, you made a dinner that I couldn't even eat."

He'd been the *only* one not able to eat it, too. That fact still dug at him. It dove, and pounded, and gagged him until he couldn't breathe.

"I don't even remember what I made," she said.

"Everything with artichokes," he said, his throat thick as if he'd eaten one right now. "Artichoke dip with toasted bread. Stuffed artichokes. Artichoke pizza. Why? Because *Ian* loves artichokes."

His voice broke on the last word, and Conrad spun away from her. "Man, I hate this. I hate coming here. I hate talking to you." Emotion welled up in the back of his throat, and he coughed to clear it.

"I know," she whispered. "I know you do. I'm so sorry. I hadn't realized."

Conrad kept his focus on the family portrait on the mantle across the room. "It's not just stuff from a long time ago, Mom. At the Halloween party just last year, I spent all morning making pineapple upside down cake for the dessert. You took one look at it and—" He couldn't go on. Her memory wasn't so fuzzy that she couldn't remember what she'd said several months ago.

"I said it was burnt," she said.

"You threw it in the trash without another word. No *thank you*. No, *it'll be fine, Conrad*. Then, you complained to everyone that we didn't have any cake for dessert, but we had plenty of candy and ice cream and that apple pie that Ginny brought. *Of course.* Everyone *loves* Ginny and Cayden."

He hated the bitterness in his voice. He loathed the way it streamed through him. He abhorred everything about this.

He closed his eyes, feeling the burn in them, and pictured Ry. He didn't hate her. He wanted her in his life. He could endure this to make sure she knew his life wasn't perfect, and that he wanted her there for every ugly piece of it.

He exhaled and recentered, using the image of Ry's flashing eyes to do it. "I love Ginny and Cayden too. I want to bring Ry to the family parties and participate with everyone. You make it so dang hard, though." He faced her again and threw up his hands. "She's not pregnant. I'm not a heathen. I'm not a loser. I work twelve hours a day, see my girlfriend every day on top of that, help Ian more than anyone, pick up any chore Spur or Cayden ask me to, and still manage to get my laundry done. I don't know what else you want from me, but I know I can't give more than I do."

"I don't need more from you," she said, her voice barely loud enough to travel across the island and into his ears.

"I apologize for whatever I did to make you dislike me," he said.

"Conrad." Her eyes filled with tears. "I don't dislike you. I love you. You're my *son.*"

"Seems like that's not true."

She came around the island and sat down heavily. "I can

see that now. I knew there was something wrong. I've known it for years." She buried her head in her hands. "You were almost the last son," she said. "In a line of boys that are so extraordinary."

"So I've heard for thirty-four years," he said, taking a seat too.

"I suppose I figured you knew how special you were," she said. "Your dad was never short on praise with you. To this day, he tells me almost daily how phenomenal you are with a horse, as if that's all that's required to enter heaven."

"We own a horse ranch, Mom," he said. "Being able to work with horses is pretty essential."

"I know," she said quietly. "Your daddy...you're his favorite, because you're the most like him. I've always thought I needed to balance him. He'd praise you up one side and down the other. He never let any of the other boys go to any trainings out of town until they were adults, but not you. You were special. He never let any of the other boys follow him around as much as you. He never let anyone touch his prize-winners until they'd done five years of training. Not you. You were training them before you even graduated from high school."

Conrad stared at her. "And you didn't like that? You don't think I should be commended and admired for that?"

"I was trying to balance your dad," she said again. "I went too far in the other direction, and I did cruel, hurtful things." Her eyes filled with tears. "I'm so sorry, baby. Please forgive me."

He did, instantly, when her first tear fell. He grabbed

onto her and pulled her into his chest. "Don't cry, Momma," he said thickly. "I'm no saint, that's for sure."

"That's the part you're wrong about," she said. "You are, and I didn't think you needed me to tell you that too."

"I need to think you like me," he whispered, his own hurt rising up and overflowing. "I want you to be my mother, not my critic."

"I will," she promised. "I'm so sorry." She wept for several seconds, and Conrad just held her, trying to hold all the pieces of himself that she'd sliced from him in place. If he could just do that, maybe they'd stitch themselves back together.

"I heard there'd be cranberry walnut muffins this morning," Daddy said, clapping his hands and rubbing them together as he entered the kitchen.

Mom straightened and sniffed, quickly wiping her face. "There is," she said in the next moment, her voice without a single ounce of nasal quality. "Conrad's been to Baker's already this morning."

Daddy met Conrad's eyes, his dark eyes shining with love and sympathy. *I'm sorry*, he mouthed, and Conrad waved him off. The last thing he needed was to make Daddy feel bad for praising his abilities over the years.

"Ian's sayin' good-bye to Stars For Eyes today," Conrad said, reaching for the box before his dad could claim it. "I want one of these for him. He'll appreciate that."

Daddy peered into the box. "That still leaves two for me."

"Jefferson," Mom warned, but Daddy only laughed.

Conrad smiled at the little ways his father defied his mom, and once they had their muffins warmed and buttered, they sat at the dining room table with coffee.

"Conrad says things with Ry are getting real serious," Mom said.

"Yes, I heard," Daddy said, glancing at Conrad. "What does that mean?"

Conrad shrugged and took another bite of his breakfast. He washed it down with a big gulp of coffee and said, "I honestly don't know. She got pretty mad at me last night, because...well, I wasn't one-hundred percent honest with her. She doesn't want to talk about happy-happy things if I don't share the hard things with her."

"No wonder you're here, talkin' to your mom," Daddy said.

Conrad exchanged a glance with his mother. "It was time anyway."

"You must love her then," Mom said. "That's when the boys have been coming to make things right with me. They want all the things in their lives to be right, and I'm just a small part of that."

Conrad finished his coffee. "You know, I don't know if I'm in love with her or not. I don't know what that feels like."

"Sure you do, son," Daddy said, his knife poised above his second muffin. "You love those horses you work with, don't you?"

"They're *horses*, Dad."

"You still know what love feels like."

"I guess."

"Think about it a little," Daddy said. "You'll figure it out."

Conrad looked at his phone and noted the time. "Yeah, I will." He was already distracted though. "I have to run. I want to be there with Ian, and his buyer should be here in twenty minutes."

"Go," Daddy said. "Tell him hello from us."

Thirty minutes later, Ian shook Dale Hammerson's hand, and the other man went to get behind the wheel of his enormous truck. Stars For Eyes had been washed that morning, and Ian himself had loaded the horse into the trailer. As they started to pull away, Conrad slung his arm around his brother's shoulders.

"Come on," he said. "Let's go back to the corner house and take the morning off. I've got that muffin for you, and I'll make fresh coffee."

"You didn't even make coffee before you left this morning," Ian said. "You ran out so fast." He tore his eyes from the retreating horse trailer. "Where'd you go, anyway?"

"Baker's," Conrad said, knowing his hard conversations for the day weren't over yet. "Then I had breakfast with Mom."

Ian's mouth opened slightly, his dark eyes getting rounder too. "On purpose?"

Conrad chuckled and said, "Yeah, on purpose. It wasn't fun, but I haven't told Ry about it yet, so you'll have to wait for the story."

"I see how it's going to be," Ian said, lightning moving

through his expression. "She's going to come before me from now on."

"Yeah," Conrad said. "She probably is, brother. I'm sorry."

"Don't be sorry," Ian said. "I've been thinking about something, but if I tell you, you have to promise two things."

"Name them."

"You can't ask me any questions." He held up one finger and then another. "You can't tell anyone else."

"Done and done," Conrad said as he followed Ian to his truck. "Does this have anything to do with a certain trainer at Glenn Marks Stables?"

Ian just shook his head, but Conrad knew he didn't mean no. He meant, *I'm not answering that, because I don't want to lie.* Which meant it was exactly about Anita Powell.

Chapter 21

Ry let out an exasperated sigh and hit the delete button on her tablet. She tapped the lines she'd been drawing with her electronic pen, and they came off as easily as she'd sketched them on. "This isn't working."

She pushed the tablet away and almost threw the pen after it in annoyance.

"Take a break," Max said. "You've been bent over that thing for hours."

"I just...I want to get the plus-size line right, but I don't know how to do it."

"I told you I could get women in here for a consumer panel."

Max had said that, and Ry had resisted it. She didn't want to take on more than she currently carried.

"All right," she said as she reached for the muffin stump on her right. She'd already consumed the top, and she hadn't eaten lunch yet, hopeful that Conrad would waltz in with her favorites from Ming Hu's. Her mouth watered just thinking about the steak and beef fried rice. She wanted a family-sized order of that right now, and she'd eat it all herself.

Her eyes felt like someone had rubbed sand in them, and she needed a shower since she'd slept in her old bedroom last night. It housed a queen-sized bed now, not the old twin she'd slept on years ago, but it wasn't the pillow top she enjoyed in her own home.

The tension between her and her parents had still be there this morning, but it had been less. Noticeably less, in Ry's opinion. So much had changed with a few tears and a lot of talking, and she wondered if she should make time for some therapy. Maybe if she spoke to a professional, she could find a way through the mess that was in her head surrounding Andy.

She picked up the card that had been with the cranberry walnut muffin. *I can't stay this morning, Ry. I'm real sorry, because you're the first person I want to see in the morning. Unfortunately, I called my mom last night, and she suggested breakfast. I'm going to talk to her and Daddy. I'll call you later, and I promise I'll see you at some point today. I don't want a single day to go by where I don't.*

He'd drawn a heart—what she assumed was supposed to be a heart—with his big, cowboy hands and signed his name.

She'd read it about twenty times that day already, and the clock had barely struck noon. Could he still be at his parents'? Did they really have that much air to clear?

A sigh fell from her mouth, and Max picked up on it. "You okay, Ry?"

She held up the card. "What do I do about this?"

"Honestly," Max said, focusing on her ledger again. She squinted at the screen in front of her and then made a check on the book. "I'm not sure why you haven't called him yet. Or why you're even here. Go see him."

"Doesn't that make me desperate?"

"No," Max said. "That makes you strong. It lets him know that yeah, you were upset with him last night, but you appreciate that he listened to you." She took off her reading glasses to focus on Ry across the room. "He *listened* to you, Ry. He's making things right with his mom."

"He's trying, at least," she murmured nowhere near loud enough for Max to hear. That only caused her best friend to get up and come closer.

She perched on the table beside Ry's tablet and tucked her hair behind her ears. "Are you worried about things not working out with him...or scared that they will?"

Ry ducked her head. "Both."

"Because of Tobias." Max hadn't asked a question. "Ry, what he said to you when you left Savannah isn't true at all."

"I know," Ry said, but she didn't. Sometimes she still felt plagued by everything that had happened in the last couple of weeks that she'd lived in Savannah. "Maybe the time just isn't right for me and Conrad."

"Why wouldn't it be?" Max said, plucking the card from Ry's hand. She read it again and added, "The only reason it wouldn't be, Ry, is because you don't want it to be." She propped the card against the muffin stump and headed back to her laptop. "That man is in love with you. He might not know it yet, but I know what it means to want to see someone first thing in the morning."

"How are things with Yarn?"

"Still slow," Max said. "It's fine. He's in physical therapy, and that takes a lot of his time and energy." She gave Ry a smile that filled her face with something lovely. "We'll be married soon enough, and then he can model for our menswear line." She went back to work, but Ry watched her for a few extra moments.

Her new boyfriend, Yarn, had been in a bicycle accident a couple of weeks ago, and he'd broken his leg in two places. The road back to walking had been painful and difficult, and Yarn had done everything asked of him. Max had too.

Ry looked at the card again. Had she?

You're running away, Ryanne.

Tobias's words haunted her as she picked up her tablet pen. She had run away from Savannah, but she couldn't even go back to the house she'd shared with Andy. She had no idea how to stay there, just like she had no idea how to drive out to Bluegrass Ranch and face Conrad right now.

She'd done that last night, and things had blown up.

You're running from us, Tobias had said. *You're running from yourself, from what you're meant to do.*

He hadn't wanted her to quit designing to run Andy and Ryan, but Ry hadn't seen another choice.

"You've done what you set out to do," she told herself, the same way her dad had last night. "It's enough." She looked up and found the posters of her designs on the walls in the sewing studio. She loved this room, with the sewing machines, the sergers, the quilting needles, the bolts of fabric, and the long wall of cupboards that held samples, styles, protocols, and one-of-a-kind items.

She'd chosen her clothes that day from those cupboards so she didn't have to wear the same thing as yesterday, and she got up and wandered over to the floor-to-ceiling cupboard. She opened one she'd looked in that morning and found a bright green coat. She'd designed this and fully constructed it from concept to shopping for fabric to the delicate pleats along the chest for one of her classes at the SCAD.

She'd been given a grant because of it. She took the coat out of the closet and started to put her arms in it. Tears flowed down her face as she did, and she didn't bother trying to hide the sobs echoing from her mouth.

"Ryanne." Max hurried toward her and wrapped her up tight. "What's wrong?"

"I m-made this coat for Andy," she gasped out. She'd worked with a local designer who did gowns and pantsuits for the rich and famous to wear to their horse races and fancy Southern balls. Some of her pieces had started to become more mainstream, and Donna Billings had been moving her designs into more ready-to-wear styles that department stores all over the country were picking up.

This coat was one of those ready-to-wear, totally unique pieces, and while Ry had done hers in the brightest peacock green she could find, she could find them in an array of colors from black to white these days.

"Oh, honey." Max stroked her hair and told her to get it all out. "Just let it all out."

Ry cried into her friend's shoulder, the same way she had last night after she'd gone to bed. She should be drained and dried out, but she seemed to just have more and more tears. The episode didn't last long, and she stepped away from Max.

"I'm okay." She brushed her hands down the front of the coat. "I don't think we'd met when I made this coat."

"Not yet," Max said kindly. "Tell me about it."

"It was for one of my final projects," she said. "A clothing design and construction class. I'd always been very good at pleating, and I wanted a coat that made Andy feel like a fairy princess." She smiled through the water in her eyes. "She loved bright colors. She always had a fluorescent pink phone, with a gaudy, blinged-out case on it."

She half-laughed and half-sobbed. "We didn't have much need for a coat in Savannah, but I wanted the challenge of making an outerwear item that could be worn on a breezy day in the autumn or spring."

She ran her fingers down the tight fabric. "Wool was out, of course. Too heavy. We didn't want it to look cheap, like a windbreaker. We didn't want it to be cotton like a T-shirt. She wanted it to have form."

Ry flipped up the bottom flap of the coat. "So I sewed in enforcements. See them?"

"Yeah," Max said, peering closer. "They looked like... plastic soda can...thingys."

"That's what they are," Ry said. "It was Andy's idea, because it gave this really flowy, flimsy silk structure. She wasn't as tall as I am, and when she wore this, she looked like the mushroom princess she wanted to be."

Ry started to take off the coat. "That was the very first piece I designed with my sister in my head. Before that, I'd been trying to think too far out of the box. I got good marks and good grades, but this... This won me the top score in the class and a grant opportunity to work with a huge designer in Savannah."

"That's where we met," Max said. "Through Donna."

"Best day of my life," Ry said, rehanging the coat in the cupboard and turning to hug Max again. "I feel like I might need to go see someone."

"Then do it," Max said. "Yarn has a great therapist. I bet I can get his number."

"I don't want to talk to a man," Ry said, the very idea turning her off immediately.

"Maybe you can get a referral then." Max's blue eyes seemed to light up the studio. So much hope poured from her. "I think it would help you. You've taken on so much, for so long. I'm worried about you."

Ry studied her fingernails, which needed to be repainted. "I'm trying to let go of her, Max. I don't know how. She seems to be everywhere. Did you know I have a stupid hat rack in my house? It's not even mine; it's hers. She bought it when she was dating that wanna-be cowboy from Alabama."

"Mike," they said together, and Max giggled while Ry scoffed. Wendell had been perfect for Andy, and the two of them surely would've been married if she hadn't died. As it was, Wendell had moved his catering company to Dreamsville once he'd finished up at the SCAD, and he didn't seem to be letting go of Andy very fast either.

"I need to make a call," Ry said.

"I hope to Conrad."

Ry didn't answer Max as she strode over to her table and picked up her phone. She didn't call Conrad, but Wendell. "Let's go to lunch," she said. "Fair warning, I want to talk about Andy."

"I need to tell you something about her too," Wendell said. "Thirty minutes? That soup place where you used to work?"

"No," Ry said, shaking her head as she left the sewing studio in favor of her office so she could collect her purse. "That's family-style. How about pizza? Sauced?"

"See you there."

Ry didn't let her stride hitch as she got her purse and left the boutique. She made the drive to Sauced quickly, feeling a bit like she was reliving last night. She'd stopped here to get the barbecue chicken pizza that Conrad loved so much. Today, though, she'd order her ham and pineapple with Alfredo sauce—the yellow brick road.

Wendell joined her in the parking lot, and Ry reached for his hand. "Hey." Seeing him calmed her, because she'd seen him and Andy together so much, she could almost see her sister standing next to him.

"Hey." He leaned over and kissed her cheek. "You look like you've been crying."

"I have been." Ry wiped her free hand down her face. "I don't want to talk until I have food in front of me."

"Let's go get food then." Wendell led the way into the restaurant, and he ordered for both of them without consulting her on what she wanted. He knew her, and she liked that about him.

The moment she slid into her chair with a Diet Coke and a big garden salad in front of her, she said, "I'm trying to figure out how to let go of Andy." She put a bite of spinach and spring greens into her mouth, along with that salty blue cheese she loved.

Wendell's eyes widened. He reached for his drink, having bypassed the salad option for his meal. He took a small sip of the lemon water and coughed lightly. "You are?"

"Have you done it?" Ry watched a storm roll across his face. More than that—a war. A downright fight between his anguish and his hope, and she felt the same battle raging within her.

"Ryanne," he said, his voice the quietest she'd ever heard it. As a chef who ran his own kitchen, the man had a loud bark, and he knew how to bellow. "I've met someone else. I've been seeing her for about six months now, and we've started talking about getting married."

Ry's fork clattered into her bowl and bounced around before coming to rest sideways over the greens. "You have?"

Wendell kept his eyes down, his fingers silently shredding the napkin in front of him. "Yes," he said. "Her name is Kodi Thomas, and she's...well, no one's Andy." He flicked a glance up toward her, not really meeting her eye but giving the idea of it. "But she's great. I fell in love with her, even when I didn't think my heart knew how to do that without your sister."

He dropped the pieces of the napkin, but Ry couldn't look anywhere but at them. "I will always love Andy, but I know she wouldn't want me to be unhappy. She wouldn't want me to pass up this opportunity to be with Kodi."

"How do you know that?" Ry asked, her voice about half the volume it usually was.

"I just *feel* it," he said. "She's okay, Ry. I'm okay. I'm going to ask Kodi to marry me as soon as the diamond I ordered comes in. Probably within the next couple of weeks. I've been trying to figure out how to tell you."

Ry nodded and picked her fork out of the blue cheese dressing. "I'm trying to let go of Andy too. It's time for me to move on as well." She couldn't walk away as easily as Wendell or her parents. She ran a company with her sister's name in it. That company had been everything to her—and to Andy.

"Good for you," Wendell said. "I wish I could help you know how. I don't know how it happened for me. I poured myself into my kitchen for a while, but it wasn't enough. I never dated, and even if I did manage to go out with friends, it wasn't fun. Slowly, things started getting put back in the right place inside me. I don't know how or when or why. It's not easy to pinpoint like that."

He looked up as a woman said their number and then slid their orders onto the table, picked up the stand with the 17 on it, and left.

"It is easy for me to see that everything started to change more rapidly once I met Kodi. I want to be with her, and if that means I have to let go of Andy, then…I did. I have."

Ry nodded, sure things had started to shift for her the moment she'd soaked that bright blue shirt of Conrad's with curry soup. "I understand."

He reached across the table and covered her hand with his. "You're not mad?"

"No," she said, feeling one piece of the anchor she'd been lugging around for so long lift away from her shoulders. "I'm not mad. I'm happy for you." She picked up a piece of her yellow brick road pizza, the mozzarella stretching out as she did. "I'd love to meet your Kodi too." Hope filled her from top to bottom and front to back. Maybe if she met the woman who had prompted Wendell to let go of Andy, she could see what he liked so much to make him want to change so quickly.

"Sure," Wendell said. "We should double with you and Conrad." He took a bite of his calzone, chewed, and swallowed. He took another drink of his water. "You're still seeing Conrad, right?"

"I thought so," a man said, and Ry very nearly choked on her slice of yellow brick road at the sound of Conrad's voice.

A somewhat flustered, barky version of Conrad's voice, but his nonetheless. She looked up into those stunning eyes as he held up his phone. "No service in here, but Max said you'd come here for lunch." He tossed a glare in Wendell's direction. "I guess I didn't realize it was a date."

Chapter 22

Conrad felt somewhat detached from his body, as if he had a bad head cold and everything around him floated somewhere he couldn't see.

"Conrad," Ry said, jumping to her feet. She grabbed onto him, and he couldn't help the way his eyes drifted closed as he hugged her back. The first time they'd met here, he'd made incorrect assumptions about her too, and he worked against the tidal wave of thoughts threatening to drown him.

"Did you want to order?" Ry asked, looking only at him.

No, he didn't want to order. He wanted to kiss her and tell her he loved her and explain about his mother. He glanced at Wendell, and he didn't want to do any of those things with him here.

"I'm going to need a to-go box," he said, standing up and walking away.

Ry watched him for a moment and turned back to

Conrad. "You guys just had a silent conversation I didn't get to hear."

"He's leaving," Conrad said. "You heard what I asked him to do."

Ry looked torn, and Conrad didn't like that. Her eyebrows pulled down. "You said we were on a date."

"I just over-reacted," he said, reaching up and pushing his hat forward. "Will you share your pizza with me?"

"Of course." She sat back down and Wendell returned to box up his pizza. She got back to her feet and hugged him, saying something that got drowned out by pealing laughter from a nearby table of women. A couple of them looked at Conrad, but he didn't even see features. He used to see every woman, and he would seek out the giggliest, cutest one and invite her to sit with him.

Ry had saved him from himself. Or a life of a constantly rotating door of women who would never like him for who he was, only how he looked.

As he sat down where Wendell had been sitting, a pull of exhaustion moved through him. He hadn't even worked that morning. *At least not on the ranch*, he thought.

Ry wore a stunning smile to go with her custom-sewn blouse and skin-tight shorts the color of his most hated food: artichokes. When she looked at him, the grin stuttered and dropped from her face. "Thank you for the muffin," she said.

"You're welcome."

She put a piece of pizza on a plate and handed it to him. "Have as much as you want. I had a salad too."

He nodded, not sure if he could eat with so many words stuffed in the back of his throat.

"How did things go with your mom this morning?"

Conrad's jaw locked and jumped, and he had to work hard to get it to release. "My mother—in my eyes—has always been a little—a lot—mean to me."

Ry abandoned her pizza and reached for a napkin.

"I can't explain it all," he said, sighing. "But she'd say cruel things to me about how I wasn't as good of a horse trainer as Ian. She'd make him cakes when we'd both gone to certification programs and returned to the ranch. Not me. Once, that summer we went to Louisville after we went to the prom?"

He cleared his throat, because that had been such a hard time in his life. "That was so hard for me, Ry. You have no idea what I was going through, and I'm not saying it's a good reason for me to have treated you the way I did, but it certainly contributed."

Ry reached across the table and covered his hand with both of hers. She said nothing, though, and the building could've started on fire, and she wouldn't have looked away from him.

"Ian and I had gone together, alone. He's a couple of years older than me, so he was a legal adult. We were gone for two months, in a brutal program where we'd both done well. We'd both earned the certificate." He cleared his throat, wishing the hurt would go as quickly as the forgiveness had come. "Mom made a huge dinner with all of Ian's favorite things. None of mine. The dinner had artichokes in every dish, and I'm actually allergic to them."

Ry's eyes widened, and he noticed that she looked like she'd been crying. His heart tore, and he wished he'd been there for her this morning.

"Are you okay?" he asked, leaning forward.

She nodded, her beautiful eyes welling with water right now. "Go on."

"I don't want to make you cry."

"You're not," she said. "Please keep going."

"Stuff like that," Conrad said, not wanting to rehash everything. "Last year, at Halloween, she asked me and Ian to bring a cake for the family party, and I did. She deemed it burnt and threw it away right in front of me. Just stuff like that. Stuff that hurt me. Comments. Things like that. So I learned pretty dang fast to avoid her. I didn't think she liked me, though I couldn't figure out what I'd done."

"Conrad." She shook her head, her lovely face crumpling as she lost the battle against her tears. "I'm so sorry. I wouldn't have pushed you to talk about this had I known."

"I don't like talking about it," he said. "I've found a way to exist inside my own bubble of confidence, and it's worked for me."

Until Ry.

"You were right, Ry."

She looked at him and swiped at her eyes. "No, I wasn't."

"You were," he insisted. "I needed to go talk to her. It's time. It wasn't pretty, and it wasn't easy, but she apologized, and she explained, and I think things will start to get better now."

She nodded and pulled her hands away. He didn't like the chill that moved across his skin with the loss of her touch. "You made me face her, and you made me realize that I did lie to you, and I have been putting Ian's feelings above yours and mine. We talked a little this morning, but he got called away to a meeting. That's not going to be an easy conversation either, though I think he knows."

He snapped his lips shut, because he'd almost said, "I think he knows I love you."

He wasn't ready to say those words, and by the tears and the turmoil in her expression, she wasn't ready to hear them.

"Thank you for being honest with me," he said. "I want us to be honest with each other. Honest and real. I want to share all the ugly things in my life with you. You are the first person I want to see in the morning and the last one at night." He didn't need to say anything more, but she might, and he gave her some space and silence to say it.

She met his gaze again, those tears back. "I'd started to push you away," she said. "You scare me to death, Conrad Chappell."

A shock moved through him like a stinging electric current. "Oh." He blinked, trying to make sense of what she'd said. "Why's that?"

"Because you're so perfect," she said.

"No," he said, barking the word. "I'm not."

"For me," she pushed on. "You're so perfect *for me*. You

support me the way my fiancé did in Savannah, and that scares me."

"Because you don't want to get married?"

"Because everything in Savannah turned bad," she whispered. "I lost everything there, remember?" She shook her hair over her shoulders and blinked the tears back into her eyes. "I went to see my parents after I left your ranch last night."

Conrad reached across the table and covered her hand with both of his. "Go on."

"It wasn't fun or easy, but it was a good conversation. Bottom line is, I'm still hung up on the past. Five years in the past, to be exact. I don't know how to let go of Andy." Her eyes turned glassy. "It's going to hurt so much, and I don't know how to do it."

Conrad got up and went to her side. He didn't care that he was blocking the aisle. He enveloped her in a hug right there in her chair as he crouched next to it. "I'll help you," he whispered in her ear. "If you'll let me."

"I can't do it without you," she said. "At the same time, I don't think I can truly move forward with you until I do."

"I'm right here," he said, hoping she heard what he hadn't said: *I'm not going anywhere.*

He wasn't, unless she told him he had to. He prayed she wouldn't, and that he could be strong enough to help her with whatever she needed.

Chapter 23

"We'll miss you, Nita," Sally said, and Nita gave her a grateful grin.

"Thank you." She wouldn't miss working two outdoor jobs, but she couldn't bring herself to be upset about the past several months. This job at the Parks Department had gotten her out of a tough spot and through what could've easily been a depressing summer.

"What are you going on to next?" Clyde asked, his second piece of cake rapidly disappearing. He still had work to do that afternoon—they all did—so Nita understood.

"Just working the stables," she said. All of her friends at the Parks Department knew she worked with horses, so she didn't need to go into much further explanation. "Having one job is going to feel like a vacation."

"I'll bet," Shane said. "We'll miss ya, for sure. We'd love to have you next summer."

"Thank you." Nita really didn't want to be back on the temporary seasonal job next summer. She smiled at her boss anyway, ate the cake Sally had ordered, and accepted all of their well wishes and congratulations.

After she finished her lawn mowing and park care for the day, she punched her last time card, put it in the slot, and went out to her pick-up

A great breath of air filled her lungs, and Nita felt like she could breathe for the first time in a year. Tears pressed into her eyes, and her bottom lip trembled. She gripped the steering wheel, as if that pressure could keep her emotions in check.

It couldn't, and she wept quietly right there in the parking lot in front of the industrial trailer that housed the Dreamsville Parks Department.

"It is done," she whispered. Not only had the job finished, but with her final paycheck from it, which she'd get next Friday, she'd be able to pay off the last of the debt she'd been shackled with. The nightmare would be over. She could return to her original plan of buying her own stable and training her own horses.

She pulled out of the parking lot, and she'd barely accelerated before her phone rang. After glancing at the fancy screen in her car, she tapped on the green phone icon to answer the call. The car always took an extra moment to connect, so she waited the second of time, and then said, "Hey, Glenn."

"Your last day," her father said. "How do you feel?"

Nita squeezed the wheel again, more oxygen entering her lungs and her life. "Good."

"Are you on your way to us? Janet has dinner almost ready."

Nita looked out her side window at a flock of geese that had chosen a pasture to settle in. "Yes," she said, deciding on the spot to go to dinner with her dad and step-mother. "I should be there in about a half-hour. I need to shower first."

"Take your time," Glenn said. "We can go over the proposal, if you'd like."

"Dad." Nita shook her head, enough frustration and resistance in that single word to house the entire conversation.

"You shouldn't buy your own stable," Glenn said. "I want you to take over Glenn Marks completely one day."

Nita's teeth clenched, and she didn't know how to respond this time, the same as she hadn't known how any other time her father had brought this up.

"If it's about your mother, Nita, it's time to let that go. This is business."

Instant fury shot to the top of her head, and Nita had to work to keep her retort from flying out of her mouth. Glenn should know better by now. "I have another call coming in," she said, her tone a freaky-calm she only used in rare circumstances. She'd been using it a lot on her dad in the past couple of years, though.

"Nita, you—"

"It's Ian," she said. "I'll call you back."

"Who's Ian?"

Nita said the first thing she could think of to get her dad off the line. "My boyfriend. I'll call you back." She stabbed at the phone icon that was red now, and the call disconnected. Relief sagged through her muscles and mind, and she continued to drive along the country roads that circled Dreamsville.

She didn't want to get too close to downtown, because then it was only a couple of turns to her dad's house. Or, a couple to her mom's. Their divorce had not been pretty, and Nita hadn't meant to take sides. They'd forced her to, though. In the trench where she'd found herself, looking up on one side to the life and career she'd always wanted as a horse trainer, or turning and gazing up at the woman who'd raised her and given her the strength and confidence to be that horse trainer, Nita had made some poor decisions.

She never should've gone out with Karlton Hoopes, that much was certain. She never should've let him live with her, eat her cereal, or have access to her purse. So much bad had come from that, and Nita had just spent nine months paying—physically paying—for that mistake.

She'd already vowed to never have another boyfriend, especially a good-looking cowboy who trained horses. Yet every time she thought of her life moving forward, there *was* a good-looking cowboy who trained horses in it—Ian Chappell.

He'd been nothing but his usual self since the lunch invitation months ago. He was salty, growly, and frowny, just like he always had been. At least he and his brother had been staying out of her stable and away from Powerplay.

Nita's chest filled with another sigh, this one filled with less freedom and air and more doubt and worry. Guilt gutted her too, because she'd lied to her father. Ian Chappell was not her boyfriend.

"My goodness," she said out loud to herself. "You're as bad as your father." Glenn had lied about his relationship with Janet Valencia for a couple of years before it finally came out that she was his mistress. Nita's mother had filed for divorce; the day after it was final, Glenn had married Janet.

Nita's whole world had been cut down the middle, but the line was treacherous and jagged. She didn't really know which side she was on, and a single step could put her in a different camp or falling straight down toward that trench again.

No matter what, she didn't want to be like her father. She pulled over and reached for her phone. She said she'd call him back, but she didn't want to talk to him again. He had a way of confusing her, telling her things that might be true—but they might not be. In that way, he reminded her of Karl, and the thought made her stomach churn around the chocolate cake she'd eaten earlier at her going-away party.

I can't come to dinner. I'm sorry. Tell Janet to save the food, and we'll have it another time. Nita studied the words and then sent the text.

We don't have to talk about the stable. You can do what you want.

"I don't know what I want, Glenn," she muttered to herself. Her stomach growled, and she knew she wanted dinner. She knew she didn't want to eat it with her dad and the woman who'd stolen him from her family.

After she'd told her dad she'd been saving to buy a stable of her own, a training practice for herself, he'd offered her a percentage of Glenn Marks. The name was well-respected around Kentucky and in racing circles worldwide. She'd learned from him, and she'd worked for her dad's company for almost twenty years already.

She wanted her name on the stables though, and they'd been collaborating about an offshoot of his stable, using her name. Glenn Marks came from two men anyway—her dad, and her father's brother. Uncle Mark had died a few years ago, and to be honest, everything about her dad had changed with his brother's death.

His life had spiraled out of control; he'd drank a lot; he'd started cheating on her mom; the stables had slipped.

Nita had stepped into a more powerful role then, and while her last name wasn't the same as her father's and no one knew she was Glenn's daughter, she'd been able to keep the reputation intact. She'd protected her father, which only made everything since the divorce even more convoluted. Sometimes, she worried that she'd hurt her mom too. They'd talked everything to the very death, and Nita was so done with talking, talking, talking.

On her phone, she navigated to her email, where the logo she'd hired out had come in weeks and weeks ago. She'd already approved it and paid for the design. GMP shone back at her, the tops of the letters rounded in the oval shape of the logo.

Glenn Marks Powell.

She pinched out to zoom in, the names becoming clear enough to read, though she knew exactly what they said. Three horses—black vectors—grazed beneath the names, and then the words "champions since 1975."

She loved this logo. She loved working with horses. She loved her name tacked onto the end of the prestigious ones that had preceded her.

She was just so worried about what Glenn Marks Powell would do to her mother. She'd already lost so much, and Nita didn't want to be the cause of any more pain in her life.

An image of the man who'd given her the name Powell filled her mind, but she couldn't capture the sound of Sampson's voice. That had disappeared in the first six months after his death. The hole that existed in her chest reopened, smaller this time than last time she'd allowed herself to think about her husband of only eight months. Smaller, but still there. She wondered if such a deep wound would ever heal. Could she even love another man again?

"You thought you loved Karl," she murmured, tapping to get away from the logo. She needed to get away from these thoughts too. Today was supposed to be a celebratory day. She'd earned enough to get out from under her bad decisions when it came to men. She only had one job now—and it was the career she wanted.

She had the proposal and the logo, and all she had to do was say, "Now," and Glenn would sign it. She'd own half of

Glenn Marks, which would become Glenn Marks Powell, and she'd sail off into the sunset in absolute bliss.

Alone, but happy.

"What should I do, Sam?" She looked up to the roof of her car, right through it, and all the way to heaven. "Tell me what to do."

He didn't, but talking to him always made her feel slightly calmer. His life had been cut too short, and their life together had been as well. "I miss you," she said, and she dropped her phone back into the cup holder and eased onto the highway again.

She just drove, though she should go to her dad's and have dinner with him like she'd planned. Maybe Janet would give her an hour instead of thirty minutes, and Nita could go visit her horses for a bit.

She tapped her phone icon on the steering wheel and said, "Call Glenn."

The car did what she asked, and her father picked up on the first ring. "I won't talk about the stables."

"I lied to you," Nita said. "I don't have a boyfriend."

Silence poured through the line, and Nita sighed, another sigh filled with frustration instead of the freedom she craved. "I'm sorry, I just...I need more than thirty minutes. Can you give me an hour? I'll be there in an hour."

"You don't need to apologize to me," Glenn said in a voice that carried so much burden it was almost pained.

Nita's own emotions rose again, always riding that roller coaster up and down. "I want to talk about the stables," she said. "We need to get moving on it if we're going to make the transition at the new year."

"We've still got four months," he said.

"It'll take time to rebrand." They'd talked about this before—always talking, talking, talking. Nita had learned to sit and listen more than ever over the past couple of years. Sometimes her mom just needed to vent, so Nita listened. Sometimes her dad liked the sound of his own voice and all of his own ideas, so Nita listened.

"True," he said. "Come in an hour. Anything you don't want to talk about, sugarbaby, and we won't."

"Thanks, Glenn." She pressed her eyes closed. "I mean, Dad." The call ended, and she continued to Bluegrass. The ranch was open almost all the time. Sometimes trainers had to sit with their horses overnight in case they casted, and Nita had endured that pain. Her horse had managed to get herself stuck too, and Nita had crawled up into the ceiling from the adjacent stall and dropped down into the one where her horse had her legs against one wall, her back the other, and panicking.

Nothing good happened when a horse panicked.

She rumbled along, all the way to the rail in front of Glenn Marks Stables and got out. Four of her horses had heard her truck, and they all hung their heads over the half-height doors. They hadn't been closed yet, which meant that someone was still here cleaning up for the night.

She looked left and right, didn't see anyone, and walked toward the end stall, which housed a horse named Precious in Pink. "Hey," she murmured to the horse. Precious's eyes drifted halfway closed as if in bliss, and Nita could only smile at her. She'd run her hard that day, which was why she was so calm.

She'd be ready to enter the big races next year, if Nita had anything to say about it. "Where's Rome, huh?" she asked, looking down the row of horses. "He hasn't put you away yet." The last stall on the row of five was empty, and that told her where Rome was—probably washing Sunday Gamble. Once the Thoroughbred was clean, he'd be back in his stall, and everyone would be closed up for the night.

Footsteps and horse's hooves approached, but it wasn't Rome who came around the corner leading the equine.

It was Ian Chappell.

Fire and confusion licked through Nita. "What are you doing?" she demanded.

He looked up, similar confusion in his eyes. "Hey, Nita."

"Hey, Nita?" She looked behind him. "Where's Rome?"

Ian threw her a sour look, and she wondered why her heart was doing this strange dance in her chest. She did not like this man. He was arrogant and too handsome for his own good. Not to mention that he overstepped his boundaries time and time again.

He's the best horse trainer at Bluegrass, she thought, her mind once again devolving into thoughts of him as her boyfriend. Maybe then, her trainers would respect her.

They'll respect you when the new logo comes out and the announcements are made.

Hopefully.

"Relax," Ian said, but that word had always had the opposite effect on Nita.

She stalked toward him as he led Gamble into his stall. "Where's Rome?"

"I expect he's to the hospital by now," Ian said, his voice darkening and echoing from inside the stall. He turned Gamble and unlooped the rope around his neck.

"The hospital?"

Ian joined her on the narrow sidewalk in front of the rowhouse. She could've backed up to put more distance between them, and Ian could've too. Neither of them did. The tension between them combusted and sparked, and Nita felt the current run down to her fingertips and then arc to her toes.

Could Ian feel that? Was she annoyed or attracted to him?

Both, she thought, and she had no idea what to do with that information.

"He fell in the wash shed," he said. "It was an accident, and I heard him calling for help. I dialed nine-one-one, because we couldn't get his head to stop bleeding, and he seemed...out of it."

Nita gasped, already reaching for her phone. "I'll call Glenn."

Ian put his hand on hers, covering the device. "Nita."

Time slowed as she lifted her eyes to his. He wore kindness there; kindness that Nita really needed in her life. With everything else that had happened today—the going-away party, the relief at being done, the pride that she'd paid off her debts, the difficult conversation with her dad, the constant worry about her mom—Nita couldn't handle the kindness from this cowboy.

She burst into tears. Ian took her phone and then took her into his strong arms and said, "Hey, it's okay. He's going to be okay."

Chapter 24

Sparks, pops, and crackles danced through Ian's bloodstream, making him feel like a real pervert. He shouldn't be so happy to be holding a sobbing woman in his arms. The truth was, though, Ian hadn't been this close to a woman in a long time. To anyone, really, though he did hug his brothers from time to time.

He had a great relationship with Conrad, though that had been shifting rapidly over the past couple of weeks. All summer, if Ian was truly being honest.

He loved spending time with Spur, and his oldest brother's advice from the last time they'd gotten together for pizza blared in his mind.

Run with it and see what happens.

He hadn't done that. He'd been dragging his feet, not running. Even if he did start to pick up the pace with Nita, he didn't even know what the first step would be. Dinner? Lunch? Holding her hand? Texting her?

He'd been out of the dating game for a long time now, and he still wasn't sure he wanted to play.

Holding Nita sure was nice, though.

He closed his eyes and stroked his hand down her hair. "He was fine, Nita. They just took him, because they wanted to make sure he didn't have a concussion."

She calmed quickly and stepped out of his arms. They fell back to his sides, utterly useless now without her in them. He frowned, because he needed someone to extract his thoughts, examine them, and tell him what they meant.

"I should go see him," she said, her voice nasally and broken. So broken.

He looked at her, sensing there was so much more to this woman than her tough exterior. He wanted to dig at her until he uncovered every piece, and that thought scared him more than anything.

"I already told him I'd close up here," Ian said, turning to do just that. "Go."

"Would you...?"

He latched the top half of the door on Sunday Gamble's stall and turned toward her. "Would I what?"

Something ran across her expression he couldn't categorize. Fear, maybe? Anxiety? Embarrassment?

She shook her head as the last of it disappeared, and Ian moved down to latch the next stall. He'd just put the lock in place when he realized what emotion Nita had worn: Desire. Hope. Longing? Attraction?

Ian felt all of the above firing through him, and firing hard, reminding him he was a man and she was a woman, and he didn't want to be alone forever. He'd thought he did. For a lot of years, he'd thought he'd be better off alone. Now...now, he wasn't so sure.

Would you...?

Go with me?

"I can go with you if you want," he said, not sure where the words had come from. Insanity, most likely. What he'd just said was one-hundred percent insane. He didn't want to make an evening trip to the hospital. He'd been planning to finish up for Rome and then shower, eat a lot of the frozen chicken enchiladas he'd warm up while he showered, and fall asleep on the couch. His usual Friday night routine.

"Would you?" she asked.

Ian locked up the third stall and faced her. "Sure." He cleared his throat. "I'm starving, though, so at some point tonight, could we get something to eat? Drive through somewhere? I'm easy to please."

"I think there's a cafeteria at the hospital," she said, her full composure back. "We could check on Rome, and then..." She shrugged, and Ian decided to look away from her. She seemed uncomfortable with the idea of eating with him, and he had to admit his stomach wasn't happy about it either.

His heart seemed to be though, and Ian closed up the last two stalls and said, "All right. Should I follow you into town?"

"Or...you could drive," she said. "I can leave my truck here and get it when we get back."

Ian looked at the elderly vehicle parked several feet away.

It felt like it belonged to a rough, tough cowboy who wouldn't give it up because it had belonged to his grandfather.

"It's a ways back into town," he said.

"I don't live in town," Nita said.

"Okay." His curiosity about where she did live could've burned a hole in his pocket. "I'm parked a couple of rowhouses over." He went toward her, so many thoughts flying through his mind. Half of them screamed at him to take her hand as he passed and see what she did. The other half clamored that he absolutely not do that. They didn't want to be too forward or get rejected, and Ian honestly had no idea what move to make—if he should make one at all.

Thankfully, Nita made the decision for him and walked in front of him until the path opened up and they could walk side-by-side without touching.

"Where do you live?" he asked as they left the Glenn Marks Stables horses behind.

"I've got a little place only a couple of miles from here," she said. "West to that road that runs south? It's just off there."

"By the windmills."

"Yes," she said. "I can see all of them from my backyard."

"Nice view of the river over there."

"There's that too."

Proud of himself for having a normal conversation with Nita that didn't involve yelling or accusations, he moved to open her door for her. Their eyes met, and Ian looked away before she could read his expression. He had no idea what he was saying with his eyes, and he didn't trust himself.

Once behind the wheel, he said, "I have to text Conrad and let him know where I am."

"Okay," she said. "I'll text Glenn."

They both got busy doing that, and Ian wondered if her text was as complicated as his. He typed, *Ran into some trouble in the stables. Rome had to go to the hospital. I'm going to see how he's doing.*

No mention of Nita.

Unease flowed through him. If he mentioned her, Conrad would call. If he didn't, Conrad would probably call. Then he'd have to tell him about Nita in person, while driving, over speakerphone...

Ian sighed, which only drew Nita's attention to him. The weight of her gaze on the side of his face didn't help his nerves. He couldn't remember the last time he'd had a woman in his truck. This specific vehicle had never seen one sitting in the passenger seat, because he'd gotten rid of almost everything he'd owned after his divorce from Minnie.

His fingers flew now. *I'm with Nita, and I don't want to talk in front of her. It's nothing. I'm fine. She's fine. I'm sure Rome will be fine. I just didn't want you to worry.*

He sent the text, which was probably laden with typos, and pulled down from the top of the screen to then silence the notifications. For good measure, he turned off the Bluetooth too. That way, if Conrad called anyway, it wouldn't connect to the truck.

He shoved his phone under his leg and looked at Nita. "Ready?"

"Ready, Freddie."

Stunned, he turned toward her. She met his questioning gaze again, shock in her eyes too. "I have no idea where that came from," she said.

Ian chuckled, the sound foreign to his own ears. The noise grew into full-fledged laughter, and he knew he hadn't done that in a while. Years, probably. All the ice between him and Nita broke and sank, especially when she started to laugh with him.

Under his leg, his phone buzzed and buzzed, which meant Conrad had gotten the message and called anyway. Ian didn't care; he could talk to his brother later. For the next few minutes, he was going to try to enjoy his time with Nita…and hope he didn't mess up too badly.

Chapter 25

Ry left her therapist's office and headed toward home. She made the drive in silence, something she'd grown to love over the past couple of weeks since her lunch date with Conrad. She still saw him every day, and she needed the quiet time to analyze her thoughts.

She liked having nothing to do except think, and she hadn't had that in so long. Right after Andy died, she'd been terrified to be alone with her thoughts, because they'd been so crooked and so harmful. Even now, when Dr. Murray had challenged her to take ten minutes each day and do nothing —her words: "Do nothing, Ryanne. Do you think you can do that?"—Ry struggled.

She hadn't been able to do it. Her mind flitted from here to there, trying to find something to land on so it wouldn't land on Andy.

In the third session, Dr. Murray had suggested Ry drive home from her appointment in silence. It was about a ten-minute drive, and all she had to do was turn off the radio. She'd done it, and she hadn't turned her radio back on. Everywhere she went now, she went in silence. She gave herself that space to just be.

It was so, so wonderful, and she understood now why Conrad loved being outside with just the breeze and the birds. A person could really think under a silent, Kentucky sky. She'd told him that, and he'd taken her for a walk along one of their quieter parts of the ranch a couple of days ago. Their time together had been simple and perfect, and she'd enjoyed it so much.

She hadn't seen him yet today, and she half-expected him to be in her driveway, a bag of something delicious for dinner with him. He wasn't, and Ry pulled into her garage and went inside her house.

The air held very still, and Ry dropped her oversized bag on the kitchen table just inside the door from the garage. She tried to match the air, and she closed her eyes and imagined what it would be like to be home all day. Would the house feel this empty? Would it be so peaceful?

In today's session, Dr. Murray had challenged her to get rid of something of Andy's that she'd kept. She'd asked, "Is there something you can think of right off the top of your head that you'd be willing to give up?"

Ry had only been able to blink.

Her eyes swept the room, and she saw so much of her sister there. Nothing she owned personally—until her eyes landed on the hat rack. Without thinking, Ry strode over to it and picked it up. Thirty seconds and several paces later, and the hat rack sat in the garbage can that stood around the corner of the house.

Her chest heaved, and she felt like she'd done something horrific and amazing all at the same time. Andy had made that hat rack in a community woodworking class as a gift for their father. She'd liked it so much, she'd kept it for herself, as she'd been dating one from Alabama quite seriously for a while there.

"She should've gotten rid of it when she started dating Wendell," Ry told her neighborhood. No one answered. No one had seen her do this difficult, disastrous thing.

Instant guilt gutted her, the hook of it so sharp, she gasped in pain. She flipped the lid back and pulled the hat rack out of the big, black can. She couldn't throw this away. Andy had *made* it with her own hands. She'd loved it.

Tears flowed down her face, the hat rack in one hand and the other clenched in a fist. She couldn't move. Everything hurt; from head to toe and all in between, she ached in a way that wasn't only physical.

Somewhere, a dog barked. An engine came to life. Someone said something, and her name might've been in the words.

Then Conrad appeared, and he took the hat rack from her and enveloped her in an embrace so tight and so tender she could only hold on and sob.

* * *

"I'm okay," she said a couple of hours later. She got to her feet and took her teacup into the kitchen. "You can go."

"I'm just fine right here," he drawled, not moving except for the muscles around his mouth. Those barely moved, and he looked calm and peaceful as if he were asleep. He'd fallen asleep several minutes ago, and that had only made Ry feel worse about herself.

She went back into the living room and leaned over him. "You are not. You're falling asleep, and you can't sleep here, cowboy."

His eyes fluttered open, and his handsomeness came alive with those eyes. "Can't I?"

"No." Ry gave him the best smile she could muster, but she was pretty sure it still turned down at the edges. "Go on, now. I don't want to have to call your mother."

Conrad groaned as he sat up. "You wouldn't dare."

"She might think I'm pregnant again." Ry's smile did manifest itself this time, and Conrad matched hers as he stood.

"You're really okay?"

"Yes," she said, her gaze fluttering over to the hat rack that he'd replaced beside the back door. "I'm fine."

"I'm worried about you." He took her into his arms and swayed with her. She went with the motion, closing her eyes and wishing they could board a plane and fly away together. She just needed to *get away*.

"Doctor Murray says sometimes it gets bad before it gets better," she said.

"Which is why I should stay," he said.

"I don't want you to," she said.

He backed up then, his eyes searching hers. He cradled her face in one hand and leaned down to kiss her. She did enjoy kissing Conrad, especially when he moved slowly like this, when he took his time, when he conveyed to her that the kiss was much deeper than it went on the surface.

He pulled away too soon and put more space between them. "Ry," he said. "Do you think we're...different?"

"No," she said, bending to pick up the pillows they'd removed so they could cuddle together on the couch. He'd made tea; he'd put something on TV; he'd kept her company all night without hardly saying anything. He'd only gotten up once to try to call his brother, but he hadn't been able to reach Ian. "*I'm* different."

He nodded, and it wasn't like him to hold his tongue quite so much. "What are you thinking?" She picked up the paper plates he'd put their French fries and burgers on and took those into the into the kitchen too.

"It's nothing," he said. "I mean, it's something, but I don't want to tell you yet."

She faced him. "Tell me what? If you're going to break-up with me, you should probably just do it."

Irritation lit his face. "Why would I break-up with you?"

"Because I'm different," she said. "I get it." She shook her head. She didn't know how to articulate the storm in her chest. "I'm not the same person I was even a couple of weeks ago. I'm miserable company. I cry all the time." The stupid tears came again now. "I had a freaking panic attack less than two hours ago, and you deserve someone better."

"Don't," he barked at her. "Don't tell me what I deserve or what I want." He came toward her, those long legs eating up distance so fast. "I *want* to be here with you. I'm not going anywhere."

She turned away from him and looked out the window. The evenings had started getting darker a touch earlier, but there was still plenty of light left in today. "What if I need to go somewhere?"

"We're going to Louisville in a few days," he said, his voice much quieter and much more reserved now. He touched her waist, and Ry leaned into him.

"What if I'm so different," she started. "And we don't make it?"

"We're going to make it," he said.

"How do you know?" she asked.

"Because I'm in love with you." The whispered words sank into her ears, burrowed into her brain, and touched her heart.

She flinched when she finally understood what he'd said to her. "What?" She turned to face him, those slate-colored eyes more intense than she'd ever seen them.

"I told you I didn't want to tell you yet," he said, half-teasing her and half-not.

"I..." She didn't know how to say it back. She'd loved Conrad Chappell for as long as she could remember. He might've broken her heart years ago, and their most recent path certainly hadn't been easy, but she'd fallen in love with him again. She just hadn't admitted it to herself yet.

"I'm going to go," he said. "You have a late meeting

tomorrow night, right?" He went around the island and back toward the front door.

"Yes," ghosted out of her mouth. She might try to get Max to take over the meeting, because then Ry could find her silence and figure out how to tell Conrad she loved him.

He put on his cowboy hat and turned back to her. "I hate to say it, but tomorrow might end our streak of seeing each other every day."

"We made it for one hundred and three days," she said.

"So I'm your boyfriend." He grinned at her, and Ry even managed a laugh. He tipped his hat and ducked out the front door, leaving her wanting another kiss and not nearly as much silence.

She followed him to the front door and locked it, then side-stepped over to the window to watch him get behind the wheel and drive away. A sigh filled her lungs and came out of her mouth. When she turned around again, her eyes landed on that blasted hat rack.

Her world spun, and she wasn't sure what to do.

I'm in love with you.

The words in Conrad's low, sultry voice filled her ears, then her mind. They pushed out doubts and fears and left room for only a new beginning.

She crossed her house and picked up the hat rack again. Outside, she lifted the lid on her trash can and put the rack inside.

This time, when she walked away from the can, she didn't have Conrad's arm supporting her, his voice encouraging her to take another step, or extreme emotions running through her.

She only felt confident and cool, and she made it back inside the house without an issue. "All right," she said. "What's next?"

She walked into the kitchen and opened her cupboard. Yep, Andy's favorite mug sat there. Ry had never used it. She put it on the counter and kept going. She loved her sister; she did. Keeping old coffee mugs, silverware that Andy had liked because it looked antique, or tea towels with her favorite sayings on them didn't prove that love.

What Ry carried in her heart did. She could dedicate a little piece of herself to her sister, but she couldn't keep living her life for her.

In order to make room for Conrad, the man who loved her, she had to get rid of Andy.

Chapter 26

"What part of *I don't want to talk about* it do you not understand?" Ian asked the moment he entered the house.

Conrad looked up from the peanut butter and jelly sandwich he'd been making for himself. He'd already eaten a bacon cheeseburger and French fries at Ry's, but that had been a couple of hours ago.

"You texted about *Nita*," Conrad said, ignoring the growl in his brother's tone. "*Of course* I'm going to call about that."

"I was with her."

"I got that when you swept me to voicemail three times in a row." Conrad capped his sandwich and lifted it to his mouth. He grinned at Ian and took a bite. Mm, his mother's peach jam was like nothing else on this planet.

Ian said nothing as he bent to take off his boots. A sigh

of relief came with each one as they dropped to the ground, and he joined Conrad in the big kitchen at the back of the house.

"So?" Conrad prompted.

"Rome is okay," he said. "They're keeping him overnight, though. He's definitely got a concussion, and they had to put in nine stitches on the side of his head."

If Conrad hadn't had peanut butter in his mouth, he'd have whistled. "What happened?"

"He slipped on the concrete in the wash shed and hit his head on the way down. We think. He doesn't even remember. He said he remembers waking up and not being able to get back to his feet. He started yelling for help. That's when I heard him." Ian shook his head and pulled down a bowl and his favorite box of cereal—Lucky Charms.

"After one look, I called for an ambulance, because the water was still running and going down the drain, but it was *really* bloody."

"Wow."

"Yep." He poured the cereal and got out the milk. "I stayed to finish up with Sunday Gamble, and lock up for the Glenn Marks Stables. That's it."

Conrad didn't think so, but he gave Ian a couple of beats of silence to keep talking. When his brother filled his mouth with marshmallow-delicious cereal instead, Conrad frowned.

"I don't want to talk about it." Ian picked up his bowl and started for the hallway.

"You're seriously leaving?"

"Yes."

"I'm in love with Ryanne Moon," Conrad said.

That got Ian to stop. He almost dropped that silly bowl of cereal. His eyes bugged wide, and he'd frozen mid-chew.

"I found her having a break-down in front of her house tonight," Conrad said, his throat so thick and not because of the peanut butter he'd been trying to cram down it. "I saw her there, and I thought, I can't do this. Then, my very next thought was, of course you can. She needs you, and you love her, so get out there and help her."

Ian blinked, probably because bodies did that all by themselves.

"I didn't want to tell her," Conrad said. "It just sort of slipped out tonight. She didn't say it back." That very real fact made his heart tear and bleed a little.

"I'm sure she will," Ian said, his voice like the rough-hewn granite they had on their bathroom wall. Conrad felt like he'd rubbed his knuckles across it, and they were bleeding profusely.

"Maybe," he said, remembering her saying that he should just break-up with her if he wanted to. He didn't want to. That hadn't even been on his mind.

At least not right then.

He'd be lying if he said he hadn't thought about it before. He had, because the past couple of weeks since she'd started therapy had been hard for him too. She seemed more withdrawn than he'd ever known her to be, and even when they were together, there wasn't much talking.

"Ian," Conrad said. "I don't want to hurt your feelings. I

have no idea what's actually going to happen. For a while there, I thought I did, but a lot has changed in the past couple of weeks."

"I've noticed," Ian said, turning and taking the end spot at the counter. Conrad went around it and joined him. "She's getting the help she needs."

"I know," Conrad said, irritated that Ian felt like he had to lecture him. "I...she's not the same, and I don't know. I miss her. I miss the woman I've spent the summer with." He shook his head. "It's stupid, and you will never, *ever* tell her I said that. She's getting the help she needs, and that's all that matters. I'm going to be right there beside her until she tells me I can't be anymore. I've already decided that."

Ian ate several spoonfuls of cereal and then said, "I'm happy for you, Conrad." He looked at him, and their eyes locked. "Really, I am."

"I know I joked about it a few weeks ago, but she does have to come before you."

Sadness crept across his face. "Yeah, I know. Surely we can still go horseback riding or something. I manage to see Spur without Olli every now and then."

"Surely we can," Conrad said with a smile. He dropped his gaze to the countertop, finding a speck of a stain in front of him. "I'm sorry, Ian."

"You have nothing to be sorry for." Ian finished his cereal and put the bowl in the sink. "Absolutely nothing, okay?"

Conrad nodded and got to his feet. He intercepted Ian

and hugged him. "You're really not going to tell me anything about Anita Powell?"

Ian pushed out his breath as if Conrad had asked him to lop off an arm. "Set a timer for sixty seconds."

Conrad grinned as he did exactly that on his phone, held it up, and said, "Go," at the same time he touched the screen to start the timer.

"We ate dinner in the hospital cafeteria," Ian said, rolling his eyes. "It wasn't a date. It wasn't even close to a date. When you're surrounded by that much antiseptic, it would be impossible to be a date."

"But you *wanted* it to be a date."

"No prompting. You just lost ten seconds."

Conrad chuckled and shook his head.

"*Maybe* I wanted it to be a date," Ian said. "I don't honestly know that. She's…confusing for me. I've been thinking about her, yes. I think she's pretty. She's always been so stand-offish, though, and she sure didn't seem to ever like me. Now…I don't know. I helped Rome like I would've helped anyone, and it just so happened to be Nita who needed a ride to the hospital tonight. It could've easily have been Judd."

"Boo," Conrad said. "You never would've willingly gotten into a truck with Judd."

Ian started to chuckle, which was a huge improvement for him already. He shook his head and said, "No, probably not." He glanced at the phone. "Time's up."

"No, it hasn't gone off."

"You lost ten seconds for prompting me. I'm exhausted and dirty. I'm going to shower and then I'm going to bed." He pushed past Conrad, who stepped out of the way to let him go.

"Wow," he said under his breath as the sixty-second timer went off. "Anita Powell. He's *thinking* about her."

Ian hadn't thought about a woman in years, and this was a huge step for him. Huge.

Conrad tilted his head back and said, "Thank you, Lord. Please bless him, and please keep Ry safe tonight."

He then followed Ian down the hall to his bedroom and closed the door. He had a ton of training to do tomorrow, and then a meeting with Spur, Trey, and Ian to go over their training schedule from now through the racing season next year. Their yearling sales were coming up, and that had be to coordinated. They needed to know how many horses they could take on, and who they could sell.

Spur had ordered a six-foot sub to be delivered to the conference room, where Cayden would meet them with some of Ginny's potato salad. Olli was donating triple-chocolate chunk brownies to the meeting, and Beth would likely send along something baked as well. Conrad just hadn't heard what yet.

He didn't have enough time to get to town to see Ry in the morning, afternoon, or evening, and he wondered how much sleep a man really needed. He really wanted to keep their streak alive, but as he settled in bed, he wasn't sure how he could do it.

Then it hit him right between the eyes. He quickly

reached for his phone on the nightstand beside the bed and fired off a text to Ry. She didn't answer right away, and after ten minutes, he had to admit she'd likely gone to bed and wouldn't see his message until morning—by which time it would be too late to do what he'd just suggested.

Chapter 27

Ry should've been tired, but she wasn't. The thermos of coffee she'd half-downed already this morning was likely helping, but she'd taken a power nap about four a.m. too.

By the time she'd seen Conrad's text about meeting him at six for a watch-the-sunrise-from-horseback ride, a few hours had passed since he'd sent it. She'd said she'd be there, and she'd collapsed for her first thirty-minute power nap.

Then she'd cleaned out another closet, and then another bedroom. Her living room and dining room looked like an army of thieves had come in and ransacked the place, only picking out things that had once belonged to her sister. Her garbage can overflowed, and she'd formulated a plan to ask Conrad to help her load everything up into the back of his truck and take it to the dump.

Maybe not today, but that was irrelevant. Ry had done

it. She'd cried—sobbed, really—she'd remembered, and she'd let go.

She'd made room for Conrad.

She also scrambled to her feet when the front door behind her opened. "I know I'm early, but—" She cut off at the sight of the wrong Chappell brother. "Good morning, Ian."

"What are you doin' here?" he asked, his eyes wide and his voice hushed. "It's five-thirty in the morning." He glanced left and right like she might have brought someone to ambush him.

She smiled. "Conrad said we could go riding at six." She turned and gestured west, though the sun would set in that direction, not come up. "See the sunrise."

"He's still in bed." Ian joined her at the edge of the steps and lifted one mug of coffee toward her. "I put cream and sugar in it. You seem like a cream-and-sugar kind of woman."

"I am." She took it from him and smiled. "I already have about half a gallon of this stuff buzzing through my veins." To prove it, a giggle came out. She didn't care, not even one whit. The Ry Moon she knew giggled. She felt like herself again, and she couldn't wait to see Conrad.

Standing with Ian on the porch was nice too. Ry had met him a few times over the past few months, but Conrad had kept him at arm's length. "I don't mean to make your life harder," she said.

"You don't," he said, taking a sip of his coffee. "I talked to Conrad last night. He's happy, and that means I'm happy." Ian even gave her a smile that seemed genuine and real. "I told him he should bring you around more often. It doesn't hurt my feelings."

"Maybe he'll listen to you," she said. "Heaven knows Conrad does what Conrad wants to do."

Ian shook his head, that smile not going anywhere. "Heaven does know that." He sobered and took a deep breath. "Can I ask you somethin'?" He glanced behind him, a covert look in his eyes now. "I know you'll tell Conrad, which is fine. Maybe just give me a day or two head start."

"Head start on what?" She set her mug on the porch railing so she could focus exclusively on Ian.

"Let's say you were talking to a man," he said, his gaze flitting all over the place, jumping up and down and around like a crazy pulse on a heart monitor. "It's casual, because you don't really get along with her. Him." He cleared his throat. "But you have a nice conversation, and it's a nice night, too. When you get back to her car, you play all gentlemanly, because you are a nice guy deep down."

She wondered if he knew he'd slipped back into using the wrong pronouns, but Ry just nodded at him to keep going.

"She looks wary, but then she grabs onto you and says 'thanks so much. I had a real nice time tonight.'" He blinked a couple of times and downed the rest of his coffee though he'd clearly had too much already too. "What would you expect from him the next day? In the next couple of days? Long-term?"

"Was this a date?" Ry asked.

"No," Ian was quick to answer. "It was an emergency."

Ry wrinkled up her nose. "An emergency?"

"Yeah, and the two of you had to go to the hospital, which is about forty minutes from here. So you're talking in the car. You do the checking-on-the-patient thing. You grab a bite to eat at the cafeteria. You don't fight, not even once, when you've argued plenty of times before..." He gestured with his coffee cup as if to say, *Then that hug happened. Now what?*

Ry drew in a deep breath of the crisp morning air and faced the view from the front porch. It was gorgeous in the flat, gray light, with the white fences classic of horse farms, and rolling green fields. Not even a speck of dust sat out of place at Bluegrass Ranch, and she knew that was because the men and women who worked here loved this land, their horses, and each other.

"That's a really hard question," she said. "Since all women are different."

"Yeah." Ian sighed too.

"She probably wants to figure out where your head is too," she said. "She probably had a really nice time—I mean, she said she did." She took a peek at him and watched as his frown deepened. "You have her number?"

"Yes," he said slowly.

"Maybe you text her today," Ry said casually, as if it didn't matter at all if Ian texted this woman or not. "Find out how the patient is. Ask her if she needs anything. If she's dealing with someone who's ill, she might need help with something."

"Yeah," he said as if he'd just now thought of that. "That's a great idea, Ry."

She smiled at him and reached for her coffee again. He had doctored it up just right. "Tell her you have food at your place, or that you can help with her dog or cat. You know, stuff like that. Stuff people have to do that can feel overwhelming in an emergency."

"I don't think she has a dog or a cat," he said.

"Offer anyway," Ry said, realizing he was looking for an exact script. "Then you'll know more about her too."

He looked at her with wide eyes, as if he'd never met anyone like her. "Thanks, Ry."

"Sure." She turned and looked at the door. "Will he really not look at his phone? He invited me to go riding at six."

"I'll go check on him." Ian took her cup from her and headed inside. Ry had been here before, but only once. Ian had been on his way out last time, and she watched as he entered the house. "You can come in, Ry. No one's gonna bite you."

She followed him into the house and closed the door. This house didn't seem nearly as still or quiet as hers. This house possessed life and laughter, men who loved each other, who *lived* full lives. She wanted a house like this, and she wanted Conrad to come with it.

Five minutes later, two voices came down the hall. Conrad came second, still pulling a shirt over his head. "Ry," he said, plenty of surprise in his voice. He scooped her right into his arms, and she laughed as she tipped her head back and let him kiss her neck.

He set her back on her feet, confusion on that perfect face. "You are completely different than last night."

"Mm." She tiptoed her fingers up the buttons on his shirt, very aware of his brother prowling around in the kitchen behind her. "I only slept for a couple of hours last night, in between all the cleaning and packing."

His brow furrowed, but he didn't let go of her, not even for an inch of space. "Cleaning and packing?"

She looked up into his eyes, the first prick of tears touching hers. Happy tears, though, and Ry gave him a wobbly smile too. "I love you, Conrad Chappell. There's been a part of me who's loved you for almost two decades now. When you told me you loved me last night, it was like this big, shiny, brass key. The one I've been looking for over the past five years. The one I needed to open my heart and let Andy out."

He searched her face, giving her the silence she liked so much.

"I cleaned out her stuff," she said. "I let her go, because I needed to make room for you." She ran her hands up the sides of his face, noting that he hadn't had time to shave that morning. "I can't lose you. I won't. But I was clinging so tightly to her that I couldn't fully have you." She lifted up onto her toes and touched her forehead to his. "I let her go, because I love you. I want you. For me, there is only you."

"For me, there is only you too," he repeated, his voice throaty and filled with emotion. "I love you too."

"Please forgive me for the past two weeks," she said.

"I don't need to forgive anything."

"The sun's comin' up," Ian said. "Better kiss 'er quick and get out there, or you're gonna miss it."

Conrad rolled his eyes, his smile calling down all the powerful lights in heaven. He took her hand and said, "Let's go saddle the horses. There's plenty of time." He tossed a glare in Ian's direction, who only lifted his coffee mug to his lips again, a dark look in those even darker eyes.

"A couple of days," he said, and Ry got the message.

"What does that mean?" Conrad asked.

"Nothing." Ian turned back to the window above the kitchen sink and gazed out of it.

Conrad led her through the kitchen and dining room—which were much bigger than hers—and into the garage. He didn't take one more step after that, though. Instead, he pushed her against the now-closed door and kissed her, much the same way he had at her house once, when his movement suggested he couldn't get close enough to her. He could never get enough of her.

She felt the same way about him, and as the passion in the kiss blazed brightly, so did the love and adoration she felt for this kind, steady cowboy who hadn't left her side when things got really hard.

"We'll miss it if we don't get goin'," he whispered, sliding his mouth along her jawline.

She said nothing, because she liked the snapping sensations against her skin from his touch. She guided his mouth back to hers and kissed him again, neither of them in any hurry to get going.

Eventually, he regained his senses and stepped away from her, nearly falling down the steps from the tiny concrete landing just outside the entrance to the house. He took her hand in his and went into the back yard, saying, "We can see it just as good from here," as he led her toward the back fence.

They both climbed up to the top rung and balanced, their eyes trained East as the golden rays of light started to greet the day. She snuggled into his side, holding him as close to her as possible.

The sun finally arrived fully, casting waves of amber in every direction. "It's beautiful," she said with a sigh. "A new day."

"A fresh start," he said.

Ry took a breath, and it felt like the first one after five years of being underwater. "A fresh start indeed," she said. A ping of sadness hit her, tinged with missing. She'd always miss Andy, but now she didn't have to carry her around everywhere she went.

"My sister wasn't a morning person," Ry said.

"Are you?" Conrad asked.

"Nope," Ry said.

"You must really love me then, to be here so early." He grinned at her, his tone full of that cowboy tease she adored.

She giggled and tipped her head back. "Mm, I think I really do."

He kissed her again, this time under the light of a brand-new day—the first day of the rest of her life with him fully embedded in her heart.

She broke the kiss and asked, "Will you come help me move all my sister's stuff out of my house?"

"Yep." He ran his hand up and down her arm, gazing out at the sunrise. "How much stuff are we talkin' about? Should I ask Ian to come help?"

"An extra truck would probably be beneficial."

Conrad turned and looked at her, but Ry watched the sun inch up degree by degree. "I could get a load of my brothers to come," he said. "This afternoon, before our meeting."

"Might be worth it."

"Ry."

"There's a lot of stuff," she finally admitted. "I didn't know what to keep or what to throw away."

"What are we doing with it?"

She smiled at the *we*. "We're going to throw it all out," she said. "Most of it I haven't touched in years. The few things I have, I'll keep, but it's like the file organizer she built for me. That's at the boutique, in my office. I kept the picture frame she made. It's little stuff. You've probably seen it and didn't even know Andy made it."

"I'll call Spur," Conrad said. "Trey can come, I know that. Ian, and Cayden too. They can't start the meeting without me, and with all of us, it'll go fast."

Relief mixed with gratitude in Ry's heart, and she snuggled deeper into his side. "Thank you, Conrad."

"Don't thank me yet," he muttered. "Dealing with more than one of us at a time is a chore in and of itself."

She giggled and sat up straight. "I think I did pretty great at the Summer Smash with all of them."

"That was a horse racing event," he said. "That we hosted. Trust me, they were on their best behavior." He started to climb down from the fence. "If I'm going to alter their plans, I best call now."

"It's six-thirty." Ry followed him back to the ground.

"Yeah, and Spur doesn't like his schedule to be changed so late in the game." He swiped, tapped, and lifted his phone to his ear.

Ry marveled at this large family, with so many moving pieces. She'd had two siblings, and now that Andy was gone, only her brother. She didn't talk to Tyler or her parents nearly as often as Conrad did his family, and on the short walk back to his house, she determined to change that. Now that she'd let go of Andy, she had more room in her life for the living.

Chapter 28

Trey Chappell picked up another box that had been hastily packed. Ryanne Moon did have a lot of stuff stacked and tossed in the kitchen, living room, and dining room of her house. No wonder she'd been up all night.

She looked like it too, though she possessed a happy glow about her too that Trey fed off of.

"Thank you so much," she drawled at him, and he could see why Conrad liked her so much. She wasn't his typical bubbling, bouncy blonde, because she was a real woman. The kind a man could take home to his family, the kind he could build a family with, the kind that could bear difficult things and put up with the hectic life of a horse trainer.

He grinned at her and started out to the trucks. He'd driven, because he'd already been in town with Beth and Fern. Another doctor's appointment. Their baby girl was almost eight months old now, and cochlear implants could be surgically inserted at twelve months. He and Beth had been exploring a ton of options, including sign language, which they'd both been learning since they'd learned of Fern's hearing impairment.

They'd looked into devices that flashed lights to get her attention, since Beth couldn't just call to her and have Fern hear.

His wife still wept some days, though she was getting stronger and stronger when it came to Fern. They owned and operated a thriving farm that only grew each day. They employed four cowboys now. Farms were a dangerous place for someone who didn't pay attention and couldn't hear. Beth had already said she wouldn't be letting Fern out of the house unless she could hear, and Beth worked the farm every single day.

Right now, she strapped Fern to her body and got the job done. The little girl was getting bigger and bigger every single day, and she'd be walking soon. Trey and Beth had already talked about hiring someone to take over her duties, because she couldn't keep an eye on Fern and muck out stalls with any peace of mind.

Frustration ran through him as he set the box in the back of the truck and pushed it forward until it met the others that had already been put there. He stretched his back and looked up into the afternoon sky. September could be a brutal month in Kentucky, with soaring heat before it finally started to cool. Today was one of those days, and he removed his cowboy hat and wiped the sweat from his forehead.

"You okay?" Duke asked as he approached Trey's truck.

Trey turned toward him and nodded. "Yeah. Okay."

"How's Fern?" Duke set the two boxes he had in his arms in the back of the truck.

Trey forced a smile to his mouth. "She's the best baby in the world."

Duke's return smile felt twice as authentic as Trey's, and he wondered what his brother saw. He'd grown closer to Duke over the past several months since he'd married Lisa Harvey. Their nuptials hadn't been entirely genuine in the beginning, just like Trey and Beth's. They'd hosted Lisa and Duke for dinner at the farmhouse several times, and Trey had seen his youngest brother mature into a man who loved his wife fiercely.

"That's great," Duke said. "Lisa wondered if we might have you guys over for dinner. The whole family. TJ's always askin' about seeing Smoking Chimney or any of the other studs."

"I'm sure Beth would love to have a night off of cooking." They ordered food plenty too, and Trey didn't expect his wife to have dinner on the table when he walked in the door from the ranch. "What's the special occasion?"

"We wanted to talk about doing a vow renewal, kind of like how you guys did last summer."

"Sure," Trey said. "Beth worked a lot with Olli and Ginny on that." They both turned to get more boxes from the house.

Spur came toward them and said, "I have to go," and he practically shoved the boxes he carried at Trey.

Trey almost dropped the boxes it happened so fast. "Go?"

"Olli called. She got her test results back for the MRI, and she was crying." He jogged toward his truck. "Tell Conrad I'll get this to the dump at some point." With that he leapt into his truck and roared away.

"Where's the fire?" Conrad asked, joining Trey and Duke on the front sidewalk.

Trey stood frozen with the boxes in his hands. "Olli got her MRI results, and she was crying." He realized in that moment, though he'd known, that he wasn't the only one dealing with scary things. He wasn't the only one battling for good health in his family.

"Crying?" Conrad asked in the softest voice Trey had ever heard him use. "What does that mean? Maybe it was a good kind of crying, and she wanted Spur there to celebrate that there's nothing wrong."

"He'll text it out," Duke said. "Or tell us at the party tomorrow night."

Trey jerked his attention to Duke and barked his name at the same time Conrad asked, "What party tomorrow night?"

Horror washed the color right out of Duke's face. "Uh..."

Trey shook his head and walked the couple of steps back to the truck to put down the boxes Spur had handed him. Behind him, Duke stuttered a lame explanation about the *surprise* party Mom had put together for Ry's birthday. Something was going on with Mom and Conrad, but Trey kept his nose out of his brothers' business, so he wasn't sure what. He knew the two of them hadn't gotten along for many, many years, and if Mom had treated Trey the way he had Conrad, he wouldn't spend any time with her either.

She'd come a long way in a short time, and she adored TJ and Fern in a way Trey had never seen from her in the past.

Trey stepped next to Duke, who looked at him helplessly. "Mom planned a party for Ry's birthday. It *was* a surprise."

Conrad looked like he'd been hit with a dead bird. "That's not happening."

"Trying to stop Mom is like trying to make the Earth spin in the opposite direction," Trey said. "She wants to do this."

"Yeah, because I got in her face about how horrible she's been to me." Conrad practically spat the words and very nearly threw the boxes in the back of the truck from where he stood. "I don't need her throwin' parties for me or Ry or anyone to make up for it."

"Conrad," Duke said, though he'd been one of the louder brothers in the past. "That's what she does."

"I don't care." He turned and strode back to the house. "Tell her to cancel it."

"Way to go," Trey said with a sigh.

"I told Mom it was a bad idea," Duke said.

"So did I." Trey wondered if she knew Conrad very well at all, and the answer stood right in front of him as he took the steps three at a time back to Ry's porch.

"Can you imagine him doing that *at* the party?" Duke pulled his phone from his pocket and dialed their mother.

"Mom, Conrad doesn't want the party." He drifted away from Trey, who let him go, because Duke was the youngest and he could sometimes sweeten Mom up to seeing things his way.

In this case, the right way.

Ian came down the steps with a laundry basket full of stuffed animals. "What's goin' on with Conrad? He is *spitting* mad."

Chapter 29

Spur Chappell burst into the doctor's office, his panic very nearly turning him into a green superhero. He wanted to pick up the nearest couch and throw it through the window, then demand to see his wife.

"Olivia Chappell?" he asked the receptionist.

Jade Nicholas rose to her feet. "Come with me, Spur."

"She called," he said, going around the desk. "She's okay, right, Jade? She was crying."

"She's all right," she said. "She's in room seven, right there. I'll let Doctor Blake know you're here. He'll be right in." She opened the door, and Spur stepped past her.

He hated that the first place he looked for his wife was on the floor. After she'd given birth to Gus, her falling episodes had disappeared, and she'd felt absolutely vindicated then. She'd just convinced him that the vertigo and dizziness and falling she'd experienced a few times during her pregnancy were related to that pregnancy.

Then she'd fallen again, three weeks ago. She wasn't six months pregnant and off-balance. She'd readily agreed to go to the doctor, and he'd ordered an MRI to check the body from head to toe to see what was going on.

She sat in a chair, looking out the window.

"Olli," Spur said, the small room suddenly so full with the two of them there. She stood, her tears starting afresh. "Talk to me. I could barely understand you on the phone."

He swept her into his arms, this woman he adored with his whole heart. He'd waited so long for a woman like her, and their baby was only eight months old. The Lord couldn't take her from him yet.

She pulled in a shuddering breath, and said, "I have a blood clot," she said. "It's little, but it's moving, and he's worried I'll have a heart attack or a stroke if it gets in the wrong place."

Heart attack. Stroke.

Spur had never known fear as gripping as the kind currently reaching into his chest and crushing the life from him.

She stepped back and wiped both hands down her face. "They're going to put me on a blood thinner. He's got ways to break it up. I might have to have surgery to put in a... something. Something that will keep the clots from going into my heart."

Spur's arms fell lifelessly to his sides. His brain whirred, trying to stay caught up to the situation. "Okay," he said, finally taking a breath that infused reason back into his life. "That's good. We can do that."

A smile wobbled on her face. "Maybe."

"Maybe? Why maybe?"

Someone knocked on the door, and Spur turned as the doctor came in. "Spur," Dr. Blake said, smiling and reaching to shake his hand. "How are you? Must've been close, because you got here fast."

"Just down the street," Spur said, trying for a smile and failing. "Helping my brother's girlfriend move a few things."

"Good, good." Dr. Blake indicated the chairs. "Did Olli fill you in? Give you the good news or the bad news first?"

Spur met Olli's eyes, and she was crying again. "I'm not really sure," he said.

"I'll go over all of it for you," Dr. Blake said, and he flipped the large computer screen toward Spur, the black and white images making no sense to him. "Your wife has a blood clot right here." He pointed to the worst place possible: her skull. "It's pressing against her inner ear, which is why she's dizzy again. It causes vertigo, and the body doesn't know where it is in space, so it falls down."

He spoke so calmly, but with every word he said, Spur's pulse sped a little bit more. Olli slipped her hand into his, and he wished he had Gus with him too, if only because the little boy brought him so much joy.

"The good news is, it's not to the brain yet, where it can obviously cause a lot of damage. The other good news is that the clots seem to be traveling away from the heart."

"There's more than one?" Spur asked.

"She has another little one—tiny in the grand scheme of things, honestly. It's barely a clot, and it'll probably break up before we can even get her started on a blood thinner. It's down here." He pinched the screen out and indicated her left leg with his pen. "It's moving away from the heart, which is good." He trained his bright blue eyes on Olli. "I don't think we'll need to go to immediate surgery."

Olli nodded, her grip in Spur's hand still so tight.

"That's good news," Spur said, glancing at her. She met his eyes and nodded again.

"And the very best news," Dr. Blake said, leaning back. "Is that your wife is pregnant." He beamed at the two of them, his smile filling the room with pure light.

Olli started to weep again, but Spur's mind had blanked. "What?" He turned toward her. "Pregnant?"

"That's what he said," she whispered, her voice somehow high-pitched and breathless at the same time.

"We weren't even trying to get pregnant," he said.

"You weren't trying not to," Dr. Blake said with a chuckle. "There's a drug called heparin that we can take while you're pregnant, Olli. It's a blood thinner. You'll want to get to your OBGYN immediately, and I'll send my notes over to them. We can treat you together. Because of your age, and these clots, this pregnancy will be something you two will have to monitor every single day. If you don't feel right, come in."

He wore a stern expression now, and Spur found himself nodding. He'd be more forceful about her health this time; no more just accepting that she left shoes out and had stumbled over them.

"You know when something's not right," Dr. Blake said. "Whether you want to admit it or not."

"You have an eight-month-old son and another baby who need you," Spur whispered, lifting her hand to his lips. "*I* need you."

She nodded again, so much concern and love on her face. "I will give you hourly updates."

"Gonna have to hire that manager."

More tears slid down her face, but she nodded. "Two babies, Spur. The Lord gave us *two* babies."

A soft smile curved his lips, and he leaned toward her to touch his forehead to hers. "A miracle, love."

"I'm going to send in this prescription," Dr. Blake said. "I want you drinking a lot of water, Olli. If you're not feeling well, low-dose baby aspirin. I want you in to your OBGYN this week, and I want to see you again in two, just to monitor the size of that clot. It'll take a month or six weeks to fully break up. But I want to see progress."

"Yes, sir," Spur said, his head spinning with all the weeks and appointments already. Olli had a calendar, though, and they'd get everywhere they needed to be. Ginny would take Gus anytime Spur or Olli asked, and everything would be fine.

"Walking will help a lot," Dr. Blake said. "Don't lay around. You're not on bed rest."

"Can I work in my perfumery?"

"Sure," Dr. Blake said. "Monitor your energy levels, but physical activity definitely helps the blood flow." He let the computer go dark. "Any other questions?"

Spur didn't know what he didn't know, so he shook his head. "You'll give us a printout or something?"

Dr. Blake smiled. "Jade's got it out front." He stood, and Spur and Olli did too. More handshakes all around, and then the doctor preceded them out of the room.

Spur couldn't remember how to walk. He looked at his wife, and it was like looking at a slice of heaven. "Another baby, Olls. You wanted two."

"I'm going to take good care of myself," she promised, wrapping her arms around him again. "Please forgive me for last time."

"I love you, baby. Nothing to forgive."

She pulled away and reached for her purse. "Now, do you want a boy or a girl?"

"Are we gonna find out this time?"

"I kind of liked the surprise in the delivery room," she said.

Spur smiled and shook his head. "I want you to be healthy and strong, and I want the same for the baby. I don't care if it's a boy or a girl."

"I'll pray for a girl for both of us then."

Chapter 30

Conrad pulled up to his mother's house, already annoyed by the other trucks there. He and Ry were going to Louisville in the morning, and he hadn't left the ranch for anything but work in years, so he was really looking forward to it.

"We can just stay for an hour," Ry reminded him.

"I'm trying not to be irritated," he said, watching the curtains in the front window flutter. "She always tries to steal the spotlight."

"I think she's trying to be nice," Ry said, repeating something she'd said yesterday and again this morning. "She's trying to make things up to you. I just know there's going to be all of your favorite things on the other side of that door." She took his hand, and he squeezed back.

"Yeah?" he asked. "What would those be?"

"Let's see," Ry said, her voice suddenly playful and light. "Bright colors everywhere. Probably in balloon form."

"It's *your* birthday party."

"Hm, we know this party is for you." She met his eyes, and she gave him that crooked smile that made his heart boom louder. "So lots of bright balloons. Plus, your mom has grandchildren, and she knows the easiest way to get them on her side is a balloon."

Conrad chuckled and ducked his head. "You've got my mom figured out."

"She likes to be everyone's favorite," she said. "Which is funny, since you said none of you boys have really gotten along with her until recently."

"She's a very strong personality to deal with," he said, his gaze moving back to the house.

"There will be those hot ham and cheese sandwiches you've told me about. Promised you'd make for me one day."

"She'll take that from me today," Conrad said, pressing against the bitterness that surged so easily when it came to his mom. He still had a long way to go to really getting along with her, though he'd taken a few crucial steps.

"Chocolate cake, of course," Ry continued. "With pudding." She stopped talking, and Conrad decided he could do anything if chocolate cake was involved.

"So that sums me up," he said. "Ham and cheese sandwiches, chocolate cake, and pudding cups."

"Hey, you're a very simple man."

Their eyes met, and fire moved through Conrad. "I love you, Ry."

She leaned toward him, her eyes drifting closed. "You are

an amazing man, Conrad. You're anything but simple, and I love you for who you are."

He touched his lips to hers, feeling the tremble from her down in his lungs. He felt the same way, and he'd never been happier to reveal who he truly was to someone who wouldn't expect him to be anyone but that man.

"Let's go in," she whispered against his mouth. "If it's terrible, set a timer, and I'll have Max call with an emergency at the boutique."

He nodded and got out of the truck. "Let me come around and get you." He did, and he took her easily into his arms as she slid out of the truck. "What do you think about carving in an hour or two to look at diamond rings while we're in Louisville this weekend?"

Ry's smile bloomed right in front of him. "I think you'll regret that offer."

He took her hand and led her toward the house. Inside, Ry had called it with the bright balloons tied to the back of every single chair at the table. The scent of chocolate filled the air, and Conrad could barely take in the mass of people standing in the kitchen and dining room. It seemed *everyone* else was already there.

"One, two, three," someone said, and the lot of them burst into *Happy Birthday*. They split into parts about halfway through, and Conrad couldn't keep himself from grinning. Everyone burst into applause after the last note, and he joined them.

Ry's face had turned a shade of red he hadn't seen before, but it went well with the deep blue—almost black—

blouse that shone with a radiance that came from within Ry. She'd called the fabric holographic, and it did almost look like the surface of gasoline, with rainbows chasing themselves along the ripples that draped around her neck and showed off her bare arms.

She wore a pair of skinny jeans with the blouse she'd designed and now sold in her boutique, and she moved away from him to hug the women who'd come forward. Lisa, Olli, Ginny, and Mariah reached her first, and he sure did like how they incorporated her right into their fold.

He stayed back by the front door and waited for Beth to bring him Fern, who he took with the widest smile he had in his arsenal. "Howdy, Ferny," he said, getting his mouth real close to her ear. She did turn toward him, and she made his whole world brighter.

"Come eat," Daddy said, appearing at Conrad's side. "Don't let your brothers rope you into holding their babies while everyone else does."

"I like holding the babies," Conrad said, hugging his dad with Fern between them.

"I know you do." He beamed at Conrad. "Mom made those ham and cheese sandwiches you love. No artichokes at all."

Conrad's heart softened again, and not only because his mother had tried so hard to put on this party for him. His family meant a great deal to him, and they were all here...for him. They'd brought their wives and children, and they let him be involved in their lives. He wanted them to be involved in his life, from now until the very day he died.

He followed his dad into the kitchen, where Daddy took Fern and said, "Come with me, little one. We'll have dessert first." He bustled away with the little girl, leaving Conrad to face Mom.

He stepped into her and embraced her, saying, "Thank you, Momma."

"I love you, son, and I'm proud of the man you have always been, and the man you are today."

Conrad pressed his teeth together to keep his tears from coming out. He gripped her tight, hoping that would be enough words to heal another piece that had been broken between them.

"Daddy's gonna give you Rolling Thunder," Ian said, his voice charred and bitter.

Conrad pulled away from his mom and looked at Ian. He too carried a plate with a thick slice of chocolate cake on it, and he took a bite as he glared at Conrad. "He is?"

"You always get the best horses." Ian rolled his eyes. "I think we should have a friendly wager for the Derby in a couple of years."

"Who'd you get?" Conrad asked, reaching for a fork. He drew off a piece of Ian's cake, which made his brother's eyebrows draw down deeper.

"Digging Your Grave."

"Oh, he's great," Conrad said. "I'd take him."

"Tell Daddy."

"The horses are assigned," Daddy called from down the counter, where he had both Gus and Fern sitting right in the middle of the island, feeding each of them tiny bites of cake.

Conrad looked at Ian, whose ire had vanished. He only liked to pretend to be upset about the horses he got to train. "I'd be game for a friendly contest," Conrad said oh-so-casually. "We can plan our training schedule to start in January, and move side-by-side."

"It's a deal," Ian said, stepping even closer to Conrad. "I texted Nita yesterday, and it sort of got out of control."

"What does that mean?" Conrad asked, his voice just as low as his brother's. No one got too close to them, but they wouldn't stay away for long.

"You tell me." He passed Conrad his phone and turned away from him. "I'll get you your own cake so you'll stop eating mine."

Conrad looked at his phone, having to scroll back quite a ways to get to the beginning of the conversation. "Holy cow," he breathed as he read the texts. Nita had been flirting with him hard core…and Ian had held his own, firing back witty comments and taking them to the next level.

It ended with his text which read, *I guess I am kind of no-nonsense. Is that a problem for you? If it's not, and you have an hour or two, maybe we could go to dinner sometime.*

He'd asked her out. A woman. Not six months ago, he'd ranted to Conrad about the unpredictability of women and how they couldn't be trusted.

He looked up from the phone and wiped the shock from his face. No wonder Ian had said the texts had gotten out of control. His brother returned, entire conversations being had as they looked at one another.

"Well?" Ian asked.

"It definitely got out of control."

"Why do you think she didn't answer?"

"Maybe she was so shocked that she dropped her phone. It broke, and now she can't."

Ian rolled his eyes. "Be serious."

"You sent it twenty minutes ago," Conrad said. "Maybe she got in the shower." He scooped up a bite of cake but didn't take it. "She'd said she was going to dinner with her dad. Maybe she'd just pulled up."

"Maybe." He shoved his phone in his back pocket. "I hate this. I feel like I swallowed a cat, and it's trying to claw its way out of my gut." He polished off his cake. "I'm gonna need more of this."

"Hang in there," Conrad said as Ian turned around again. "She's going to say yes, based on the flirting that happened before you asked."

Ian grunted, but Conrad was still trying to wrap his head around the fact that his brother had asked a woman on a date. A real date.

Ry looked toward him, her gaze edged with panic, and Conrad moved toward her instantly, arriving just as Duke's loud voice lifted into the air. "Before we really sit down to eat, Lisa and I have an announcement."

"Quiet down," Mom yelled. "You boys are so loud. Hush now. Hush!"

Conrad smiled down at Ry and tugged her away from Olli, who'd been asking her for her favorite scents. "She likes to make perfumes for specific people," he murmured as the last of the conversations faded into silence.

With the spotlight on Duke, he beamed at his wife, pure love in his face. "Lisa and I are going to do a vow renewal at our farmhouse in October, kind of like Trey and Beth did. We want you all there." He glanced at Mom. "Mom's going to send out the invite in the next week or so. Lisa has an assignment for y'all."

All eyes turned to her, including Conrad's. "We're going to have a suggestion box there," she said, her voice not nearly as loud as Duke's. It also broke on the last word. "For gender-reveal ideas. Duke and I will find out if we're having a boy or a girl just after Christmas, and I need something awesome to post on social media, because I'm really bad at that kind of stuff."

She reached up and wiped her eyes, that single moment all she got before the congratulations and cheers started.

Conrad looked at Spur, who smiled and clapped along with everyone else. He didn't step forward to make any announcements, though, and neither did anyone else. Mom said, "Let's eat. Jefferson, who's going to pray?"

Chapter 31

Ry stood on the sidewalk in Louisville and turned her face toward the sun. There was no better place to be, in her opinion, and she was so glad she'd returned to Kentucky from Georgia. At the time, she hadn't thought that, but once again, her life had been turned upside down when she hadn't even seen it coming.

All because Conrad had gone on a miserable blind date to the restaurant where she'd been working at the time.

"I miss you, Andy," she breathed into the sky. She still thought of her sister every single day. The simplest of things reminded Ry of Andy, like the scent of roses or the color green. Andy had loved both, and Ry had the thought that her sister had been so full of life and found joy in the simplest, most mundane things while she'd been alive, because she wouldn't get much time here on Earth.

She sensed someone behind her, and she opened her eyes and twisted to see Conrad stepping out of the jewelry store.

He carried a little blue bag with elegant lettering on it that seemed far too delicate for his big cowboy hands to hold. She reached for it, but he pulled it away.

"This is mine still," he said, grinning at her.

"I told you we didn't need to buy one today." Especially not in the first store they'd gone in. She had seen a ring she liked—a whole lot. It was probably love at first sight, truth be told—and he'd pulled out the platinum card. She didn't even know cowboys used credit cards.

"It was too expensive," she mused.

"Billionaire," he muttered under his breath as he slid his free hand along her waist. "All that shopping made me thirsty. Can we find a smoothie shop or something?"

"We went in two stores, and only one of them with diamonds in it," she said, glancing at him. "It's been an hour since breakfast. I take longer than that to pick out a single fabric for a blouse."

"This is why you're the fashion designer and I'm the horse trainer," he said, steering her down the sidewalk, where there was a smoothie shop a few doors down.

"When am I getting that ring?" she asked.

"When I give it to you."

"No hint?" she teased.

He cocked one eyebrow at her, no smile in sight. "Do you *want* to ruin it?"

"I want to tell my mother so we can put a date on the calendar," she said. "Or at least find out what her schedule is."

Conrad paused, right there in the middle of the outdoor

mall. On a Saturday afternoon, people streamed around them, and Ry glanced at them as they went by before nudging him off to the side. "What? Why'd you freeze?"

"Women usually have a plan for their wedding," he said, clearly having just thought of that right then. "What's yours?"

"No plan," she said honestly. "When Andy died, I stopped making plans that went further than the next thing I wanted to accomplish."

Her answer only made his brow furrow more. "You stopped dreaming?"

"Yes," she said simply. "There was only Andy and Ryan." She sighed, because she knew how unsettling that sounded. "I'm getting better. In fact, I dreamed about *you* last night."

The eyebrows shot up now. "Oh, really? Do go on."

She giggled and patted his chest. "You're so arrogant. I'm not telling you a thing." She turned and blended back into the crowd.

Conrad caught her quickly, taking her hand and anchoring her to the world. "Will you if I give you the ring?"

"That reminds me," she said. "Ian asked me about Anita Powell the other morning when I came for the sunrise. He said I should give him a couple days' head start, but then I could tell you what we talked about."

"Yeah, I know about Nita," he said. "He asked her out after this super-long, two-day texting session. Last I heard, she hadn't answered him."

Ry grinned. "Texting, huh? How did he start that?"

"I don't know," Conrad said. "Something about Rome and if she needed help at the stables."

She nodded, satisfaction driving through her. "That's great. Good for him."

"He wasn't happy this morning when I left to get you. I guess she hasn't answered him still. I wonder if she has by now. It's been almost a whole day."

"Why is this such a big deal?" Ry asked. "I know you said something about his divorce, but I don't get why he's so scarred."

"That's not my story to tell," Conrad said. "His marriage and divorce was very difficult for him, let's just say that. Like, think of the worst thing you think can happen in a marriage, and then double it. That's what Ian went through with a woman he thought loved him."

Ry studied Conrad, but he didn't hold an ounce of joviality in his face. "That's terrible."

"He hasn't dated in ten years," Conrad said. "I think he forgot women existed. That's how walled-off he's been."

"No wonder you wanted to protect him." She linked her arm through his. "I'm sorry I tried to take that from you."

"Don't," he said. "I lied to you. We don't need to go over it again. It's worked out. Done."

She nodded, because he was right. No sense in hashing through past things they'd already resolved. "I think Kentucky in the springtime is beautiful."

He chuckled and ducked into the smoothie shop. "Noted."

* * *

Their time in Louisville went far too fast in Ry's opinion. He took her to Churchill Downs, where they spent the afternoon watching horses run. He educated her on the trainers, how horses learned to do things, and specific moves jockeys performed to get their champions to win. She could admit that going to a horse race was ten times more fun than she'd thought it would be.

She'd enjoyed the museum on the history of racing and the history of the Kentucky Derby. All the dresses, men's fashions, and hats had stirred something creatively in her that had been dormant for a while.

They went to the theater on Sunday evening, and Conrad could pull off slacks better than any horseman she'd ever met. She felt glamorous and extremely lucky to be on his arm, even if he had nodded off in the second act.

They'd gotten up late, met for breakfast in the hallway outside their hotel rooms, and now he turned down her street.

She knew instantly that something was going on at her house. "What's going on?"

"What?" Conrad asked, his voice somewhat distracted.

She flicked a glance in his direction, unable to look at him for long because of the chalkboard placard that had been placed on her front porch. She used that to announce sales at Andy and Ryan, and it usually went on the sidewalk in front of the boutique after Max hand-lettered the steal-of-the-day that would bring in customers.

Today, it sat on her porch, and it had been erased clean. She didn't see anything else amiss in the neighborhood, though her mind rioted at her to find the person who'd put that sign there and demand to know what they'd been thinking.

Conrad pulled into her driveway, and she didn't wait for him to get out of the truck. She bolted from it, but he still beat her to corner of the truck. "You're panicking."

"That's from my store."

"I know," he said. "I had Max bring it over."

She tore her eyes from it and looked at him. "You did? Why?"

"Come see." He took her hand and she swore he moved deliberately slow, taking her up each step in a painstaking process. He flipped it around, and Max's delicate calligraphy sat there.

Will you marry me?

Ry sucked in a breath, pressed both hands to the bucking beat beneath her breastbone, and looked at Conrad.

She didn't have to look up nearly as far. He'd dropped to his knees right beside the sign, and he had the ring box open already. How long had she stared at the sign?

"I love you, Ryanne Moon," he said. "I love your kind spirit, and I love your creative mind, and I love your attention to details I don't even see. I will work my hardest my whole life to be the man you deserve, if you'll say yes. Will you marry me?"

She blinked down at that huge diamond ring she'd been pulled toward at the store in Louisville. A square cut, the diamond protruded up from a thin, gold band that let the gem shine in its purity. She'd never been into gaudy things, and simple worked for her.

Just like this proposal. He'd known she wouldn't want a huge audience. She wouldn't want it to happen somewhere she could never visit again. He'd used part of Andy and Ryan to do it, and her very best friend in the whole world.

Tears filled her eyes, and she said, "Yes." She bounced on the balls of her feet. "Yes, yes, yes! I'll marry you!" She took his face in both of her hands and kissed him, the scent of his cologne, the cotton in his shirt, and the chalk from the sign filling her nose and becoming the scent of pure joy.

He laughed as he pulled away and got to his feet. His fingers didn't shake even the tiniest bit as he slid the ring on her finger. "I think you'll be able to pick a date with your mom that will work for me. The Derby is in May, though…"

"How about April?"

"If you do April, that would be great," he said, clearly relieved. "We race a lot from May and through the summer. The big, high-stakes races."

"It won't just be me, silly." She admired the ring on her finger. "We'll get married in April. The beginning, so we can go on a honeymoon."

"Mm, yeah, I like the sound of that." He ran his hands along her waist and brought her close to him. "I love you, Ry."

"I love you too, Conrad."

He touched his mouth to hers, and this kiss turned every

other kiss on its head—because she was finally kissing the man she was going to marry.

* * *

Keep reading for a bonus sneak peek of the next book in the Bluegrass Ranch series, **CONVINCING THE COWBOY BILLIONAIRE. Now available in paperback.**

Sneak Peek! Convincing the Cowboy Billionaire Chapter One:

Ian Chappell's hands slipped, and the hay bales he'd been carrying tipped. "Whoa!" he yelled as he felt himself tipping to the right. He stumbled that way, abandoning the bale he'd started to bobble.

The window loomed right there, and he had a flash of himself falling out of it, tumbling three stories to his death below. He managed to hurl the hay bale onto the conveyor and catch himself as his hand came down against the wall.

"Comin' your way!" he called just as he bashed his shin against the side of a metal beam in the loft. All kinds of swear words streamed through his mind, but none came out of his mouth. Mom would be so proud.

He instantly took all the weight off his right leg, realizing that idiotic beam had probably saved him from going out the window, but holy-mother-of-pearl, it had just injured him something fierce.

"You okay?" someone asked, but Ian had forgotten who

he was working with in the loft. He definitely took his turn doing chores around the family owned and operated ranch, and he'd never minded loading hay onto the conveyor belt to get it out of the loft and where it needed to go.

He blinked, the pain still shooting up into his hip and radiating down into his foot. His toes tingled, as if he'd hit a nerve, and he steadied himself against the wall of the barn and pulled in a breath. He didn't dare put any weight on his foot, though.

"Yeah," he managed to say, glancing over to Lawrence, one of his brothers.

Someone yelled from below, and Lawrence turned to see what they wanted. They were probably mad about the double-bale coming on the belt, but Ian *had* warned them. His fingers ached from the way he'd been clenching them around twine and lifting fifty-pound bales for the past hour.

He tried putting weight on his right leg, but his shin gave a violent protest in the form of another blinding wave of pain. He groaned and collapsed onto the nearest thing—which of course, was the bale of hay he'd had in his left hand. He'd been injured dozens of times on the ranch. Spur, his oldest brother, barely had any feeling left in his fingertips for how often he touched hot things. Blaine, the second oldest brother in the Chappell family, had once broken his leg and then worked on crutches for eight weeks. Daddy sure didn't see a reason not to be out in the fields or stables, broken legs or not.

He *had* taken a break a couple of years ago when he'd

had hip surgery, but Ian suspected his mother had enforced that more than his father would've.

"Ian got hurt," Lawrence called down from the big window where they'd positioned the belt.

"I'm fine."

The belt started to slow and then stop, and Ian's mood worsened. He didn't want the spotlight on him. Now that he was the last remaining brother to get engaged or married, it seemed to be shining directly in his eyes at all times. He'd been one of the first to get married originally, but that relationship had been such a disaster—and he hadn't even seen it until it was too late.

Almost too late, he amended silently. He'd gotten out of the marriage without any children and without having to pay a whole bunch of money. It helped that it had only been six months old, and that Minnie had been a pathological liar.

"You are," Lawrence said. "Your pantleg is soaked with blood." He crouched in front of Ian, who looked down at his leg. He moved his foot further from his body, but even that slight motion sent stars into his head. Sharp, steel stars that sliced at his senses harshly.

His vision went white along the edges, but he still managed to see the bloodstain on his jeans. "Great," he said. "I just washed these." His attempt at humor fell on deaf ears in Lawrence, who hadn't looked away from Ian's shin.

"I'm going to pull it up," Lawrence said as Blaine yelled from below. Neither Ian nor Lawrence answered him. Lawrence met his eyes, and Ian reached up to grab a bar that had been nailed into the wall. Probably a steadying bar, which he could've used as he was falling toward the open window.

He nodded, quick little pulses of his head. "Okay," he said. "I'm ready."

Even moving the jeans around his wound made his teeth grind together and a groan come out of his mouth. "Holy heavens," he said, the words bursting from him in mostly air. "What did I do?"

Lawrence didn't answer, and that wasn't a good sign. He whistled a warning like *I can't believe what I'm seeing, you're in so much trouble*, and stood. "I'm getting everyone up here. You've got to get to the hospital, and you're not putting any weight on that to get down the ladder." He moved over to the window despite Ian's protests.

As he yelled for Blaine and Trey to come up and help, Ian took a deep breath and closed his eyes. He wasn't exactly squeamish about blood. He could deal with horse injuries, Conrad—the brother he currently lived with in the corner house on the ranch—cutting his hand while washing a glass, and any other number of slices and scrapes…as long as it wasn't his *own* blood.

There was something eerie and really disturbing about seeing his own blood leaving his body, and he hissed through his teeth as Lawrence returned and started to pull his pant leg down. "We'll want to cover that," he said. "You don't want it getting any dirtier than it already is. I'm gonna call Spur and let him know we can't finish up here. Maybe he can send over a few guys."

"It's that bad?" Ian asked, his heartbeat suddenly

freefalling through his body. He was supposed to be taking Anita Powell to dinner that night. Their first real date, one he'd thought would never happen.

He'd texted her a lot over the course of a couple of days, and then suggested they could get dinner together. She hadn't answered for two more days, during which time he'd imagined every terrible thing that could've happened to her or her phone, and then he'd started in on himself for being so bold and so assuming.

He'd asked women to dinner before. Lots of men did it. It wasn't like he'd proposed.

No, that honor had gone to Conrad, who'd gotten engaged only a week ago.

He looked down at his leg, a shocked gasp flying from his mouth.

"No," Lawrence said, pawing at his pantleg now. "Don't look, Ian."

It was too late. Ian had seen the bloody mess that was his shin, with long, weeping fingers of red liquid moving down his leg to the top of his boot. The hay loft started to spin. He groaned, and Lawrence knelt in front of him and said, "I'm going to kill you for looking. Don't pass out on me."

He closed his eyes, but the image of his bone—so snowy white and so jagged—right in the middle of all that blood didn't go away.

"I'm sorry," he slurred, because he was definitely going to pass out.

"Help!" Lawrence called. "Blaine, get up here now!" He braced himself against Ian's chest, and the last thing Ian heard was Blaine's voice mingling with Trey's as they arrived in the loft. He passed out before he heard or felt anything else, not a single thought in his head at all.

* * *

"There he is," Blaine said, and Ian's eyelids fluttered again. "I told you he wouldn't be out long."

"How long?" Ian asked, his tongue so thick in his mouth. He wasn't on the hay bale anymore, but lying on the floor of the loft, looking straight up at the pointy part of the roof. Bales had been moved to block the window, and he wished for a breeze to come cool him down. In the next breath, he trembled with cold or pain, he wasn't sure which.

"Maybe three minutes," Lawrence said. "Come on, we still have to get him down."

"Maybe he could ride the conveyor," Trey said.

Even Ian gaped at him. Daddy had said he'd tan their hides if he ever found them treating the bale conveyor as a toy.

Trey shrugged. "I know it's not ideal. It's not something we'd normally do, but TJ does it at our place. He hasn't died yet."

"TJ is six years old," Lawrence said. "Ian weighs at least ten times as much as him."

He groaned and closed his eyes again as the roof above him began to spin.

"And can't stay conscious," Blaine added. "No, he has to go down the ladder."

Lawrence: "He'll pass out from the pain."

Trey: "Call Spur."

Blaine: "What's Spur gonna do? He's not a doctor."

Ian just wanted them all to stop talking. Didn't they know their voices were driving a wedge between the halves of his brain with every word they spoke? He opened his eyes and sat up, though even that seemed to pull on his shin bone and send a wave of pain through his body. "I'm fine. I can go down the ladder."

"How?" Lawrence demanded. "You cannot, in any way, put weight on that leg. I'm pretty sure you cracked your shin. It could splinter."

He really didn't have time for a broken anything. Helplessness cut through him, because even moving his leg left to right with no weight on it hurt.

"I'm calling Spur," Trey said, and he paced away from the three of them to do it.

"Moving me is going to hurt," Ian said.

"I'm calling an ambulance," Blaine said. "There's no way we can drive him to the ER. He'll be bouncing all over." He stood and started tapping.

"I don't want an ambulance."

Lawrence crouched in front of him again. "Ian, you're in a bad way. Let us figure this out."

"I'm sorry," Ian said again, and Lawrence wore understanding in his gaze. They were only fourteen months apart, and he'd been close to Lawrence growing up. Once Conrad had shown his skill with the training, though, Daddy had always partnered he and Ian together, and Lawrence had gone his own way.

"It was an accident," Lawrence said. "They happen."

Ian nodded, pressing his teeth together in frustration and pain.

Blaine: "The ambulance is on the way."

Trey: "Spur and Duke are on their way. They're gonna grab Conrad from the family stable."

Lawrence: "I'm texting the work thread."

"That's everyone on the ranch," Ian complained. "Everyone doesn't need to know."

"Yes, they do," Lawrence said, his fingers flying only inches in front of Ian's face. "They need to move vehicles and we might get some volunteers to come help finish the loft."

All Ian could think was that Nita would get that text. Lawrence would push it out to everyone who worked at Bluegrass, as they had a lot of people come and go on the ranch. They ran one of the biggest boarding stables and training facilities in the Lexington area, and Nita worked as a trainer with one of their long-time rowhouse renters.

Within sixty seconds, more voices filled the air, and Ian consigned himself to his fate. No one suggested moving him, and when the paramedics got there, they took one look at his leg and then each other, the deathly still expression in their eyes speaking volumes to Ian.

"All right," one of them drawled. "We're going to strap you to a board." He stayed down on his knees, close to Ian, his voice calm and oh-so-even. He knew exactly what he was doing, and Ian trusted him. "It's like a stretcher, but it'll hold your head still—and that leg. Then we'll send you down the belt. It's going to be fine."

Ian nodded, those short bursts happening again. "All right."

Spur: "Daddy's here."

Blaine: "Don't let him climb the ladder. They're bringing him down."

Trey: "I'll get everyone away from the conveyor and go get it moving again."

Movement happened around Ian, but he didn't twitch a muscle. He said nothing. The paramedics used the belt to get their "board" up to the loft, and they sent everyone except Conrad and Duke down.

"It's okay, brother," Conrad said, reaching for Ian's hand. They gripped each other's fingers, and the paramedic said, "Good. Hold on tight, cowboy. This is going to hurt."

Both of them moved him then, and Ian yelled out as white-hot waves of pain cascaded through his whole body.

"It's okay," Conrad said on his left, Duke on his right.

Ian panted, the echo of his scream still caught in his head. He felt wild, frantic, and he needed some meds *now*.

"When we get him down, we'll start a drip," the first paramedic said. "Morphine and fluids. We can only take one in the ambulance."

"Don't come," Ian said through gritted teeth. "I'm fine. Daddy can come."

"I'll go talk to Daddy." Conrad left, because he was

closer to the ladder. Ian looked at Duke, who wore such a sober look on his face.

"All right," the paramedic said. "Easy now. You've got that side?" They inched him over to the belt, and it was smooth as butter as they laid him on it. He couldn't watch the sky flow by, as it made him dizzy and nauseous, and thankfully, keeping his eyes closed also meant he didn't have to see how many people were staring at him coming down that blasted conveyor belt out of the hay loft.

The belt beneath him started to slow, and Trey said, "It'll stop in time."

Ian opened his eyes as it did indeed stop, but he could only stare straight up. The paramedics hadn't made it down the ladder yet, but he felt like he'd just landed on the moon —he'd just taken one giant step for mankind—by getting from the loft to the ground.

Spur appeared above him. "Okay?"

Ian couldn't nod, so he employed his voice to say, "Okay."

He leaned closer. "Nita wanted to know if you'd like her to bring dinner to your room tonight." His dark eyes sparkled with something Ian couldn't name. He wasn't teasing Ian, because Spur didn't do that. He sure seemed happy though. "She asked me real privately, and no one overheard."

Ian normally would've nodded, but once again, found he could not. "Okay," he said again, and the paramedics arrived.

The crowd started to applaud in reverence—there was

no whooping or hollering as could often be heard among cowboys—and Ian could definitely see out of his peripheral vision.

Nita stood right at the bumper of the ambulance, and their eyes met. She wore worry in hers as Ian's humiliation and embarrassment doubled and then tripled.

"Sorry," he muttered, to which she said, "See you at six."

The had been the last text she'd sent him, right after she'd given him her home address so he could pick her up all Southern-gentleman-proper.

As he got loaded in the back of the ambulance and Spur helped Daddy climb in with him, Ian couldn't help smiling to himself.

See you at six.

He hoped they wouldn't give him so many drugs that he couldn't enjoy his second hospital experience with the lovely Anita Powell.

Sneak Peek! Convincing the Cowboy Billionaire Chapter Two:

Anita Powell suspected she'd throw up on her next breath. When she didn't, she thought, *The next one.*

Nope.

Next one.

She managed to keep her breakfast where she'd swallowed, though that had been hours and hours ago. She'd skipped lunch when she'd gotten the text about an injury on the ranch, and she'd spent the afternoon cleaning stalls and organizing paperwork—anything that didn't require too much mental energy.

All of that was currently going to Ian Chappell.

She'd texted him right after Lawrence's text had hit her phone, and he hadn't responded. Word spread fast on a ranch, even a big one like Bluegrass that housed boarding stables and training facilities. Besides, everyone knew Ian. He was a god among trainers, the last three horses he'd devoted his time to going on to win huge money prizes in some of the biggest races around the world.

Most people knew about three races: the Belmont Stakes, the Kentucky Derby, and the Preakness. They were, by far, the most popular races in the US. But Australia had massive money prizes, as did the UK and the United Arab Emirates.

Even if Ian didn't stay with them throughout his career, she knew he consulted with the new owners of the horses he'd raised and broken. The ones he'd taught initially. She'd been around Bluegrass enough to know how they worked, and they were a breeding, working, training ranch that specialized in Thoroughbreds.

Now that they'd started their own race, the Chappell's had only been adding to their pool of money, and everywhere she looked at Bluegrass, she saw dollar signs.

"Fifty-four," a man called, and Nita looked down at her receipt. She was fifty-four. She held up he receipt and stepped through the to-go crowd to pick up her barbecue dinner. "Family rib meal," the man said, pushing everything toward her in Styrofoam and plastic bags.

"Thanks," she said, and she tucked her receipt in her pocket and picked up her food. She couldn't *believe* she was headed to the hospital. The last time she and Ian had been there together, they'd gone to see one of her fellow Glenn Marks trainers, a man named Rome.

She was fairly certain Ian hadn't planned on taking her back to the hospital cafeteria for their first official date. He'd told her that he didn't count the meal they'd shared a few minutes before the cafeteria had closed as a date. Tonight, though, would've been. That much had been clear to Nita.

She was still shocked Ian had asked at all. She'd felt sparks for hours after he'd delivered her back to her truck the evening they'd gone to see Rome. Every time her phone dinged, her stomach swooped, because it could be Ian.

She hadn't thought she'd caused the same—or even a close-to-similar—feeling inside him. They did spend a lot of time talking about horses, but she knew he loved authentic Kentucky barbecue sauce and mashed potatoes with plenty of country gravy—not brown. She could definitely take him a good meal tonight, and that thought alone got her back to her truck and on her way toward on the tallest buildings in Dreamsville—the hospital.

Her father called as she pulled into a parking space out front, and she tapped on her screen to answer it. "Hey, Dad." She'd met with him last week to go over the proposal, contracts, and final logo. His new wife, Janet, hadn't seemed overly enthusiastic about the splitting of Glenn Marks, but Nita didn't much care what her dad's new wife thought. This was something she'd been talking about with Glenn since her uncle's death. They both wanted her to take over the stables, and Janet really had no say in the matter.

"Where you at, sugarbaby?"

She looked toward the half-circle entrance to the hospital that stuck way out from the main building. "Taking dinner to a friend."

"I heard there was an accident at Bluegrass today."

"Yeah," she said. "Ian Chappell got hurt in the hay loft. I

haven't heard if he broke his leg or what, but they strapped him up tight to a stretcher and sent him down on the conveyor belt."

"That's terrible," he said. "I'll call Jefferson as soon as we hang up."

Nita should probably tell him that she was about go inside the hospital and see what Ian needed. If he was really as injured as a broken bone, she wouldn't be able to take care of him the way he had her. He'd come over to Glenn Marks a couple of times to help keep the horses fed and clean and healthy. Now, when she saw Conrad or Ian talking to one of her champions, she smiled and thanked them, and she'd started to feel like a part of the community at Bluegrass where she'd always felt on the outskirts.

"Okay," she said, not mentioning the family barbecue rib meal on the seat next to her. She didn't need to get anyone's hopes up—least of all, hers. She knew tonight's dinner was intended as a fishing expedition for Ian. He wanted to see what a real date would be like, and if she didn't meet his standards, she felt certain she wouldn't hear from him again—at least not about personal matters.

With Ian, a person usually only got one strike. She'd shown up at his house and yelled at him to stay out of her stables, and she'd still gotten a second chance to bat. She knew she wouldn't get a third.

"Casey said he'd have the paperwork ready to sign in the next week or two."

"Okay," Nita said again. She didn't want to think about taking half the stables from her dad right now. The weight of that might crush her lungs, and she just wanted to try to enjoy her evening with Ian. If she was lucky, it would last an hour, as neither of them seemed all that loquacious. She'd actually made a list on her phone of things she could ask him, because it had been a long time since she'd been out with a man, and certainly forever since that man had been as talented and as handsome as Ian.

"I can tell you're busy," her dad said. "I'll let you know if we're going to do something for the Chappells."

"Sounds good," she said, only because she didn't want to say *okay* for a third time. The call ended, and Nita decided she didn't want to waste any more time. If she didn't go in now, she'd drive the family meal back to her perfect little house on the edge of some woods and eat the whole thing—even the country gravy she didn't particularly like.

She collected the bag and got out of the truck, her mind running through the mundane tasks she needed to do when she got home to that perfect little house on five acres, with a gorgeous view of the river from the front porch and the windmills from the back.

She needed to switch her laundry from the washer to the dryer, and if she didn't give her little dog a bath soon, the both of them were going to be paying for it.

"Nita?"

She looked up, her pulse skyrocketing at the disgust her name had been said with. She looked right into Judd Rake's eyes, and a groan pulled through every muscle in her body. "Judd." She said his name with as much respect as she could muster, which admittedly, wasn't much.

"What are you doin' here?" His gaze slid down to the plastic bag in her hand. Thankfully, Blue Barbecue cared more about their flavors than having fancy sacks to carry it in, and she could've been taking in groceries for all Judd would know.

"Nothing," she said, though Judd would hardly let that stand. No one just came to the hospital for fun.

"Did you hear about Ian Chappell?" he asked.

"Yes."

"We just saw 'im," Judd said.

She really wanted to ask him who "we" comprised. As far a she could see, only he stood in front of her. She clamped the remark behind closed lips and nodded.

"You're not here to see him, are you?" Judd asked, moving out of the way as a mother and her two small children exited the hospital and couldn't quite get by him.

"It's really none of your business," Nita said. "I have to go. Excuse me."

Judd narrowed his eyes at her, but Nita walked away, choosing to enter the hospital by one of the side doors, instead of having to shuffle along in that rotating automatic door. She couldn't shake Judd's eyes until she stepped onto the elevator that would take her to the second floor, where she'd learned Ian's room sat.

Her nerves assaulted her again, but she kept her feet moving, one in front of the other. Room two-eleven loomed in front of her, the door open. At least she wouldn't have to wonder if Ian was taking visitors.

She slowed as she arrived and she peered into the room.

There was no one there, and sharp disappointment hooked through her at the same time a hint of relief soothed it.

"He's down in x-ray," a nurse said as she stepped past Nita. "You can come in. He won't be long."

"No?"

"Nope." She gave Nita a warm smile. "This one's popular. He's had people here with him all day." She started removing the sheets from the bed. "I'm just going to get him set up for the night." She kept working, and Nita felt stupid standing there watching her work in the tiny room. She put the food on the built-in desk that Ian could reach from the bed. A TV had been mounted to the wall above the door, and the world's tiniest recliner sat on the other side of the bed. Behind that, a slim window let in natural light and another door led into the bathroom.

The nurse finished making up his bed, and she bustled out of the room. Nita sighed as she sat down in the recliner, surprised she fit though she wasn't a very tall or very wide woman.

You're not here to see him, are you?

"Why can't I come see Ian?" she asked the empty hospital room. "Judd had. I'm no different than Judd."

She was, though, and she knew it. She wasn't here out of brotherly love for a fellow trainer. She wanted to see Ian so she could feel the sparks he sent through her whole body with a single look.

"Here you go," a man said, and a wheelchair came into the room, Ian riding in it. He wore the darkest look she'd ever seen on his face, and she immediately got to her feet, the fireworks going off like the Thunder Over Louisville, which was a massively huge fireworks show that kicked off the Derby season here in Kentucky.

"Looks like Shanda got the bed switched out," the man said, looking at Nita with a wide smile. "Let me lower the bed, and then we'll get it where you want it." He set about doing that, and Nita felt in the way in this microscopic room. She couldn't even imagine being trapped in here, with the door closed, with just her and Ian.

You won't be trapped, she told herself. *You want to be here.*

Ian hadn't said anything, and she fell out of his sight to make room for the nurse helping him get the bed as low as possible so he could just move over from the chair to the mattress. Working together, the two of them managed to get Ian into bed with only a slight groan.

"All set?" the man asked.

"Yes," Ian clipped out.

"They serve room service from the kitchen until ten," he said, bustling around the room to get out an extra blanket from the tiny closet in the corner Nita hadn't seen. "The menu is right there on the desk. You know how to call me or Shanda?"

"Yes," Ian said again.

"Anything you need right now?" He looked at Nita. "Either of you want water?"

"I'll take some water," Ian said, and Nita nodded to indicate she'd like some too.

The man smiled and nodded. "Be right back." He left, pulling the door closed behind him.

The moment it clicked closed, Nita flinched. It went well with Ian's sigh.

She wanted to offer to leave, but she couldn't bring herself to do it. "Sounds like you've had a busy day," she started with.

"Beyond." Ian leaned his head back and closed his eyes.

"Is the bed where you want it?"

"Not even close."

She reached for the remote. "I can do it. Higher? More laid back?"

"Higher for sure." He spoke with the timbre of wood mouse now—soft and meek and almost pleasant to listen to. "Then I can put my dinner on that tray right there."

"All right." She raised him up and rolled the tray into position. With her hands busy, she didn't feel so nervous. "I got barbecue ribs from Blue's. Mashed potatoes with country gravy. I got the sweet corn, because my momma taught me to always eat a vegetable with my barbecue."

She told herself to stop talking, because she'd started to rush and ramble. She set the food in front of him.

"What did you get?" he asked, his eyes turning a touch softer as he looked at her.

"Ribs," she said. "Same as you." Panic streamed through her when she realized she'd have to eat like an animal in front of this man she could barely look at. "But I like the brown gravy, so I got baked beans. There's cole slaw too, and that's technically a vegetable. Cabbage, you know."

A smile ghosted across his face, barely lifting his lips. "I know what cole slaw is made of."

Nita slicked her hands down the front of her jeans. "Okay."

He reached out and because the room was so dang small, he was able to reach her hand easily. She froze, every cell her body combusting, putting itself back together, and then re-exploding. Over and over.

His touch did things to her no man's had ever done before.

She had no idea what that meant. What she knew was that she'd drifted closer to him somehow, and that his other hand had reached up toward her face. She leaned down, and because the bed had been lifted so much, and she wasn't very tall, it wasn't that far of a dip to get close to him.

His hand curled along the back of her neck, and he whispered, "Thank you for making this dinner date happen. I've been looking forward to it all day." With that, he brought her mouth to his, his fingers insistent and yet soft at the same time, exactly like his kiss.

Nita hadn't been kissed in oh-so-long, and she hadn't expected to do this tonight either. She couldn't help sinking into his touch, and breathing in when he did, and sighing in pure bliss when he pulled back only a few seconds after the kiss had begun.

Wow, was the only thing she could think. *Wow, wow, wow.*

Someone knocked on the door, and she spun toward it

and then immediately away when Judd walked in. "Hey," he said. "I think I left my keys here somewhere…"

She hurried to the back window, wishing she could leap through it and disappear. Ian said something in a voice that didn't make it through the rushing in her ears, and Judd responded.

"See ya, Nita," he said.

She turned toward him. "Yep. 'Bye."

Their eyes met, and Judd narrowed those eyes again. He knew too much about her, and she hated that. He also knew there was something going on here, and she wished he didn't. Instead of him blurting out the secrets she'd been keeping for years, he nodded curtly, said good-bye to Ian, and left.

"Sorry about that," Ian said.

"About what?" Nita asked.

"Didn't you hear him?"

"No."

"He asked if we were dating. I said no." Ian looked up at her, and Nita felt a knife go right through the fleshiest part of her heart.

She nodded and sat down in the recliner, though she'd left her food on his tray, out of her reach. "I guess that kiss was a mistake." She should've known better. Men like Ian Chappell weren't interested in women like her.

Familiar bitterness and fire flamed through her. "I'll just go."

"No, wait," Ian said, but Nita wasn't going to wait to be

made a fool of again. She pulled open the door and nearly rammed into the nurse who'd gone to get their water.

"Sorry," she mumbled and kept going. It wasn't until she'd made it into the silent elevator that she thought she'd heard Ian say, *It wasn't a mistake. Don't go.*

She couldn't go back now, though, and Nita let her humiliation and foolishness propel her out of the elevator car at full speed.

"Anita," a man said, holding up both hands as she nearly plowed into him.

She came to a halt, her chest heaving.

"Anita Powell?" He smiled, and she recognized him as the nurse who'd brought Ian back to the room. A woman burst out of the door to the left of the elevator.

Shanda. Ian's other nurse.

"Praise the heavens," she said panting. She pressed one hand to her pulse. "Can you imagine having to go back to his room if we hadn't caught her?" She looked at the male nurse, and Nita just kept volleying her gaze between them.

"Come on," the man said, his smile not slipping even a centimeter. "Ian asked us to come get you and escort you back to the room for dinner." He stepped to her side and linked his arm in hers.

"How did you get down here so fast?" Nita asked as Shanda pushed the button to call the elevator.

"We have secret passageways just for nurses," he said. "My name is Marty, and Shanda and I won't bother you or Ian for at least an hour." He glanced over to the other nurse as the elevator dinged. "Right, Shanda?"

"That's right." She led the way into the elevator. Nita wasn't sure if she'd entered an alternate reality or not. She knew Marty didn't release his grip on her arm at all, and Shanda's words echoed in her mind.

Can you imagine having to go back to his room if we hadn't caught her?

Ian *could* be a beast of a man. Nita knew that…and yet she still found herself smiling, her own pulse kicking out extra beats at the thought of dining with him—and maybe even kissing him again.

* * *

She'll do anything to keep her dignity…even convincing the saltiest cowboy billionaire at the ranch to be her boyfriend.
Read *CONVINCING THE COWBOY BILLIONAIRE* in paperback today.

BLUEGRASS RANCH ROMANCE

Book 1: Winning the Cowboy Billionaire: She'll do anything to secure the funding she needs to take her perfumery to the next level...even date the boy next door.

Book 2: Roping the Cowboy Billionaire: She'll do anything to show her ex she's not still hung up on him...even date her best friend.

Book 3: Training the Cowboy Billionaire: She'll do anything to save her ranch...even marry a cowboy just so they can enter a race together.

Book 4: Parading the Cowboy Billionaire: She'll do anything to spite her mother and find her own happiness...even keep her cowboy billionaire boyfriend a secret.

Book 5: Promoting the Cowboy Billionaire: She'll do anything to keep her job...even date a client to stay on her boss's good side.

Book 6: Acquiring the Cowboy Billionaire: She'll do anything to keep her father's stud farm in the family...even marry the maddening cowboy billionaire she's never gotten along with.

Book 7: Saving the Cowboy Billionaire: She'll do anything to prove to her friends that she's over her ex...even date the cowboy she once went with in high school.

Book 8: Convincing the Cowboy Billionaire: She'll do anything to keep her dignity...even convincing the saltiest cowboy billionaire at the ranch to be her boyfriend.

CHESTNUT RANCH ROMANCE

Book 1: A Cowboy and his Neighbor: Best friends and neighbors shouldn't share a kiss...

Book 2: A Cowboy and his Mistletoe Kiss: He wasn't supposed to kiss her. Can Travis and Millie find a way to turn their mistletoe kiss into true love?

Book 3: A Cowboy and his Christmas Crush: Can a Christmas crush and their mutual love of rescuing dogs bring them back together?

Book 4: A Cowboy and his Daughter: They were married for a few months. She lost their baby...or so he thought.

Book 5: A Cowboy and his Boss: She's his boss. He's had a crush on her for a couple of summers now. Can Toni and Griffin mix business and pleasure while making sure the teens they're in charge of stay in line?

Book 6: A Cowboy and his Fake Marriage: She needs a husband to keep her ranch...can she convince the cowboy next-door to marry her?

Book 7: A Cowboy and his Secret Kiss: He likes the pretty adventure guide next door, but she wants to keep their relationship off the grid. Can he kiss her in secret and keep his heart intact?

Book 8: A Cowboy and his Skipped Christmas: He's been in love with her forever. She's told him no more times than either of them can count. Can Theo and Sorrell find their way through past pain to a happy future together?

Texas Longhorn Ranch Romance

Book 1: Loving Her Cowboy Best Friend: She's a city girl returning to her hometown. He's a country boy through and through. When these two former best friends (and ex-lovers) start working together, romantic sparks fly that could ignite a wildfire... Will Regina and Blake get burned or can they tame the flames into true love?

Book 2: Kissing Her Cowboy Boss: She's a veterinarian with a secret past. He's her new boss. When Todd hires Laura, it's because she's willing to live on-site and work full-time for the ranch. But when their feelings turn personal, will Laura put up walls between them to keep them apart?

About Emmy

Emmy is a Midwest mom who loves dogs, cowboys, and Texas. She's been writing for years and loves weaving stories of love, hope, and second chances. Learn more about her and her books at www.emmyeugene.com.

Printed in Great Britain
by Amazon